The Days of
Anna Madrigal

The Days of
Anna Madrigal

A Novel

Armistead Maupin

HARPER LUXE

An Imprint of HarperCollinsPublishers

This is a work of fiction. The characters, incidents, and dialogue are drawn from the author's imagination and are not to be construed as real. Any resemblance to actual events or persons, living or dead, is entirely coincidental.

HarperCollins books may be purchased for educational, business, or sales promotional use. For information, please e-mail the Special Markets Department at SPsales@harpercollins.com.

FIRST HARPERLUXE EDITION

HarperLuxe™ is a trademark of HarperCollins Publishers

Library of Congress Cataloging-in-Publication Data is available upon request.

ISBN: 978-0-06-229872-0

14 ID/RRD 10 9 8 7 6 5 4 3

For Olympia, naturally
and once again for Chris

The way to love anything is to realize that it may be lost.

—G. K. CHESTERTON

Some people drink to forget. Personally, I smoke to remember.

—ANNA MADRIGAL

The Days of
Anna Madrigal

1
Leaving Like A Lady

S ummer had been warmer than usual this year, but the heat that throbbed in the East Bay was already coaxing pale fingers of fog into the city. Anna could feel this on her skin, the chilly caress she had come to think of as "candle weather." She had not owned a fireplace since her landlady days on Russian Hill, but to her mind the proper application of candlelight carried all the primal comfort of a campfire.

She grabbed the purple plastic firelighter on the sideboard in the parlor. Her legs, however, weren't cooperating, so she steadied herself for a moment, slouching ludicrously on one hip, like Joan Crawford in 1940s gun moll mode. This thing in her wobbly old hand *was* disturbingly gunlike, complete with a trigger and a barrel.

Mustn't think of it as a gun. Think of it as a wand.

She aimed the lighter at the top of a candle, a stately pillar whose rim had grown satisfyingly wavy with use, though she did not recall having seen it before. She wondered, optimistically, if her companion Jake had been burning it in his room.

"Stop!" Jake sprang from the sofa, having just noticed her above the top of his magic slate. "Not that one!" The alarm in his voice suggested someone arriving at a gas chamber with a last-minute stay of execution from the governor.

Anna dropped her firearm, surrendering on the spot. "Sorry, dear. Saving it for a special friend?" This was naughty of her, since Jake was easily embarrassed, but she liked the notion that he might have found someone worthy of candlelight.

"It's for you," he said placidly, shaming her with his teddy-bear dignity. "Got it at Pottery Barn this morning."

"Ah. Very thoughtful." She was still confounded by that melted rim.

"I can get some more, if you like it."

"I do . . . yes." She hoped this sounded sincere; there was not much you could say, really, about a plain white candle. "And why am I not allowed to light it?"

He took the pillar in his hands, fidgeting with something on the bottom, causing it to glow, candle-like, from within. "Wa-lah!" he crowed.

"Oh my," she said, unable to manage anything else. Was there nothing on earth this child could not replace with inscrutable electronics?

"You don't have to light it," he said. "And you don't have to blow it out."

Anna widened her eyes at him comically. "And you don't have to burn down the house."

"That too, yeah." Jake smiled without losing his aura of parental resolve—an achievement, really, from someone almost sixty years her junior. How could she blame him for fretting about this? One afternoon last winter, after the first cold snap, he had come home from the gym to find her asleep in her chair, the remains of an amethyst candle dripping off the end table like a Dalí clock. She had not heard the end of it.

"Here's the cool part," he added brightly, soldiering on. "It's on a timer! You can make it turn on and off whenever you want. Amazeballs—right?"

She had wearied of this "amazeballs" business, but she let it pass; she was touched by the effort he'd put into this campaign. She regarded him benignly until she caught his gaze. "So this is the end of candlelight?"

He hesitated. "Well . . . if you wanna put it that way."

"How would you have me put it?"

"Jeez, Anna—the End of Candlelight? You just can't light stuff when I'm not around, that's all."

"I understand," she said calmly, because she did; some of her old playthings now required adult supervision. Her days were full of such small surrenders—why make a fuss over them? You could see them as loss, or you could see them as simplification. Her daughter Mona would have called this an act of faith, this Zen letting-go of familiar pleasures. Anna chose to think of it as leaving like a lady.

"I have bade farewell to flame," she declared, lifting her hand in a fluttery theatrical wave that she hoped would disguise any actual melancholy on her part. "And I am so much lighter for the journey."

He sighed with relief. "Thank you, but you have not . . . 'bade farewell to flame,' or whatever. There's gonna be plenty of flame in your life. Trust me."

This sounded so strangely purposeful that she was taken aback. "What on earth does that mean?"

"Nothing." Jake was blushing beneath his stubble, obviously mortified at having said more than he'd intended. He was helplessly chameleonic, this boy, forever blending in with his emotions. "It doesn't mean anything," he said.

"I'm not expecting a funeral pyre," she said.

He scowled at her. "That's not funny."

"Well, what does 'plenty of flame' mean?"

"It's just—you know, a figure of speech."

She knew Jake to be many things, but metaphorical was not among them.

They read in the parlor until bedtime, as was their custom. Anna was reuniting with an old friend from childhood: *Richard Halliburton's Book of Marvels.* Even now its bulk was downright biblical; it must have overwhelmed her as a child. She turned the yellowed pages slowly, past murky black-and-white photographs of Machu Picchu and the Taj Mahal, a dirigible tethered preposterously to the top of the Empire State Building. The illustrations had never impressed her, but the author's kinetic prose had more than compensated. His description of Iguazu Falls was a waterfall in its own right, a torrent of subordinate clauses that spilled off the page in a sibilant white mist. Mr. Halliburton, for all his swagger, had been something of a queen, and Anna had responded to that subliminal fact long before she had identified her own particular brand of royalty.

"Whatcha reading?" Jake was looking up from his magic slate.

"Halliburton."

He grimaced. "Dick Cheney's company?"

"No." She shuddered at the thought of that horrid little man invading her beloved tome. "The adventurer. Richard Halliburton."

No reaction from Jake.

"You know—who had himself declared a ship so he could swim the Panama Canal?"

He shook his head. "Nope."

"He was very handsome." She peered down at the image on the page, a sunburned blond sitting astride a camel. "He wasn't even forty when he died."

"What happened to him?"

Anna shrugged. "His junk disappeared."

"What? You mean . . ." Jake's brow was furrowed in confusion. "He was like . . . T or something?"

"No, dear. He was not 'like T or something.' " She leaned on the letter to convey her disdain for Jake's latest relabeling of their once-exotic species. "What on earth does that have to do with this?"

Her companion shrugged. "You said 'junk.' I thought . . ."

"Yes." She remained patient, assuming a more deliberate tone. "He was sailing a Chinese junk from Hong Kong to the World's Fair on Treasure Island. It was 1939. There was a typhoon at sea. They never found them."

"Them?"

"He had a captain and a crew. And a beau, Paul something, who wrote the books with him. They traveled the world together. I guess you could see it as wildly romantic. Two men deeply in love, lost at sea."

"How do you know they were deeply in love?"

"They'd better have been."

"What do you mean?"

"Well, it's preposterous otherwise. A Chinese junk? What on earth was the point? It wasn't a world record. They were just being *vivid*."

He gave her a lopsided smile. "But not if they were in love."

"It would help," she told him. "I'd be far less impatient with them." It was difficult, at her age, not to be a little put out with *everyone* for leaving.

Jake was silent for a moment. "How long have you had that thing?"

He meant the book. She ran her palm across it, as if comforting an old cur. "Since before I was me," she said. She lifted the book to her nose and inhaled the scent lingering in its cardboard bones: a hint of rosewater and Lysol that instantly genie-summoned the Blue Moon Lodge. It was Winnemucca condensed, this book, the only thing she owned that could still predictably take her from here to there.

Bet your book can't do that, she thought.

But she knew that Jake wasn't reading a book. She had heard the telltale cackling of his favorite game, the one with the evil birds and the catapults. The sound of it had bothered her until she'd learned to connect it to Jake himself, to his endless coltish curiosity. There were times, in fact, when she found it almost comforting, like a music box in a nursery. It meant that Jake was there.

"Are you winning?" she asked.

"You don't exactly win," he replied.

"Ah," she said, as she returned to her book.

No, you don't, she thought. You just get to the end.

Notch, her old rescue cat, sauntered into the room and climbed onto her lap. They dozed off together for a while. When she opened her eyes again, Jake was stretched out on the sofa. In the light of his magic slate his cheek was gilt-edged, Rembrandtesque. He seemed to be reading now, so she assumed it was his latest, a book called *American Gods* by an author with whom Jake had once tweeted in a state of delirious fandom. He had even read to her from this book, a passage about a man being swallowed by a giant vagina that had amused them both for entirely different reasons. Or perhaps, come to think of it, the same reason.

That was the lovely thing about Jake: he had come such a long way to meet her. For most of her life she had tried to imagine the company she'd be keeping at the end. There had been both men and women in those anxious/

hopeful visions (an ex-wife, a couple of old beaux, and the long-lost daughter she had found and then lost again), but she could never have imagined Jake. He had arrived out of nowhere, like a unicorn in a forest, this man-child who knew her journey as clearly as his own.

She fretted about him, though. He should be having his own life, his own evolving dream of last companions. He was well into his thirties and, since his hysterectomy two years earlier, had become a far more sociable creature. He even brought friends by the house these days—a varied ensemble, to say the least, some bejeweled of brow and brilliant of plumage, others swaggering in Elvis haircuts or prim as movie librarians, pop approximations of their psyches. They seemed fond of Jake, she was glad to see, and some of the ones with boys' names stayed the night.

That's what she fretted about: whether she was cramping his style.

"You know," she said, "the chair in my room is much more comfortable."

He glanced up at her distractedly. "What?"

"It's just as easy for me to read in my room."

"Now, you mean?"

"No, dear—when you have company. You should be able to entertain without having an anthropological exhibit in the corner."

He rolled his eyes. "Read your book."

"Do you understand me?"

Jake grunted.

"And you should know that when you have visitors in your room, I can't hear a thing. These old plaster walls are thick. There's no need to whisper. Just go about your business."

Jake's eyes narrowed suspiciously. "How do you know we're whispering? If you can't hear a thing."

"Don't talk back to your elders," she said.

Just before bedtime, Jake brought out the Volcano, a contraption that never failed to amuse Anna in every phase of its nonsensical operation. It was silver and squat—cone-shaped, like a mouse-size space capsule—and its purpose was to deliver the herb, superheated and free of smoke, into the clear plastic bag writhing above it. Once inflated, this voluptuously bobbing bladder would be removed and handed to Anna, who would puff (only once) on a mouthpiece that looked as if it belonged on a wind instrument of some sort, possibly a bagpipe. Jake invariably conducted this ritual with deadpan solemnity, so Anna, out of respect, tried to follow suit, though she could never shake the feeling that they were engaged in an East European clown act, or a fraternity prank involving rubbers and a tank of helium.

The Volcano had been a Christmas gift from a friend, a former tenant at her old house on Russian Hill. Mary Ann had spent her middle years in the East with a well-to-do Republican husband, only to return to the city on the brink of sixty with a pocket full of alimony and a heartbreaking need to ingratiate herself to the past. Jake had only to declare within earshot that fancy vaporizers of this ilk were "seven hundred fucking dollars," and Mary Ann was off and running. She'd presented it to them almost formally during a picnic lunch she'd organized at Occupy San Francisco. They had no place to plug it in, of course, so full appreciation had been postponed.

"What *is* this?" Anna was holding the valve of the balloon now. She half expected that, if released, it would fly around the room making farting noises.

"What is what?"

"The name. I enjoy the names."

"Oh." He picked up the shiny gold packet from the cannabis club. Its sleek design evoked something you might find in a Japanese grocery store. "Blue Dream," he said, reading the label. "Same as last time."

She inhaled the sweet smokeless cloud and held it for a moment. "Lovely," she said at last. "I think it's my favorite. The Purple Tush was a little oppressive."

Jake chuckled. "Kush."

"What?"

"Purple Kush, not tush." Jake took the balloon from her. "Purple tush—ugh."

She finally caught his gist. "*Oppressive* purple tush, no less."

He laughed like a child who had just been tickled.

"They must have an ointment for that," she added, wanting to prolong his mirth, but was promptly interrupted by the cricket chirping merrily in his jeans. He tugged his phone from his pocket and examined the surface. "It's Brian," he told her.

"Hey, dude," he said into the phone. "Yeah . . . where are you? . . . yeah, the Volcano . . . I know, right?" Jake laughed and turned back to Anna. "He says we're busted."

"Tell him I have a damn prescription," she said.

Jake handed her the phone, grinning. She held it up to where she thought it should go; she was no longer confident about these things. "It's Mary Ann's fault," she said. "We'd hurt her feelings if we didn't use this infernal contraption."

"Oh man," he said. "I miss you."

Those few words, gruffly uttered yet warm and familiar as buttered toast, were all she needed to construct an image of her former tenant: the emerald eyes and snowy hair, that sandpaper dent in his chin. "Where are you, dear?" she asked.

"Pacifica. Winnie can't go any further."

Who?

"The Winnebago," he explained, reading her silence. "I'm in an RV park."

"Ah."

"Our connection is shitty. I can barely hear you."

"Oh—all right then. I'll give you back to Jake."

"No, I wanna come visit. There's someone I want you to meet."

She knew what that *usually* meant, but with Brian you had to wonder. Could it be that the senior member of her brood, this perennially roving bachelor of (good heavens, no) sixty-seven, had finally found someone worthy of a permanent cuddle? The last time she had spoken to him (when he was parked somewhere in the Great Smoky Mountains), he had seemed placidly committed to his solitude. She had come to believe that his divorce from Mary Ann had forever soured him on cohabitation. Not to mention the fact that Brian had a lovely grown daughter from that marriage, and—to hear him tell it, at least—Shawna had always been family enough for him.

"Is this a new thing?" she asked.

"Yeah—fairly." He seemed amused by the thought. "Not really, though. We just sort of . . . picked up where we left off."

"Someone I used to know?"

"No . . . actually. Come to think of it."

"Now you're just being mysterious."

He laughed. "We'll make a date soon as I'm hooked up."

"Hooked up?"

"At the RV park! Gotta run, Mrs. Madrigal."

He was gone, so she handed the phone back to Jake.

"What's up?" he asked.

"He has a lady friend. He wants to bring her by to meet us." She fiddled with the cuff of her Chinese pajamas, pondering this enigma until she finally spoke it out loud: "It's someone he used to know. That I don't know."

"Does that bother you?"

"It puzzles me."

As soon as Jake had helped her into bed and doled out her pills, she found herself wondering why Brian had called her Mrs. Madrigal on the phone. It was an echo of her landlady days, curiously out of time, and she could only surmise that he had reverted to this formality for the benefit of his listening lady friend. These days she was on a first-name basis with all the members of her logical family, since the ever-shrinking distance between the middle of life and the end of it encouraged a level of informality. She had never been a Mrs. anyway. The honorific had been her way of further musicalizing her new name—the pleasing rhythm of "Mrs. Madrigal"—though she sometimes told those who had yet to learn of her past that single women are less likely to be harassed if they are thought to be widows or divorcees.

That was true enough, but there had been another motivation. She had assumed the Mrs. upon her return from Denmark in the 1960s not only to imply a respectable history but also to invent a shadow companion for her daunting new journey. She had married herself, in essence, so she would not be alone in her skin. "There never was a *Mr.* Madrigal," she used to tell her new tenants at 28 Barbary Lane, and that had certainly been the case from the very beginning. There had only been scared-silly little Andy Ramsey, the lone male resident of the Blue Moon Lodge and no one's idea of a mister, least of all his own.

Funny, she thought, sinking deeper into the folds of a wilting cannabis balloon. Blue Dream is not that far from Blue Moon.

Then, somewhere beyond the window, out in the white mirage of a desert afternoon, she heard the most curious thing.

It was the sound of a chicken squawking.

2

A Proper Gentleman

The chicken was in the pen out back, and the ruckus it was making woke Andy from an afternoon nap. They had not kept poultry for some time, so he figured Margaret was turning a trick with the Okie from down the road who sometimes paid in livestock. He wondered if Violet had heard the chicken and if she would be ugly about it at dinner and hurt Margaret's feelings again. Andy couldn't see why doing it for a good hen was any less respectable than doing it for a couple of bucks.

He rolled on his side and gazed at the window shade. It had darkened to amber during his nap, and the acacia bush swam against it like mint in a glass of iced tea. These hot afternoons made him languid and dreamy. They made him think about the Basque boy at the drugstore, with the raven locks and long eyelashes.

"Listen up, ladies!"

Margaret's voice. Addressing the various cabinettes.

"Who nabbed my Lysol?"

Not a good time to open the shade.

"Do you hear me, ladies?"

No reply.

"If I get knocked up—"

Explosive laughter. Probably Sadie's.

"I mean it," yelled Margaret.

"You ain't havin' no baby, Grandma." This time it was Violet being mean. Margaret was forty-five, the oldest girl at the Blue Moon, older even than Andy's mama, who ran the place, so the other girls could be spiteful. Andy figured they were jealous that Margaret had repeat customers. She was even asked for by name when college boys drove in from Reno, drunk as lords on casino gin.

Violet's wisecrack brought raucous laughter from the cabinettes, but there was no response at all from Margaret. Andy felt bad for her, so he cupped his hands and yelled through the shade. "There's a bottle of Lysol in the crapper."

Another silence, then Margaret spoke in a more subdued tone. "Now there's a gentleman."

Andy knew where this was leading. "Want me to get it?"

"Would you, lamb? If I move an inch, this tapioca is gonna make its way to glory." The urgency of the mission was underscored by the clanky flatulence of a jalopy coming to life just beyond the cabinettes. The customer was already leaving.

Andy hurried out to the crapper and found the bottle. By the time he got to Margaret's cabinette with a basin, there was only a distant plume of dust trailing out to the highway. Margaret was sitting on the edge of the bed in her peach camisole. She looked weary and resigned when he set the basin down beside her on the bed.

"That's gotta be watered down," she said.

He nodded. "Already done it."

"You *have*?" She touched the pee-colored solution with a look of tender amazement, as if he had just presented her with the Hope Diamond. "If that don't beat all," she murmured. "Where can I find one like you, Andy?"

He shrugged, since it wasn't really a question.

Margaret grabbed a sponge off the nightstand and dipped it into the basin, turning away from him as she began to scrub vigorously between her legs. Andy headed straight for the door, eyes to the floor, but Margaret was still talking.

"I swear. What did ladies do before Lysol?"

Another shrug.

"I ain't takin' any chances. That Okie has thirteen kids of his own."

Andy knew that already. Two of the girls were classmates at Humboldt High, compulsive gigglers who lived with their aunt on Mizpah Street. One of them had flirted with Andy on the bus the day before. He wondered if she would be trouble.

"Anyway," said Margaret, "we'll have us some eggs for breakfast."

"That'll be swell," he mumbled.

Margaret was still scrubbing away. "I know you like your eggs," she said.

Margaret knew lots of things about Andy. She knew things that happened before he was born, back when Mama was teaching piano in Rapid City and Margaret was her friend, working at the five-and-dime. Margaret had always claimed that they were both ready to get out of there, and the opportunity presented itself when Mama got pregnant by a piano pupil whose father was, in Margaret's words, "a big muckety-muck in the Chamber of Commerce and a hotheaded Greek to boot." Margaret's mean-as-a-snake husband had keeled over dead at the cement plant a week earlier, so she paid her debt to the Almighty by helping Mama through her ordeal. "She was our salvation in our flight from the Pharisees" was how Mama had put it, implicating the unborn Andy in this biblical-sounding event, but it would be years before he would learn that their midnight motor trip to Nevada had been paid for with cash Margaret had lifted from the notions counter at the five-and-dime.

He would learn this from Margaret, mind you, not Mama. Mama, when pressed on the matter, had said only that Andy's father was a "a hero of the Great War who succumbed to his wounds"—an explanation that, even at nine, Andy had found unconvincing, since he knew the radio show she was referencing. They had listened to it together, in fact, him and Mama, down in the parlor on a slow night. A doughboy and a crippled Irish girl finding true love in New York City, if only briefly.

It embarrassed Andy when Mama's lies became this bold, but he could see how a casualty of war would be easier to explain than some horny fifteen-year-old she had taught to play "Clair de Lune." Even now, Andy's paternity was vague in his mind, since he had never been able to put a grown man's face to that nubile phantom. Sometimes he would study the boys in the lunchroom at Humboldt High, other sophomores with vaguely Grecian features, and imagine them in

Rapid City with a younger version of Mama, but it led nowhere. Nowhere comfortable, at least.

Mama had been straight with Andy about her business. She was proud of *that* story. She and Margaret would tell it in tandem sometimes, playing to a crowd of rowdy customers in the parlor, Mama banging out the funny parts on the piano, shaking everything she had. They had been "two sweet-ass gals flying on a wing and a prayer," though, truthfully, that prayer had not been uttered until their third night in a Bridge Street hotel, when a railroad man, "a perfectly nice gent in a suit," offered Margaret five dollars to go upstairs and give him a blow job. Margaret had been a knockout back then, a genuine Swedish blond with cornflower-blue eyes who never forgot her makeup. It had been a natural mistake, Mama had insisted, what with all the plug-ugly women out here in the desert, but maybe it had also been a sign from heaven. Maybe a nice girl mistaken for something else had just been shown her true calling in life. Especially if she had gone upstairs as readily as Margaret had.

Their initial agreement had been simple: Mama would find the johns and take their money, and Margaret would "haul their ashes." There were already a few girls working in cribs on Bridge Street, so Mama took them under her no-nonsense wing, promising a steady income and protection from the johns. By the time Andy was born at Humboldt General in the spring of 1920, Mama was offering six ladies (including Margaret) and setting her sights on a big private spread out on the road to Jungo. The old house was already there, so Mama added the cabinettes, a semicircle of cinder-block huts painted with tall organ pipe cacti, though there was nothing remotely like them growing on that barren expanse. Folks just naturally expected "a touch of the Old West" when they drove out for pussy in the middle of nowhere, so Mona Ramsey intended to oblige them. (Mama used the third person when she got really fired up, as if she were talking about someone else entirely.)

Andy's first memory was not of the house, or even the huge neon moon Mama had erected by the highway, but the cool, vaulting interior of the Catholic church on Melarkey Street. At four, Andy was a little old for a christening (and Mama wasn't even Catholic), but St. Paul's had just been completed, and it was the grandest place in town, a Spanish-style edifice with towers like a castle. Mama wanted folks to see that her son was being raised a proper gentleman. To that end, Margaret had made him a christening outfit with Irish lace she ordered from Denver. Technically, it was a dress, since she had simply enlarged a McCall's pattern meant for babes-in-arms, but Andy had not complained. He had worn it all day, in fact, chasing a billy goat around the yard. He could still remember how fine it felt against his skin, and the flinty look in Mama's eyes when he refused to take it off.

When hard times came and poor folks headed west in droves, Mama never lost faith in the business. There were rumors in town that gambling was about to be legalized in Nevada, and she reckoned that was a good thing, since the fools who went bust at the tables would be even more needful of female consolation. She had been right, as usual. The Blue Moon Lodge thrived, gaining a fresh coat of paint and a scarlet slot machine in the parlor, shiny as a new Hudson and emblazoned with an Indian head. Customers came from as far away as Boulder City, where thousands of workers, predictably starved for ladies, were building a colossal new dam.

Lately, Mama'd had her mind set on gold. She had heard from old Mrs. Austin, whose husband ran the general store in Jungo, that Mr. Hoover himself, the former president, had arrived in a private railway car with an oilman from San Francisco and inquired about George Austin's claim in the Slumbering Hills. It was common knowledge, Mama said, that old George and his college-boy sons had been poking

in the ground up there. They had recently shipped
two bags of gold ore to the mint in San Francisco.
Everybody in town was talking about it, but Mrs.
Austin had been tight-lipped with Mama, saying
only that Mr. Hoover had been a regular feller and
that she had grown accustomed to famous folks when
she was a nurse in San Jose.

"The nerve o' that woman!" said Mama, wielding
her fork like a saber at the dinner table. "There she is,
sellin' chaw tobacco to the goddamn section hands, and
she's actin' all high-and-mighty with *me!*"

A tiny fleck of mashed potato flew off Mama's
fork and hit Violet square in her hennaed spit curl.
Margaret winked at Andy; Violet had not even
noticed.

"The ol' biddy is about to get filthy rich on that
claim," Mama added sourly. "And she don't even have
the decency to say so."

"What were you doin' in Jungo?" This was Delphine,
the back-talking Cajun girl, but Andy was wondering the same thing. Jungo was over thirty miles up
the road, a pissant little railroad junction that made
Winnemucca look like Gay Paree.

Mama was glowering now. "Hush up, Delphine."

"If you're lookin' to buy property, there ain't that
much poontang in Nevada."

"Delphine, I mean it. Another word out o' you and you're gettin' that fatty from Battle Mountain the next time he comes in for a dry bob."

Delphine stared down at her plate as a cautious silence fell over the table. Andy knew from experience that it was in everyone's interest to change the subject. None of these girls wanted to give a dry bob to the fatty from Battle Mountain.

"What famous folks?" he asked.

Mama frowned at him.

"Mrs. Austin," he explained. "Who did she know?"

This brought a grunt. "Some feller named London. Who cares?"

"*Jack* London?"

"I reckon. Yeah."

"Wow," Andy said under his breath.

"You heard o' him?"

"He wrote *The Call of the Wild*. We read it for English last year."

Mama stabbed a sweetbread with her fork and poked it into her mouth. "Well, don't go tellin' that ol' battle-ax. She's already too big for her britches."

A smile flickered at the corner of Margaret's mouth, but she managed to conceal it by turning toward Andy. "How was school, lamb?"

He shrugged. "Okay."

"You pass your history test?"

"A-minus."

"Get you," said Margaret, beaming. "You're heaps smarter than the rest of us."

Mama shot Margaret a crabby look. "Where do you think he got it from?" Mama had finished high school, while Margaret had dropped out early to go to beauty school in Rapid City. Mama used that dubious advantage to lord it over Margaret whenever they squabbled. Lately, there had been more squabbles than usual, though Andy was not sure why. Maybe Mama was just worn out.

"I saw the Watson girl at the post office today," Mama offered, reassembling her face to look more pleasant for Andy. "She asked after you."

He doubted this was true. If anything, Mama had probably raised the subject herself, since Gloria Watson's family was known to be well fixed. Her father was a doctor—a widowed doctor to boot—who had once conducted the monthly exams at the Blue Moon. Mama's coquettish overtures had failed to get a rise out of him (and most likely scared him off the job), so now she was working on his daughter.

"I think she's taken a shine to you, Andy."

Andy sighed so she could hear it.

"What's the matter with Gloria Watson?"

"Nothing. She's very nice. She's dating the class president, that's all."

"Well, that don't make no never mind."

Margaret glanced at Mama sideways. "Leave him be, Mona."

"Andy's a damn sight better-lookin' than any class president."

"Mona . . ."

"Well, look at him, Margaret. He could get any pretty girl he wants."

Andy rolled his eyes. "You're a stitch, Mama."

"Don't you sass me, kid. You know I'm right."

He stayed calm and smiling as he rose and took his plate to the sink. Half the time Mama was just spoiling for a fight, so he had learned not to engage her.

"I've got homework," he said, heading off to his room.

By nine o'clock the yard was full of cars, so Andy stayed in his room, reading under a lampshade printed with a map of the world. Down below he could hear the usual music from the Victrola, the usual howls from the customers and counterfeit squeals from the girls. Not an awful sound, really, just an awfully familiar one, and the wrong accompaniment to *Richard Halliburton's Book of Marvels*. He wondered if Mama truly wanted to go on like this forever, selling good-for-all-night tokens unto death, or if she ever dreamed of being somewhere else entirely. That would be fine with him, unless her escape plan involved the acquisition of a wealthy daughter-in-law, in which case leaving would be just as grimly unimaginable as staying.

He had just turned sixteen, though. There was still time to figure it out.

"You there, lamb?" Margaret was cooing from outside his door, so he invited her in. She was wearing a calf-length green velvet gown that was balding in places like the arm of an old settee. Her palomino hair was now loosely corralled on top of her head with bobby pins. She was holding a parcel about the size of a shoe box, wrapped in the funny papers and tied up with twine.

"Guess what's playin' at the American next week."

"What?" he replied, before snatching an answer out of the blue: "Charlie Chan."

She sat down on the edge of the bed, setting the parcel beside her. "Much better—Jeanette MacDonald!"

"Oh," he said, remembering. "*San Francisco*." He had passed the glass-encased poster on his way to Eagle Drugs, but the chance of laying eyes on the Basque boy again had dulled its impact considerably. "With Clark Gable."

" 'Together for the first time,' " said Margaret, quoting the poster.

Andy did not much care for Clark Gable, with his big tombstone teeth and wooden ways, even if he *had* starred in *The Call of the Wild*. (It was the dog that Andy had most admired in that film.) Jeannette MacDonald, on the other hand, was ladylike elegance itself and not to be missed under any circumstances.

"Wonder if she sings," he said.

"I expect so." Margaret gave him a winsome smile. "Wanna go on Saturday?"

"Sure."

" 'Less you've got a chum you'd rather take."

"No."

She clamped her hands on her knees and stood up. "Well, then—okay. It's a date." She headed for the door, leaving the parcel behind on the bed.

"What's that?" he asked.

She stopped in the doorway and silenced him with a finger to her lips. "Happy birthday, lamb. Latch the door behind me."

His heart was pounding wildly as he obeyed her order, pushing the metal hook into the rusty eye on the doorframe. He had used this latch hundreds of times before without giving it a second thought, but now, with the din of strangers rising from the parlor, it struck him as woefully inadequate for any secret worth keeping.

He went to the bed and sat where Margaret had sat, pulling the parcel into his lap. It was soft and squishy, obviously fabric, but lighter than the woolen shirt she had made him last Christmas or even the seersucker suit of an earlier birthday. The twine on the parcel was so tightly knotted that he finally gave up the effort and tore a hole in the news-paper—a *Maggie and Jiggs* comic in which Maggie, as usual, was chasing Jiggs with a rolling pin. Within seconds he had liberated the contents, a billowing cloud of lemon silk chiffon printed with roses in pale pinks and greens.

The betrayal blooming in his lap made his eyes dart to the door again. The latch was still firmly in place, but true reassurance came in the fact that Mama had turned off the Victrola and started play-ing the piano. That meant folks would stay put for a while. She was playing her favorite song, "Smoke Gets in Your Eyes."

He rose and went to the corroded mirror on the back of his closet door. The gown was long and sleeve-less. There were cape-like flounces at the shoulders and hand-rolled seams at the neckline, all of it diapha-nous as a dream from which he was sure to wake at any

moment. He slipped it over his head as Mama began
to sing.

They asked me how I knew my true love was true
I of course replied something here inside cannot
be denied . . .

The tissue-fine silk slid down Andy's body like a
lover's whisper.

3
One Guess

The RV park was a patch of asphalt wedged between the highway and the Pacific. Shawna found her dad's Winnebago easily enough, since he had rescued it from beige anonymity by slapping a Grateful Dead decal on the back. The RV was pointed toward the ocean, practically hanging ten off a crumbly cliff, and its view of the surf was clearly the reason he had chosen this particular park. There was not much to be said for Pacifica itself, a fog-bruised little suburb-by-the-sea, fifteen miles south of San Francisco, that seemed resigned to its mildew and plywood.

She rapped on the door several times, but no one responded, so she pulled her cell from her bag and called him.

"Hey, baby girl. You here?"

"Yep. Where are you?"

"In the laundry room."

Shawna chuckled. By his own account, her dad had once made a practice of picking up women in Laundromats. In fact he had picked up her mom in one, her biological mom, that is—the legendarily louche Connie Bradshaw—though Brian was not her biological father. (That honor fell to some dude Connie had met at the Us Festival, whatever that was.) Brian and his wife Mary Ann had inherited Shawna—and that was the right word—after Connie died of eclampsia in the hospital. Knowing she was dying, she had left her little girl to her "best friends," though their credentials had been skimpy at best. Brian had slept with Connie a few times, and Mary Ann, a fellow Clevelander, had crashed at Connie's apartment upon arrival in San Francisco. They both liked her, but she had never been their best friend. Brian, however, had fervently wanted a baby, so he regarded the infant Shawna as a seren-dipitous wonder. Mary Ann, not so much. After seven years of trying, she gave up completely and made Brian a single dad. A happy one, eventually.

Strangers tended to find this history confusing, but Shawna valued it greatly, and ached to know more about Connie. Mary Ann remembered little beyond the fact that Connie overused the word *fantabulous*. Brian said Connie cried after the sex the night they met, since nobody knew it was her birthday. He had cheered her up by sticking lit matches in a peanut butter sandwich and calling it a cake.

Her dad was a very sweet man. Always had been.

"Doing laundry?" she asked teasingly. "Did you get lucky?"

"Har dee har har."

"Shall I come there?"

"No. I'm on the way. Hang tight."

In less than a minute he was rounding the corner with a nylon laundry bag slung over his shoulder. That bag and his creased face and the muddle of snowy curls gave him the air of an old salt home from the sea—which, in effect, he was.

He dropped the bag and enfolded her in his arms. She mumbled "Hey, Dad" into his shoulder, catching a whiff of wet wool and some piney-smelling shampoo. She felt a curious sense of homecoming here on this unfamiliar bluff. She hadn't seen him for over a year, when he had parked the RV in Petaluma on his way to Cabo.

"So where is she?" she asked, wondering if her dad's new squeeze was cowering in the RV at this very moment, having chosen not to admit her.

"Taking a hike," he said.

She raised an eyebrow. "So soon?"

He did not find this funny in the least. "It's good for us," he said soberly, unlocking the door and leading the way into the RV. "I do it all the time myself. This buggy gets a little cramped sometimes. Even if you're—"

He cut himself off. *In love*, she thought. He wanted to say it, but it would have been too embarrassing at his age to put that enormity into words. He had survived one happily-ever-after, but just barely, and Shawna knew better than anyone how love-shy Mary Ann had made him. Even after all these years.

"I've got fizzy apple juice," he said, dropping the laundry bag and opening the door of his mini-fridge.

"That's okay. I'm fine." She collapsed into one of the beige swivel chairs.

"You sure?"

"Yeah."

He settled in the other chair. "I talked to Anna last night. She sounded good."

Shawna shrugged. "She's okay."

"What the matter?"

"She's ninety-fucking-two, Dad."

"She's not sick, though?"

"No—just kinda . . . packing up."

He took that in glumly, saying nothing.

She stroked the arm of the chair, comforting something inanimate in lieu of the more vulnerable human alternative. "We have to honor it, Dad. Anything else would just make her feel alone. We have to—"

She didn't finish, so he did it for her. " 'Drive her to the station and wave good-bye.' " He was quoting Mrs. Madrigal herself. Their long-ago landlady had hit them with that sobering train metaphor a few years back. They were not to make a fuss, she had told them, but she wouldn't mind having "family on the platform."

Shawna sighed. "How can she be more chill than we are?"

Her dad shrugged. "Always has been. About everything."

There was a long silence before she said, "Got anything stronger?"

"Stronger than what?"

"Apple juice."

"Oh . . . sure, kiddo." He sprang to his feet and pulled a bottle of scotch from the cupboard, filling a couple of café glasses and handing one to her as he sank back into the chair. "Number four on the *Times* list. Worth celebrating!"

She knew he meant that, but something in his smile made her wonder if they *both* had something to share today. If so, it was probably best to let him go first.

"I wanna tell you about Wren," he said.

Oh shit. Here we go. She's younger than I am. She's painfully shy. She's a raving fundamentalist who was horrified by my degenerate novel.

"Beautiful name," she offered at last. "Wren, like the bird?"

"Yeah." He took a slug of his scotch. "We hooked up on Facebook."

"Mmm . . . racy."

"Just shut up and listen, smarty-pants."

"Okay . . . sorry."

"Here's the deal: I met her years ago—when you were still a kid, and I was with Mary Ann. We never—you know—did anything, but . . . we had a moment."

She seriously doubted this. Her dad had a princely heart, and certainly more than a few "moments" over the years—but they had traditionally come *after* he bagged someone, not before. "C'mon, Dad. I don't care if you did anything."

"You may not care, but I want you to know why we didn't. Sex was the last thing on my mind. I thought I had AIDS, and . . . Wren was wonderful about it. Gallant, really. I never forgot how kind she was."

That stopped her cold. "Why did you think you had AIDS?"

"I was sleeping with someone who had it. Who died of it." He hesitated a moment. "It was nothing serious—for either of us. She was just—you know . . ."

"A fuck buddy."

"Yeah."

"Did she know about it?"

"Did who know about what?"

"Did Mary Ann know about the fuck buddy?"

"No, never—as far as I know. I was planning to tell her, but . . . she left me. She left *us*. It was kind of a moot point by then."

"So why have you never told me?" This was what bugged her: he had violated their full disclosure contract. There was nothing he didn't know about *her*, after all, thanks to her former blog, *Grrrl on the Loose*. He knew about her playmates, male *and* female, during her undergraduate days at Stanford. He knew about her stint selling dildos at Mr. S Leathers, and the peep show in North Beach where—briefly, very briefly, for journalistic purposes—she had dressed as a Catholic schoolgirl and diddled herself in a booth for the pleasure of customers at the Lusty Lady. He knew about her bout with chlamydia, for fuck's sake. It wasn't fair. His unnecessary little secret left her feeling oddly betrayed.

"I'm not some delicate flower, Dad." She took a sturdy sip of her scotch, as if to prove the point.

"I know. I should have told you, but—there was very little reason to bring it up. I thought that chapter was closed forever."

"Until—what? You saw her on Facebook?"

"YouTube, actually."

"Doing *what*?"

"She was on *Johnny Carson*—once upon a time." He gazed at her like a soulful spaniel. "Do you even remember Johnny Carson?"

"I'm twenty-nine, Dad, not twelve. What was she doing on Johnny Carson?"

"She was a model. A big one. A large one, I mean." He made an expansive gesture with his hands.

"Like—plus size?"

"Yeah, except they didn't have 'em back then. Wren was sort of a pioneer. She was all over the tube for a while. *Carson*. The *Donahue Show*. They called her 'The World's Most Beautiful Fat Woman.' "

She was certain he was fucking with her. "Shut the front door."

When Shawna was a kid, her dad had claimed that there were miles of secret tunnels under Chinatown, that some of the city's wild parrots were over a hundred years old, that Coit Tower had been designed to resemble the nozzle of a fire hose. These were widespread San Francisco myths, so her dad had left them blithely unchallenged. He had been more committed to her amusement than to the truth.

"I'll show you the YouTube," he said flatly.

There was no arguing with that. "So . . . where did you meet her?"

"At the Russian River. I was waiting for the results of my AIDS test. It took a couple of weeks back then, and I didn't wanna . . . I mean, it would have been awkward with Mary Ann, since we were still very . . . you know, sexually active."

She left that alone.

"So Michael took me under his wing. He had already tested positive himself, so we went up to the river together. He met Wren at a gay resort."

"She was bi, you mean?"

He shook his head. "She just liked being recognized. She was very big with the gay guys."

"So to speak."

"That's just the sort of joke *she* would make."

He was sounding a little defensive, so Shawna tried to make amends. "She sounds cool, Dad. I'm not throwing shade."

Pokerfaced, he regarded her for a moment. "I'm sure I'd find that comforting, if I knew what it meant."

She smiled and translated: "I wasn't trashing her, Dad. C'mon. I used 'throwing shade' in the novel."

"You used lots of things in that novel. I just don't speak Elvish."

She flinched, since some reviews of *pvt msg* had been similarly snide. Mostly the boomer critics, of course, who had come late to the party, and were pissed off that someone so young and unknown had written a novel composed entirely of text messages. They mocked the cryptic slang and the soullessness of the lowercase abbreviations as if those devices had been totally unintentional. She had hoped, at the very least, to be recognized as a new experimentalist, but they had treated her more like a Kardashian than a Kerouac.

"Did you really hate it?" she asked.

Funny how his opinion still mattered the most.

"C'mon, Shawna, I loved it. I couldn't stop reading it. I told you that already. I just don't understand all the words."

She was feeling way too needy now, so she let it drop. "Anyway, I think it's great that you've found someone. I'm thrilled for you."

A slow, sleepy smile from the old man. "Totes?"

"Yep . . . totes."

"See? My lingo's improving."

"Did you learn that in *pvt msg*?"

He gave her a crooked grin. "You think people talk that way around here?" He gazed out the window at the sea where the fog was finally lifting. The pewter skies were slashed open along the horizon, revealing innards of startling blue. Turning back to her, he said, "So what do you think? Do I look like a husband?"

She saw her opening and took it. "More like a grand-father, actually."

He drew back. "Well . . . thanks for that."

"No," she said, smiling. "I mean . . . how would you like that?"

His brow was still furrowed in confusion.

"I'm gonna have a baby, Dad!"

She'd been prepared for any number of reactions, but not the look of abject horror that transformed her father's face before he snatched the glass of scotch from her hand. "What the hell are you doing, then?"

"No, no." She found his panic attack endearing. "I'm not pregnant now. I'm just planning on it."

"Planning on it," he echoed, collecting himself.

"I wanna be a mom, Dad. And I wanted you to be the first to know. I think I'd be good at it . . . and I've made enough money from the novel to support us."

"Us being . . . you and the baby?"

"Yes."

"Is there a boyfriend I don't know about? A girlfriend?"

"Nope." She smiled placidly. "Not a one."

"So . . . not the clown guy."

"No. That's been over for years. And, for the record, he wasn't a clown guy, he was a clown."

This was followed by a silence that could genuinely be described as pregnant. Finally her dad said, "So . . . we're talking . . . insemination?"

She nodded. "Thanks for not saying 'artificial.' I hate that."

"No . . . it's just as real as the other kind, I guess. Just more purposeful." He was trying his best to be hip about this, and Shawna was touched by the effort.

"Anyway," she said. "It's not like I'm afraid of single parenthood. I know I'd be good at it. I had the best role model in the world."

He shrugged off the compliment, then gulped down the rest of his scotch. "So how do you go about this? A sperm bank or something?"

This was another term that sounded clinical and old-fashioned to Shawna's ears. "These days," she said gently, "it's more like a private deposit."

"A friend or something?"

"Yeah. But I haven't asked him yet, so . . . it's nothing definite." She thought it prudent to refrain from elaboration. "I do know *where* I want it to happen."

"Where you want *what* to happen?"

"The Eurovision Song Contest . . . Dad, c'mon! Are we on the same page here?"

He was squirming a little, she realized. "You've picked a place for your insemination?"

"Yes! And you've been there!"

"Well . . . that's a relief."

She laughed. "You're no fun! C'mon, guess!"

"This is not my idea of a parlor game."

"Well, it's not much of a parlor either. C'mon, one guess. There's a big fire involved. And it's very flat and dusty."

His answer, when it came, was equally flat and dusty. "Burning Man."

"Awriight."

"No, not all right. That's a terrible idea."

"Why? You've been there yourself! You couldn't stop raving about it. You said it was a deeply spiritual experience."

"Six years ago! It's completely out of control now. It's a fucking mosh pit in the desert! It's gonna be eighty thousand people or something."

"Sixty," she said. "And this year's theme is Fertility 2.0. It's perfect!"

"Perfectly unhygienic."

She sighed noisily. "It's a conception, Dad, not a delivery."

Her father tilted his head in defeat. "Whatever. You're right."

"I want to mark the moment, that's all. I want my child to know that it was—you know—completely intentional. And there will be friends around, so—"

She was interrupted by the *whack* of an opening door. The woman who climbed into the RV was fiftyish and luscious in a blowsy Wife of Bath kind of way. Her gray hair was gathered into a ponytail, her waist cinched with a wide green belt that caught the color of her eyes and hoisted her ample breasts into full display.

She wasn't especially fat, but she wasn't thin either.

"I'm Wren Douglas," she said, extending a small, pink-varnished hand to Shawna, "and you're my new favorite writer."

Shawna could feel herself blushing. "Well . . . thanks."

"And guess what?" Brian blurted. "She's gonna make you a grandmother."

Shawna glared at her father with teen-style indignation until simple astonishment won the moment. "You're *married*, you mean?"

"Last week in Santa Fe." Wren waggled a finger wrapped in a turquoise-and-silver ring. "He wouldn't put out until we made it official." She laughed throatily.

"He said, 'If you want it, then you better put a ring on it.' "

Her father's grin was sheepish but without shame. "That's sorta true."

"So you're pregnant, huh?" Wren had moved on jauntily without missing a beat. "That's great! What a gorgeous child you're gonna have!"

Further elaboration would have been much too intimate with this stranger, so Shawna just widened her eyes in mute appreciation.

There were times when she seriously wanted to clobber the old man.

4

Darkwad

"So what's the book about?" Ben asked pleasantly without lifting his eyes from his sewing machine.

It already seemed like "his" machine, Michael realized, though they had bought it only yesterday at Serramonte Mall, and Ben had never sewn so much as a trouser hem in all his forty years. But that had not stopped him from leaping into the mysteries of bobbins and threaders with the same bravado he'd no doubt brought to outboard motors and snowmobiles in his adolescence.

Michael, by contrast, was still intimidated by the Kindle in his hands.

"A bunch of high school girls," he answered, describing Shawna's new best-seller. "It's all done in text messages. So far, they're nasty little shits."

"Doesn't that get old?"

"Well, yeah. Nasty little shits do."

"I mean, the text messages."

"Oh—you'd think so, but . . . you get used to it. It becomes its own language. The cruelty is more pronounced because everything's abbreviated."

Ben just murmured, absorbed in his sewing.

"It's creepy as hell," Michael added, "but it's hard to put down."

"They kill one of their classmates, right?"

Michael winced and rolled his eyes. "Not. That. I. Know. Of. Betsy Ross. Thanks for the spoiler alert."

Ben grinned, exposing the gap between his two front teeth. "Sorry. Just read it in a review."

"That's why I haven't read the reviews."

"Shit, fuck, piss!"

Michael checked to make sure this outburst of Tourette's had not been directed at him. Ben, to his relief, was addressing his sewing machine, thereby validating the possessory pronoun. He and Mr. Singer were having their first fight.

"This fucker is supposed to be heavy-duty. The clerk told us it could handle EL wire."

There was nothing useful Michael could add. He had only just learned about EL wire—electroluminescent wire, the magic plastic filament that made clothing and bicycles dazzle like Christmas trees. Ben was sewing a coil of it on the back of a patchwork jacket they had bought at a Tibetan shop in the Castro.

"It's this cotton," Ben added in a calmer tone. "It bunches up, and the needle gets stuck."

"You know," Michael offered, "I like the jacket on its own. It doesn't need anything on it. And I could wear it after Burning Man."

Ben wasn't buying it. "You have to be lit, baby. It's dangerous otherwise. It's pitch-black out there on the playa."

"But won't all that stitching fuck it up?"

Ben looked up. "It'll fuck *you* up if you get run over by an art car."

Michael had already seen enough photos of Burning Man to imagine himself being mowed down by a disco bus full of half-naked hippie chicks—reduced to a grease spot on a vast Nevada alkali flat. He could see that quite easily.

"You don't want to be a darkwad," Ben added.

"A what?"

"That's what they call people who don't light themselves."

Michael cringed inwardly. *Darkwad.* They had *names* for their miscreants, just like at summer camp or on *Survivor.* This temporary city of liberated souls, for all its "radical self-expression," had rules out the ass. Some of them made sense, like Leaving No Trace (cleaning up after yourself) and Decommodification (not selling things to each other), but Michael sensed a creepy expectation of allegiance. It was like school spirit back in high school. He didn't have it then, and he didn't have it now. To him, the biggest advantage of being queer was being queer.

"Come," said Ben. "Try this on."

Michael followed orders, holding his arms akimbo while Ben adjusted the wiring. The jacket was tight around the waist. He felt tubby and preposterous, like Wavy Gravy being suited for the Fourth of July parade in Bolinas. Ben, of course, had looked as smart as a tin soldier when he tried on his metallic silver jacket at a retro shop on Haight Street. Get over yourself, thought Michael. He's always going to be younger than you. Have eight years of marriage taught you nothing?

"That looks so cool," said Ben.

"Does it?"

"Here, check it out." Ben led him, tethered, to the hall mirror so he could see the amber mandala glowing ecstatically on his back. It *was* cool. And all the more so because Ben had made it for him, toiling for two nights at this genteel sweatshop on the crest of Noe Hill. "That's amazing, sweetie."

Ben studied his handiwork, skimming his hand across the top of his sandy brush-cut head. "It's not bad, is it?" He handed Michael the controls, a small oblong box. "Keep it in your pocket. You can turn it off and on or make it blink."

Michael was now preoccupied by a niggling, high-pitched sound, like a mosquito keening in his ear. "What's that?"

"What?"

"That noise."

"Oh. You won't hear that when you're there."

"Why won't I hear it when I'm there?"

"Because it's kinda . . . noisy. A lot of the camps play music all night. The sound of the EL wire will blend right in. You won't even notice it."

Swell, thought Michael.

"I've bought us earplugs for sleeping. And we can take the wave machine with us."

The wave machine, with its faux-oceanic lullaby, made its home on Michael's bedside table. That's where it belonged, he felt, forever and ever. Why should they have to import the sound of crashing surf to the middle of the Black Rock Desert?

"Will I have a place to plug it in?" he asked feebly.

"It works on batteries too. Why are you being so grumpy?"

"Have I said anything?"

"Yeah. More or less. You have." Ben caught his eye in the mirror. "I thought you wanted to do this?"

"I do."

"But?"

"I dunno . . . it sounds more and more like a party I can't go home from. I've never liked an all-nighter, Ben, and this is . . . an all-weeker. I get tired of people and noise. Even when I was young, I went home early to Barbary Lane."

"You said you left the baths at dawn sometimes."

Michael shrugged. "That was different."

"Oh, yeah?"

"It wasn't noisy."

Ben laughed.

"Not in that way," Michael added with a smirk.

Ben slipped the jacket off Michael's shoulders like a tailor done with the fitting. "It's really peaceful on the playa. We can ride our bikes out there and be totally alone. It's like being on the moon or something. Just the two of us."

The image was seductive, except, of course, for the bike part. Michael hadn't ridden one in years, so he was already concerned about looking clumsy on the pink clunker Ben had found for him on Craigslist. Add to that the presence of large menacing vehicles and thousands of other bikers who assumed he knew what he was doing, and you had a recipe for abject panic. At least it'll be flat, he told himself.

"Which reminds me," said Ben, returning to his sewing machine. "We should go on the Naked Bike Pub Crawl."

All Michael could manage was a snort.

"Seriously, honey. Wouldn't that be fun?"

"No. It would not."

"Why not?"

Michael returned to his armchair before composing his answer. "Okay, first of all, naked—my flabby white ass on a bicycle seat. Second of all, pub crawl—*drunk* on a bicycle, right? Naked and drunk on a bicycle. Tell me when we get to the fun part. I'd kill myself, honey. In a hot minute. I'd die an ignominious death."

Ben smiled. "I bet Shawna will do it."

"Oh, well, there's a safe enough bet. She'd do that in the *city*."

"You sound like a prissy old uncle."

True enough, thought Michael. He had known Shawna since she was a baby. He had become a sort of coparent, in fact, when his old friend Mary Ann made a single dad out of his old friend Brian. He and Brian had doted and fussed and fretted over that child—and later the teenager—to such a degree that the fretting had never stopped. Ben regarded Shawna simply as a hip woman less than ten years his junior. The thought of her naked on a bicycle didn't make him nervous in the least.

"As I recall," Ben added, "you used to get naked all the time."

"When?"

"You know . . . at the nude beach. Devil's Slide. With Mona. You told me so."

"That was before you were born . . . practically." Michael felt a pang at the mention of his old roommate. Cynical, loyal Mona, with her rusty Brillo Pad hair and thrift shop finery. Mona who took no shit and took no prisoners. She'd been gone for a dozen years, her ashes scattered on a Cotswold hillside, but she was right there in the room with him, breathing taunts in his ear, wondering how he'd turned out to be such a scaredy-cat—*such a fucking pussy*—in his twilight years.

"It was Mona who got naked at the beach," he said, correcting Ben. "I wanted a tan line."

"What about three years ago in Tulum?"

"What about it?"

"You got naked then."

"That was around the pool."

Ben grinned. "So a body of water is required for your nakedness?"

"An absence of *family* is required, Ben. Shawna is family. It feels . . . borderline somehow."

"We'll have our tent. We'll have privacy. Anyway, Shawna has friends in at least three other camps. We'll probably never see her."

Michael looked down at the Kindle aflame in his hands, considering its twisted tale and the bright young woman who had somehow brought it to life.

It made him proud and nervous at the same time.

"I've been thinking," said Ben, later that night in bed.

Michael's gut clenched. "I've been thinking" was often the preamble to change of some sort, and Michael didn't much care for change. He had his life the way he wanted it, more or less. He was happily married; he was still surviving the plague that had wiped out half the people from his past; hell, he was still surviving the meds that had given him a future. He didn't want that messed with. At all.

"Don't leave me," he said, hoping that his darkest fear could convincingly masquerade as total flippancy.

Ben chuckled, pulling him closer. "This bed really sucks."

"What do you mean? It's a Tempur-Pedic."

"I know what it is, and I know how much we paid for it, but it's just not cutting it, honey."

Thank you, Jesus. It's the bed. It's not me.

"What's the matter with it?" Michael asked. "It's memory foam. It's comfy as all get-out. It molds to your body."

"It molds to *your* body."

Michael still didn't get it. "And yours too, right?"

"Yeah, but . . . when people cuddle all night the way we do . . . and when one of them is—no offense—heavier than the other . . . it forms, you know, a trench that the other one sort of . . . falls into. It's not a good thing."

There was so much about this explanation that Michael found charming, but he went for the obvious: "*No offense?* Like I don't *know* I'm fatter than you are?"

Ben chuckled. "Well, yeah, of course you do, but . . . I didn't know if you were aware of—"

"The Trench," said Michael, capitalizing it for extra drama.

"Yes." Ben grinned. "The Trench from Hell."

"Damn. That bad?"

"Pretty much."

Roman, their Labradoodle, loped into the room and sprang onto the bed between them. He knew their nightly routine as well as they did, maybe even better. Michael scratched him behind his ear, where dense charcoal hair, despite their best efforts at grooming, was clumped like an old fisherman's sweater.

"You don't feel a trench, do you, Mr. Dood?"

"Give Dad a kiss," Ben told the dog.

Still standing on the bed, Roman accepted this assignment with quiet resignation, dragging a broad pink tongue across Michael's ear. How and when Ben had taught him this trick was lost in the mists of time, but it still retained its charm. Roman knew exactly who "Dad" was (at least in this instance), and he'd been known to bestir himself from a comfortable chair across the room, stopping only for a downward-facing fart, before planting a single perfunctory kiss on Michael's face.

"We can't afford a new mattress," said Michael.

"I know," said Ben.

Of course he knew. Ben was the one keeping them afloat, the one who had stalled foreclosure on their mountain property in Pinyon City and footed the bill on Michael's recent dental implant. Ben's furniture company, thanks to a lone Twitter executive with a passion for *tansus* was their most reliable source of income. Michael's gardening business wasn't exactly belly-up, but it wasn't thriving either. His younger partner Jake Greenleaf had done most of the grunt work lately.

Gardeners aged better than athletes, but their bodies betrayed them the same.

"Can you handle the trench a bit longer?" Michael asked.

Ben smiled sleepily and pecked him on the mouth. "Long as it takes, bambino." He pushed his foot through the sheets, across the very trench itself, twiddling his toes against Michael's in an act of reassuring monkey-love.

"I'll lay off the jam in the morning," Michael told him.

Ben chuckled, then fell silent until he suddenly remembered something. "Oh—did you get the message from Shawna?"

"No. On the machine?" Lately, like everyone else he knew, Michael had lost the habit of checking the landline. "What did she want?"

"Dunno. Just said to call her. I figured it was about Burning Man."

This didn't seem very likely to Michael. "Why would she call me? You're the boss of that."

"Is that right?"

"I didn't mean it like that. We're in this together. I just—"

"Whatever." Ben was obviously hurt, but his fallen features stopped short of a pout.

Michael felt awful. Ben had wanted this to be a communal effort, a grand adventure that would change their lives forever, but Michael's careless words had divorced him from the effort. There were times, he felt, when he didn't deserve this man at all.

"Don't listen to me," he said, apologizing with his toes. "I'm just a darkwad."

5
Home Free

There was a restaurant near Anna's apartment in the Duboce Triangle, so Brian took Wren there before their visit. It was a corner place with a French staff, a bistro with an alchemical blend of silk lampshades and dark red walls. They looked out on lush summer sycamores turned rusty under the streetlights.

"Seems like her kind of place," Wren observed, popping a *pomme frite* into her mouth. "From what you've told me about her, anyway."

Brian was thinking the same thing, having already felt certain echoes of Barbary Lane. "I invited her," he said with a shrug. He liked Wren's face in this light, the way her own glow fused with the room's. "She said to join her for dessert."

"She's not that mobile, huh."

"Yeah, but mostly I think she wanted to receive you at home."

"Ah."

"Sort of a tradition for newcomers."

"Now you're making me nervous."

He reached across the table to squeeze her small, well-manicured hand. His own hand was piebald with spots, most of them too freeform to be written off as freckles. Liver spots, his dad had called them, back when Brian was still in law school and the old man was feeling his age. *Liver spots.* There had to be a better term, something that invoked a life robustly lived. Steak spots? Burger spots?

"Don't worry about Mrs. Madrigal," he told Wren. "She'll get you, I promise."

"I feel like I'm meeting your mother," she said.

In a way, of course, she was. Not the mother who had died of cancer when he was barely thirty—the Irish housewife from Harrisburg who collected spoons from every state—but the mother who had surreptitiously given him a home in a new city when he was too strung out on women to notice. Anna had been his stealth mother.

Wren fussed with the low neckline of her blue velvet dress. "You sure this outfit's not too much?"

"Are you kidding? It's right on the nose. She was raised in a Nevada whorehouse."

Wren raised an eyebrow, but it was comically intended and more in curiosity than indignation. "And why have you never told me that?"

He shrugged. "Thought I had." The truth was, he thought he'd told her everything. He *wanted* to tell her everything. His new aim in life was to tell her everything. "She ran away when she was young," he explained. "Sixteen."

"Why?"

Sort of an odd question, he thought. "If you were a boy who felt like a girl, would you want to grow up in that environment?"

She pondered the issue for a moment. "Seems as good as any. Depends on the whorehouse, I guess."

Her cavalier tone made him smile.

"Seriously, women as a rule are kinder than men. Sorry, babe, but you know it's true. A kid like that would do much better in a whorehouse than . . . you know, a military academy." She picked up another *frite*. "Did she have family there?"

Brian sawed on a corner of his filet mignon. "Her mother was the madam."

Wren absorbed that for a moment. "Did she love her?"

"Did who love whom?"

"Either one. Mother or daughter. Son, whatever."

"Not for a long time. Maybe. Who the hell knows? They didn't reunite until the seventies. Mona bumped into her on a bus to Reno and got a job answering phones at the Blue Moon. When she figured out their lineage, she brought the old lady back to Barbary Lane. Sorta forced the issue. It wouldn't have happened if—"

"Wait! Bumped into the mother? The madam?"

"Yeah, the mother, the madam." He knew this was bound to take a while, so he popped a morsel of steak into his mouth and chewed it.

"And Mona was Anna's daughter? The one who married the English lord and . . . passed away in England?"

"Yep."

"So she bumped into her own grandmother on the bus to Reno?"

"Right."

"And reunited her with Anna, who used to be . . . Mona's father."

"*Exactemente.*"

Wren tilted her head and widened her tigress eyes. "Jesus Christ, you people are complicated." She reached out with the corner of her napkin and, delicately, did minor repairs to the corner of his mouth.

"You realize most brides have an easier time sorting out their in-laws?"

He smiled. "It makes more sense if you've lived it."

Anna's parlor (as she liked to call it) had been prepped for their arrival: pillows plumped, lighting adjusted, a silver tray of sherry and shortbread laid out on the coffee table next to a red lacquer bowl full of joints. Brian had expected Jake to greet them at the door, since that had been the custom lately, but there she was in all her bohemian glory, spiffed up in Chinese pajamas and wobbling precariously. He hadn't seen her for months, so the hug he gave her was part reunion, part rescue.

"It's all right, dear," she said, patting his back. "I've got it."

With that, she tottered toward her chair. Brian saw Wren move to offer assistance, but he stopped her with a glance and a shake of his head.

"You're lovely," said Anna, still inching away from them.

Wren looked thrown. "Me?"

"Yes, dear. Brian doesn't like it when I call him lovely."

Wren chuckled nervously and glanced at Brian as Anna pivoted slowly and free-fell into her chair.

(The lavender fabric on its scalloped back had grown shiny from many such landings.) Anna took a moment to catch her breath before lifting her hand to Wren like a dowager empress. "What the hell took you so long?"

Wren, who had dialed down her usual megawattage, looked almost mortified as she took Anna's hand. "Sorry. They were a little slow with the check."

"What?" Now Anna looked confused.

Brian scrambled to restore communications. "I think," he said, glancing at Wren, "she meant that remark in the broader sense."

"I meant," said Anna, gazing up at the velvet-sheathed hourglass whose hand she was still gripping for punctuation, "this boy has been a tramp. A *vagabond*. I've been worried about him. You took your time getting here, dear."

Brian tried to translate: "Not you *specifically*, of course—"

Anna shot him a withering look. "Yes, her specifically. She's *exactly* what I pictured. The hair, the shape, the placement of the eyes, everything."

"Well . . . good," Wren said awkwardly as her hand was released. "That's great to hear."

"She gets kinda spooky about that shit," Brian explained.

Wren glanced at him slack-mouthed, unfamiliar with his longtime sparring partnership with the rail-thin old woman in the chair.

"Before you know it," Brian added, "she'll claim she conjured you up with a love potion and some juju dust."

Anna gave Wren a weary sisterly look. "He's so tiresome sometimes. Sit over there, Brian, and have a joint or a cookie or something. I want to talk to your wife."

She had unbalanced him exactly the way she wanted. "How did you know we were married?"

"A soothsayer," Anna said curtly. "How do you think?"

Shawna, thought Brian. Or Michael had heard it from Shawna and told Anna. Brian had not yet spoken to Michael, so he hoped he approved, that Michael's memories of Wren, all these years after that week at the river, were good ones.

Anna had turned her attention back to Wren. "How was L'Ardoise?"

"Scrumptious," said Wren, pulling up a chair to Anna's throne. "I eat way too many fries when they have a fancy French name for them."

Anna nodded. "What does that mean, anyway, 'L'Ardoise'?"

Wren screwed up her face, pretending to ponder the question. "I think it's the feminine form of *lard-ass*."

An odd chortle, uncharacteristically male, erupted from the back of Anna's throat.

Brian realized with a rush of relief that Wren was already home free.

In the old days Mrs. Madrigal had named her home-grown pot after strong women she admired. There was one in particular Brian remembered—a certain Miss Stanwyck—that could knock his socks off and keep them off for hours until he returned to 28 Barbary Lane from his vulpine prowls at Thomas Lord's or Henry Africa's. If Mrs. Madrigal was still up and about (as she often was, reading or even watering her garden in the dark) she would join him for a toke of Miss Stanwyck. She wasn't smoking with them tonight, but she had not forgotten her manners.

"So who's this lady?" he asked, passing the doobie back to Wren.

Anna smiled. "You've forgotten her name already?"

Brian laughed. "Not *that* lady. The one in her hand."

"Oh . . . I didn't name it," Anna said. "Jake bought it at the medical pot place. They come with their own names when you buy them. Like tea. Or hookers."

"You're funny," said Wren.

"What did I tell you?" said Brian. Even as he spoke, he knew how overeager he sounded, like a little kid showing off an old friend to a new one.

"I grew up with hookers," Anna added. "I assume he told you that."

"He did, yes."

After an interlude of silence, Anna said, "Lysol."

"What?"

"The whole damned place smelled like Lysol." Wren's nose wrinkled, but she ended with a shrug. "Better than the alternative, I suppose."

Anna chuckled and looked at Brian. "This one's no shrinking violet."

"I'm no stranger to hooking either." Wren was on a roll now, he realized, obviously feeling the pot. "I mean . . . long as we're sharing."

Anna's eyes widened. "Do tell."

Brian was starting to squirm a little. "She only did it once."

"Once is all it takes," said Anna. "Go on, dear."

"He was a nice old guy who liked his ladies big, so . . . he made an outright offer. It paid for my vacation, and he had a good time. I'm not sorry."

"That's how she met me," said Brian.

Anna's brow furrowed. "You were the nice old guy?"

"No, no!" Brian laughed. "She was up at the Russian River with him. I was up there for a week—"

"—with Michael," said Anna, finishing the thought. "Back in the eighties."

"So he's filled you in?" Of course he has, thought Brian. How could he restrain himself?

Anna nodded. "He's excited about seeing Wren again. He was quite a fan, apparently, even before he met her."

Good, thought Brian. Michael approves, and Shawna approves, and Anna knows Wren had a career outside of hooking. He was checking off the members of his family one by one, letting the pieces fall into place. (His ex-wife Mary Ann would be a tougher sell—not because she was his ex but because Wren had once been a guest on *Mary Ann in the Morning* and remembered her interviewer as condescending and uptight— an impression that would not have been off the mark twenty-five years ago. Brian liked Mary Ann these days, but he had never been in the same room with both his wives and did not intend for that to happen anytime soon. Why risk it? *Start with easy ones, man.*

"Where's Jake?" he asked Anna. "I thought we'd see him tonight."

"He's out with his friends, being deeply mysterious."

"How so?" asked Wren, expelling smoke.

"If I knew, it wouldn't be mysterious."

Wren chortled, clearly honored that Anna had dispensed with etiquette.

"It's a project of some sort," Anna added. "They come around in overalls and tool belts, all smudged and sweaty, but they just . . . clam up whenever I ask them what's going on." She paused to sip her sherry. "Maybe they think it would shock me." She set the glass down again. "I can't imagine what that would be."

Wren smiled, then leaned forward to underscore the next question: "Did you ever get back to . . . your childhood home?"

Anna shook her head. "But lately I've spent some time there." She set her glass down with stately deliberation. "It's something old people do . . . apparently. Dwelling on unfinished business. Old ghosts. It's tiresome, really. No point in it whatsoever. Especially when . . . what did Gertrude Stein say? . . . 'there is no there there.' "

Like most seasoned San Franciscans, Brian recognized the quotation. "But she was talking about Oakland, right?"

"Yes, but . . . her *home* in Oakland. It had been torn down, so she had no reason to go back. She wasn't mocking Oakland. That's a common misconception."

Wren was still focused on her original question. "But how do you know it's been torn down when . . . you haven't been back?"

"I've *seen* its absence," Anna told her. "There's nothing but a parking lot and an ugly casino they built in the nineties. It looks like a mall. I've been all around it."

"But . . . I don't understand."

Anna shrugged. "I'm spooky that way—ask him."

Brian was tired of paying for that remark, so he scowled at Anna like a grumpy vulture. "Google Earth, I'm guessing."

She gave him a sly smile. "I think that's the name, yes."

"Did Jake show you?"

A somber nod. Suddenly the joke was over, and a palpable melancholy had taken its place. "There is no there there," she repeated.

Wren wasn't giving up. "But the town is still there, right?"

"Winnemucca," said Brian, trying to make himself useful.

A crooked smile from Wren. "Seriously?"

"Yes."

"It was named after an old Indian," Anna said. "Back in the last century. Or—you know—the one before that. I can't keep up with them. He hung around town wearing only one moccasin, so they called him Wunnamocca."

"I don't know whether to believe that or not," Wren said jovially.

Anna carefully arranged one of her fragile long-fingered hands over the other. "I don't make up things, dear. The truth is hard enough to sell."

A long silence before Wren asked: "Would you go back?"

"To Winnemucca?"

"Yes. I mean . . . all things being equal?"

Anna gave her a bittersweet smile. "All things are not equal, dear."

Brian already recognized the purposeful gleam in Wren's eye. His mother (the one with the spoon collection) would have called it "a bee in her bonnet."

"Why not?" asked Wren. "Gimme one good reason."

They were winding along the coast highway in their rented Ford Focus, heading back to the RV park in Pacifica. The air was still, bordering on balmy. The moon was just a sliver above the dark sea, the tart remains of a lemon Life Saver.

"She's old," said Brian. "She's had several strokes. She falls down all the time. There's three good reasons."

"She won't fall down with us around. She'll be safer than usual. We'll make her cozy in the big chair. She can have the private bedroom."

"What if . . . something happens?"

"What if something happens *anywhere*? It's just three or four days. And we'd be with her the whole time. I'm sure Jake could use a break."

Brian turned and looked at her. "What's gotten into you, anyway?"

"I dunno, pumpkin." Wren smiled wistfully. "I just wanna know her better. I didn't expect to like her this much."

They were silent for a while as the car ribboned along the ocean.

"The point is," said Wren, sliding her hand onto his leg, "you know she wants to do it. You heard what she said about unfinished business."

Brian had heard all right, but it made no sense to him. Who could Anna possibly know in Winnemucca after seventy-five years? And what difference would it make?

"Old ghosts," said Wren, reading his mind.

6

Scorcher

Jeanette's MacDonald's coat was slinky satin trimmed in marabou, but Andy had only a moment to admire it before the room shook and the balcony cracked and people began screaming bloody murder. He usually saved a few Milk Duds for after the movie, just to prolong the experience, but he gobbled every last one of them in the three minutes it took for the city of San Francisco to collapse into rubble.

"My goodness," said Margaret as they spilled out of the American Theater into the unglamorous daylight of Bridge Street. "You were wolfin' down those Duds like gangbusters. Scared the hell out of you, huh?"

"It was sure realistic," Andy replied, though truthfully he had been more shaken by Clark Gable's treatment of Jeanette than by the ensuing earthquake.

Gable had just *humiliated* her onstage, after all, evicted her from his club and his life, this blustery brute who couldn't recognize true love when it came along. It was almost as if he had *caused* the earthquake. Andy had seen plenty such men, and so had Margaret, but Margaret, oddly, trembled only in the face of collapsing buildings.

"I ate all mine too," said Margaret, holding up an empty box of Red Hots. Andy expected her to blow on it and make it honk like a goose, and that's just what she did, prompting an old lady standing by the ticket booth to jump, then turn and frown at them. He smiled a sheepish apology. Margaret could be childish sometimes.

"I love the song," he said, hoping at the very least to keep Margaret from attempting a second honk while there were people around.

It worked. Margaret puffed up her ruffled bosom, shook her loose platinum hair, and began to sing: "*San Francisco, open your Golden Gate—*"

Andy took it from there. "*You'll let no stranger wait, la, la, la, la.*"

They burst into laughter and joined in a duet, heading down the dusty sidewalk like some goofball vaudeville act. "*San Francisco, here is your . . . la, la, la . . . saying I wander no more. Other places only make me la, la, la—*"

"Okay, that's enough!" Margaret brought an end to their routine by yanking on Andy's arm.

"What?"

"You were twirling."

"I was giving it some pep."

"We're making a scene," she whispered. She nodded in the direction of two men in dirty overalls scowling at them from the alley by the five-and-dime.

Andy shrugged. "Big deal."

"You can twirl at home, lamb. Just don't do it here. Folks will get the wrong idea."

Andy could have told her that an old chippie honking on a Red Hots box was making just as big a scene as a boy twirling on the sidewalk, but he kept his mouth shut because he knew what she meant, and because he could hurt her feelings more than she could ever hurt his. They took care of each other in different ways. She did it with movies and tender conspiracies. Sometimes silence was all he could offer.

Margaret glanced at him as they passed Kossol's Kosy Korner. Even there, in the dim glare of the diner on a sober Saturday afternoon, people seemed to be watching them through the streaky glass, including old Kyle Kossol himself. "Did you like your birthday present?" Margaret asked him.

"Uh-huh."

"I thought you'd like those colors."

"I did. Yeah." His face was aflame with mortification and unarticulated gratitude.

"You can't tell your mama, Andy."

"I know." This was not news to him. There was not much of anything he could tell Mama these days. Sometimes he wondered if Margaret actually preferred it that way, since it made him more like her own son and less like Mama's. In that sense it felt like a betrayal of Mama—a form of desertion, even—but there was nothing he could do about it; his very nature, after all, was the ultimate betrayal.

Margaret had a customer back at the Blue Moon, so she left Andy at Eagle Drugs with the remains of their milkshake. He was stalling for time now, drawing petroglyphs on the frosty canister until the Basque boy showed up for work.

"Want another one?" asked Mr. Yee. He was wearing the same garnet bolo tie he had worn since Andy was a little boy. Andy figured it was to prove he was a cowboy, even if he was an old Chinaman who ran the Rexall. When Mr. Yee was a boy there had been lots of Chinamen in Winnemucca—thousands, even, according to Mama—but now his kind was rapidly dwindling, and that meant he had to fit in.

Andy waved away the offer of a milkshake.

"Hunky-dory, huh?"

"Yes sir."

"He should be here pretty soon."

Rattled, Andy pretended not to understand.

"Lasko," said Mr. Yee, explaining himself. "Your buddy, right? He's got baseball practice until four. You're welcome to stay."

"Oh, right . . . thanks." Andy's heart was thumping with anxiety and hope. He wondered if Mr. Yee, through canny oriental powers, had detected his infatuation with Lasko, or if Lasko himself—and here's where the hope came in—had told Mr. Yee that he and Andy were buddies. In either case the jig was up. Andy poured the rest of the milkshake into his glass and stared at a postcard taped to the mirror.

Lasko. It suited him perfectly—exotic and roughneck at the same time. While his name was officially Belasko (Andy had seen it on a roster at school), the shortened version was all he ever used. Lasko's father was Mexican, but his mother (a cook at the Martin Hotel and the daughter of a sheepherder) had insisted on Basque names for their children. Lasko had been extremely lucky in that regard; there were no awkward intrusions of x's and z's in his name. He had a brother who'd been saddled with Xalbador, and even worse, a sister named Hegazti, which sounded less like a name to Andy than some sort of muttered gypsy curse.

The summer before, Lasko had danced in Pioneer Park at his grandfather's birthday in traditional Basque garb. (Only foreigners were described as wearing "garb," Andy realized, never Americans.) Lasko was as much of a local boy as Andy, but seeing him that day, dashing in his black beret and red-sashed white pajamas, Andy felt every gallant, grueling mile of the journey that had brought Lasko's people from the Pyrenees to Chile and, finally, to the high desert of Nevada. Andy had not been invited to the birthday party, of course—he didn't know these people, and his mother was widely known to run a whorehouse—but he watched, entranced, from a blanket spread under a nearby cottonwood tree. It was hot as the hinges that day. Lasko was dancing hard, so his white pajamas had turned gray in the places where sweat had stuck them to his strong, hairy legs.

"That's the Rexall train!"

Andy nearly fell off the stool when Lasko's voice broke his reverie. Then a hand landed on his shoulder, firm as an accusation and warm as a caress. "Pretty snazzy, huh?" Lasko's other hand was pointing to the postcard on the mirror, but Andy still wasn't seeing it. All he could see was their reflection: one of them seated, the other standing, both looking straight ahead, like a couple in an old daguerreotype.

All too soon the hand abandoned Andy's shoulder, and Lasko was behind the counter, wrapping an apron around his gabardined loins. He yanked the strings so tight he might have been a wonderful Christmas parcel in need of extra protection. "It's gonna be a big deal," he said. "She's comin' through every state in the union."

The train, thought Andy, trying to concentrate. The train on the postcard.

"Why is she doing that?" he asked feebly.

Lasko shrugged as if the answer were obvious. "To let folks know about Rexall. Spread the word. The Depression is over. Ain't she a beaut?"

The train on the postcard was a streamlined cylinder that seemed to stretch on forever, the horizontal cousin of a Buck Rogers rocket ship.

"She's stopping in Winnemucca next month. For a whole day." Now Lasko was wiping the counter with a towel, his naked forearms circling hypnotically.

"But . . . why?"

"So folks can come on board and look at it. See all the Rexall products."

Andy still didn't get it. There were plenty of Rexall products to be seen right here: corn plasters, enema bags, mysterious-looking trusses for old people.

"And it's air-conditioned," Lasko added. "All twelve cars."

Now *that* was something. Nothing in Winnemucca was air-conditioned, not even the movie house. Andy had experienced that supernatural coolness only once in his life: when Mama took him on a trip to Reno so she could interview a blackjack girl named Irene. They had dined on chicken salad sandwiches and cherry pie in an air-conditioned coffee shop next door to the casino. He had never forgotten the sensation, that instantaneous release from the blast furnace of summer.

"Do you have to get tickets?" he asked Lasko.

"Not if you're a Rexallite."

"What's a Rexallite?"

"*He's* a Rexallite," Mr. Yee piped up from over at the pharmacy counter. "You talk nice to him, I bet he'll pull some strings."

Lasko laughed. "He's a Rexallite, too. And you don't have to talk to nobody."

But I want to, thought Andy. I want you to pull strings for me. I want you to take care of everything.

"When is it coming?" he asked. "I mean she." Trains had a gender, apparently, so Andy thought it best to follow Lasko's lead.

"We ain't got the schedule yet, but I could let you know. I could show you."

Andy knew better than to give him the phone number for the Blue Moon. Mama had always been clear about that. It interfered with business, she said. "Maybe at school," he said. "I sit two rows behind you in Geography."

"I know," said Lasko. "You brought in that book one day."

Andy nodded, exhilarated by the knowledge that he'd been remembered. "*Richard Halliburton's Book of Marvels.*"

"With the pictures of the new bridge in San Francisco."

"Yep. That's the one." Andy almost never said yep, but he knew how boys were supposed to talk to each other, especially boys like this one.

Lasko, scrubbing a glass with a brush, looked over at Andy. His nose was indelicate, broken-looking, his eyelashes so long and luxuriant they might have been painted on, like Robert Taylor's on the cover of *Screenland* magazine.

"Could I look at that sometime?" asked Lasko.

"Uh . . . what?"

"The book."

"Oh . . . You bet. . . . I could loan it to you, even."

"I liked those pictures," said Lasko. "And the ones with the Panama Canal."

"Yeah, me too. Pretty nifty."

Nifty. Something else he never said.

"I could bring it by tomorrow," he added, barely able to breathe.

Lasko shook his head. "Sundays I help my mama out."

"At the Martin Hotel? I could bring it to you there."

"Okay . . . sure. Swell." Lasko's dark brows furrowed. "How did you know where she works?"

Andy panicked for a moment, then shrugged. "Everybody knows where she works. Her roast lamb is world-famous." This was laying it on thick, but it was the best he could manage under the circumstances. "World-famous lamb" was actually painted on the side of the Martin Hotel, so it seemed a safe enough choice. And it was better than telling the truth, that Lasko had been under polite surveillance ever since Andy had seen him dancing in the park in those sweaty pirate pants.

Lasko nodded, acknowledging the fame of his mother's lamb. "Come after dinner," he said. "We can eat something in the kitchen."

"Sure. Swell."

An awkward silence followed while Lasko washed spoons. Andy wondered if either of them had a clear understanding of what had just been negotiated.

Finally Lasko said, "Scorcher today, huh?"

Andy whistled—*whew*—and tugged on his shirt collar, a gesture that didn't come off nearly as natural—or as manly—as he had planned.

"Want some shaved ice?" Lasko asked. "No charge."

"Sure."

In one practiced movement Lasko yanked a paper cone from a dispenser, slapped it into a chrome holder, and filled it with shaved ice, glancing briefly in the direction of Mr. Yee, who was occupied with his ledger. Then, as if to say *This is our secret,* Lasko pressed a finger to his lips before hitting a tap and squirting cherry syrup into the cone. Andy smiled as the nectar bloomed in the ice like a rose.

He left the Eagle as soon as he had finished the shaved ice. It wouldn't do to hang around. Lasko was popular, and popular boys always knew when other kids were over-eager for their company. Besides he seemed to like Andy (or at least his book), and Andy had just been invited to dinner at the Martin Hotel. Well, sort of invited, if eating in the kitchen counted. The invitation to the train was less clear-cut, since it could have been done to impress Mr. Yee, but an afternoon of air-conditioning with Lasko, whatever the reason, was nothing to sniff at.

By five o'clock Andy was hitchhiking home on Jungo Road. A breeze had rolled down from the mountains, warm and velvety. Andy felt buoyed by nature and a wondrously unthinkable thought: I have a date tomorrow. He may not know it, and he may not even know my name, but I have a date for the first time in my life.

A beat-up Packard pulled over and stopped, so Andy ran to catch up with it. The driver was a skinny bald man in an old brown suit.

"Where you headin', son? Jungo?"

"No. Just a mile or two down the road."

The man squinted at him. "The Blue Moon Lodge?"

Andy hesitated, then uttered the all-important "Yep."

"Ain't you too young for that place?"

No, thought Andy, I'm too old for it.

"You ever been there?" asked the man.

"I live there."

A slow nod. "You're Mona's boy."

"Yes sir."

"Get in."

Andy did as he was told, and the car sped off down the road.

"You're growin' up like a weed," said the man.

"Yes sir," said Andy. "I am."

7
The Stuff of Home

This house, thought Shawna as she passed through the rose-heaped gate at the crest of Noe Hill, feels like the family seat now. There was a mature garden here, and curling brown shingles, and an air of tatty antiquity that evoked her childhood home at 28 Barbary Lane. Shawna's new home (a crisp bamboo-floored condo near the Greek Orthodox cathedral on Valencia) was handy to her life— well, her *night*life, at any rate—but it still felt more like a base camp. Mrs. Madrigal's flat in the Duboce Triangle was no more than a charming last stop on her journey, and Shawna's dad's RV was a journey in itself, hardly the stuff of home if you didn't actually live in it.

But this house, oddly enough, this cluster of "temporary" shacks built for refugees of the 1906 earthquake, felt steeped in permanence. On the nights when she joined Ben and Michael on the sofa for takeout burritos and *Boardwalk Empire*, the lights in the valley below seemed designed to twinkle for all eternity. They had made it that way, the two of them, with their reverence for domestic detail.

Including, of course, this dog, this big Muppet of a Labradoodle galumphing toward her down the garden path. As usual, when she was wearing a flowy skirt, he made her feel merry and girlish, like Heidi coming home from the hills. Right up to the moment he stuck his big Muppet nose between her legs.

"Stop that, Roman!" Michael was yelling from the front door.

"Please," she said. "I can use the attention." (Not true. That particular part had received plenty of attention the night before, and she was pretty sure Roman already had the scoop on that.) "He's the one I'm worried about," she added. "One day he'll get his nose stuck on my vajazzling, and it won't be pretty."

"Be stern with him," said Michael. "Push him away. He took classes to learn not to do that."

"I remember," she said. "Labial aversion therapy."

Michael kissed her on the cheek as she reached the front porch. "Not just for that. He's an equal opportunity sniffer."

"Hey, I can dig it." She found herself sounding strangely retro whenever she was around Michael. It wasn't something he actually required of her, so it was possible she just liked doing it. Maybe, in fact, that was what having a "gay uncle" was all about for her: to take the sting out of having missed the 1970s.

"I was half expecting a fashion show," he said, leading the way into the house.

"Why?"

"I dunno. You mentioned Burning Man on the phone. I thought maybe you were gonna model an outfit."

She could see why he'd think that. Their living room looked like backstage at Fashion Week. There were bolts of fabric everywhere, a veritable planetarium of EL wire on the table, some fuzzy shit on the floor like shrapnel from a lime-green bomb.

"Actually," she said, "I haven't started on my outfit."

Michael just shrugged. "You don't need to, do you? You've already got a closet full of costumes."

She loved that he knew that. That he had actually *seen* the whorish snarl of scarves on the back of the door. Not to mention the mysteries within: the tutus and bustiers, the baseball uniforms, the Catholic schoolgirl fetish wear. He knew her as well as anyone, this dude in the white mustache and untucked Pendleton.

"It's all Ben's doing," said Michael, looking around the room. "You'd think sewing had just become another event in the decathlon."

She smiled—partially because that was funny, and partially because she had just pictured Ben, tanned and gleaming and yoga-sculpted, running out of the waves to grab a seat behind a sewing machine.

"That is so cool," she said. "Is there anything he can't do?"

Michael widened his eyes at her. "Guess not."

There was a brief squirmy silence between them. She had not meant the question as a leading one, and he almost certainly hadn't taken it that way, but she was still uncomfortable. She scrambled, tellingly, to back away from the subject.

"Dad's new Facebook bride is awesome," she said.

"Isn't she? At least she used to be. I'm glad to hear she still is."

"So down-to-earth, you know. A real broad."

"You know they called her 'The World's Most Beautiful Fat Woman'?"

"Mmm. I checked her out on YouTube."

"She really was a knockout." He chuckled suddenly at a surfacing memory. "Brian told me he had already jerked off to her before we met her up at the river."

"What?"

"Am I oversharing, little one?"

"Of course not! Where? On the Internet?"

He rolled his eyes with a sigh. "A picture. In a book. It was something we had back then. A bunch of pages you could turn." He flopped on the sofa like a flung-aside teddy bear, then motioned for her to follow suit. "Is she still hot?"

She took a seat, curling her legs under her ass. "Would I fuck her, you mean?"

"No, I did not mean that."

"Well, I would—I mean, I *wouldn't*, of course, but I would . . . if I met her at a Litquake party, say, and she asked me out for a drink or something."

He arched an eyebrow. "My, aren't we getting specific!"

Shawna shrugged. "She liked my book. She said so when I met her. I was just putting it into a believable context."

He smiled. "Everybody liked that book."

She reached over and patted his denimed knee. "Thanks for tweeting about it, by the way."

"Sure. I meant it. I couldn't put it down."

"Still . . . thanks for spreading the word."

"To all seventy-six of my followers. You don't need my help, sweetie. I just saw your picture in *USA Fucking Today*."

Oh God, that picture. And even worse, that dress: a short high-waisted number intended as a friendly nod to Lena Dunham in *Girls*. Huge mistake. The end result had been more like Little Lulu. Note to self: dress like self.

"Actually," she said, curling up on the sofa, "I'll be glad to *stop* being everywhere for a while."

"Burning Man," he said without much enthusiasm. "Why is that not part of being everywhere?"

"No cell phones. No cars. No airplanes. No schedules." The litany was already lulling her. "It's the opposite of a book tour."

"I guess so," he murmured. "How about sofas?"

"What?"

"Do they have sofas?"

She chuckled. "They do, actually. Lots of them. In the strangest places."

"Good. I have a feeling I'm gonna need 'em."

She was relieved to see the rueful twinkle in his eye. He was starting to get with the program. It was vital to her agenda that Michael feel fully connected to this grand adventure. "That should be your playa name," she said. "Sofa Daddy!"

Michael groaned. "Do we really have to have playa names?"

"No . . . but it's fun, Uncle Grumpy. Being someone else for a while. Flying our freak flag. No one I know takes it too seriously."

"What's yours, then?"

"My playa name?" Oh shit, he *would* ask that. On her last Burn she had dubbed herself Loosey Goosey while slinging Cosmos at Celestial Bodies, but that would *not* work for an insemination. She needed something grounded and classic, something she could conceivably—so to speak—share with her child someday.

"I haven't decided yet," she told Michael.

He scrunched up his brow with sober professorial interest. She remembered him using that expression when she was seven years old and brought him riotous finger paintings from the Presidio Hill School. It proved that he cared.

"What do you want the name to convey?" he asked.

And there was her opening.

She shrugged. "The theme of Burning Man, I guess. Fertility 2.0."

"What's that mean? 2.0?"

"I know—right? Confusing as all fuck. They had one before, apparently. This is the second one."

"So—just Fertility, then."

"Yes."

He mused briefly. "Tillie T."

She rolled her eyes. "Cute. But that's a waitress in a diner."

"Okay, then . . . Fecundity."

"*Fecundity*?" She swatted him with a throw pillow. "That makes me sound like a swamp!"

"Are you pregnant?" he asked, instantly scuttling their game.

She shook her head. "I wanna be, though. You know that."

He nodded with a beneficent smile. She had suggested as much a month or so earlier when the royalties started coming in from the book, when she could finally lay a claim to adult responsibility. Michael had told her he wanted no part of raising a kid, but he wouldn't mind having one nearby. He wouldn't mind that at all.

"And the clock is sort of ticking, you know."

"C'mon. Twenty-nine is not old."

She shook her head. "I meant Anna. I want it to happen while she's still with us." She avoided Michael's eyes by fidgeting with her skirt. "I dreamed last night that we were at Barbary Lane. Only it looked like it was when I was little, before those dot-commers made it look like a five-star B and B. But it was now present-day . . . because you and Ben were there . . . and Anna was there, too, but she looked really young and . . . you know . . . fresh . . . younger than I can remember even. And she was touching my belly. And when I woke up, I knew it was time to get pregnant."

Michael smiled sleepily.

"The thing is," she added, "I want it to happen at Burning Man."

The smile curdled noticeably. He was obviously thrown, but trying not to show it. "Well . . . I'm sure you'll find plenty of takers."

She rolled her eyes at him. "Oh, Michael, not *that* way."

"Oh, you mean . . ." Mysteriously, he pressed his fingers to his thumb as if he were operating the mouth of a hand puppet.

"What the hell is that?"

"Turkey baster."

"Oh, right . . . exactly. Bingo."

The relief bloomed on his face. "Thank God. I was picturing some grotesque variation on speed dating. With me and Ben in the tent next door."

She chuckled.

"You know it's an eight-hour drive, don't you?"

"What do you mean?"

"Well . . . that stuff doesn't travel very well. You'll need one of those super coolers—"

"Michael—"

"Oh . . . right. You have a supplier *there*."

She nodded. "A possible one. A sweet guy from my Conscious Dance workshop. He has no interest in being a father, thank god, but he's totally fine with . . . you know, giving it up for me. I've checked him out. No schizophrenic parents or anything. Clean and sober even. He's got a hammock over at Chakralicious—"

"I have no idea what that is, Shawna."

"Just another camp. Not far from ours. Sharon, this friend who works at Zynga, has offered to be the runner."

"The cum runner."

It was less of a question than a not-so-funny joke, but she confirmed it with a nod. "He's a decent guy, but I don't feel close enough to him to . . . you know, have him in the tent while it's happening." It sounded odd to put that into words, but it was exactly what she meant. It was important to be clear from here on out.

"So Sharon is gonna—"

"—run it, yeah . . . from Chakralicious."

Michael took that in for a moment. "You know," he said, "if you were a guy, you'd know it's not all that easy to jerk off in a hammock."

She laughed. "I'll leave it to him to figure that out. Assuming, of course—" She cut herself off.

"Assuming what?"

Another excruciating silence. "The thing is . . ." She realized that this was the second time she had said The Thing Is in the last minute. She was not the sort of girl who touched her throat and said The Thing Is. As a rule, she said just what she wanted without batting her eyes in supplication.

"—you and Ben are my family."

"I know that, sweetie."

"I mean, Dad too, of course . . . but now that he and Wren are settling in New Mexico—"

"They are?"

"He didn't tell you?"

Michael shook his head, frowning. "I guess he was waiting until he saw me in person."

"But . . . *anyway* . . . Caleb will be perfectly fine for this—"

"Caleb?"

"The guy from Chakralicious."

"Oh—right."

"—but you would have been my first choice."

"Your first choice for . . ." It took him a moment, but he got it. "Oh, Shawna, honey . . ."

"Am I weirding you out?"

"Just a little, yeah." His flashing stoplight of a face confirmed this.

"I'm sorry. I just wanted you to know that . . . I would have been thrilled for my baby to have something of you. Something of your sweetness and wit and your . . . huge capacity for love. I know it can't happen, since you're HIV-positive, but I want you to know that I would have asked you, everything else being equal. I would have, Michael, in a fucking heartbeat. So there—I said it. Shoot me."

For a moment she couldn't tell if he was deeply touched or just grossed out. Then, when he reached for her hand, she saw the tears shellacking his cheek.

"No one's gonna shoot you, honey."

"But shut up, right?"

"Yes, please. Immediately."

"It's not like we're related."

"But it is, sorta." He quickly swiped at his cheek. "It *is* sorta like that. Even if I weren't positive, it wouldn't be appropriate. We're different generations."

She shrugged. "You and Ben are different generations."

"Well, yeah, but—"

"David Crosby did it for Melissa Etheridge, and he was like a hundred and eight."

He gave her a crooked smile as she squeezed her hand. "Believe me, the invitation means infinitely more than the dance."

She squeezed back. "Good. That makes me feel better." She exhaled. "It depressed me for a while, you know. Knowing it wasn't possible."

"Oh, frevvinsakes."

"I know, right? But then I saw how silly I was being. Fuck HIV. And fuck some guy I barely know from Chakralicious. We're family, so this baby should be about us. All of us. And it still can be, Michael! About you and Ben even!"

Michael's mouth was agape. "How can it be about that?"

"Okay," she said, her heart struggling in her chest like a small bird stuck in a chimney. "This is what I called about. I thought you and I should talk first."

His face revealed that they were finally on the same page, though it might have been an obituary page, or a notice of imminent nuclear annihilation.

"Do you think Ben would be up for it?" she asked.

8
The Art Car

"Do you think she'll be up for it?" Jake asked the visitors.

They were standing in a derelict warehouse in Emoryville, a place chosen for its wide-open spaces and ready access to the freeway. Jake's upstairs neighbors, Selina and Marguerite—both transfolk—had just arrived on a trans-bay BART train from San Francisco. Kinda funny, thought Jake, since Trans Bay was the name of his camp in Black Rock City, but Selina and Marguerite were way too ladylike for a Burn.

They were here to see if the art car passed muster.

"It does look comfy," said Marguerite, craning her neck, "but how on earth would you get her all the way up there?" A math teacher at the Harvey Milk Civil Rights Academy, she was prone to asking questions.

And since she was as short and waddly as a pigeon, practically everything she encountered in life struck her as too-high-up.

Jake was prepared. "There's a detachable ramp, see? We can roll her up there, if we have to. And once she's in place—wa-la!—all she has to do is sit there and watch the world go by!"

Marguerite frowned. "But, surely, when it's out on the highway . . ."

Selina Khan, a tall and deeply practical Canadian who advised people about their investments, shot a weary glance at her flatmate. "You don't seriously think this thing is going out on the highway, do you?"

"Well . . ." Marguerite screwed her face into a pout. "It has wheels, Selina. It looks very strong to me . . . with all that metal and . . . welding."

Jake tried to soothe Marguerite's feelings. "A natural mistake. "It *is* a vehicle . . . technically. It's already registered in the Mutant Vehicles Parade."

"It's a giant tricycle," Selina said flatly. "So what do you do between here and the desert? Disassemble it or something?"

"There ya go!" Jake fired his forefinger at Selina as if she had just picked the right answer on *Millionaire*. He knew he had to placate both of them if this was ever going to happen. As members of Anna's caregiver circle, these ladies had a serious say in the matter. "We're packing the parts onto a flatbed truck," he said, "and reassembling it on the playa. Anna won't even see it until we're there."

"She won't have to pedal it, will she?" Marguerite again, with her questions.

"Nope. These three pods are the only ones that have pedals."

Selina grabbed one of the pods and shook it, apparently testing its sturdiness. "And three people—just pedaling—can make this thing move?"

Stop calling it a thing, thought Jake. This is my baby—the Monarch. It took nine whole months to make, in fact, so have some respect.

"Want a demonstration?" He tried to say it without defiance, but wasn't sure that he'd succeeded. "It's really simple."

"That's what I'm afraid of," said Selina.

Three of the other guys from Trans Bay, including Jake's boyfriend Amos, were huddled in a circle on the other side of the room, possibly smoking weed. Jake weighed the pros and cons of summoning them, then stuck his fingers in his mouth and whistled. "Yo, bitches! Magic Time." Within seconds they had all come running, scrambling into their pods like firemen mounting a hook-and-ladder.

"Oh my," said Marguerite, pressing her hand to her chest as soon as the art car began to rumble across the concrete floor. "Should we get out of the way?"

"You're fine," said Jake. "They've got it under control."

A section of plastic tubing fell off Amos's pod and clattered noisily to the floor, making Marguerite jump back several feet.

"That's just decorative," Jake hastened to explain. "We're not finished with that part yet. The hardscape is totally solid."

"It's quite something," murmured Marguerite, obviously trying to say something supportive. "It's like an old-timey carousel."

Selina arched an eyebrow at her. "Pray tell, Marguerite. How is it like an old-timey carousel?"

"Well, it goes up and down as much as it goes around and around."

"It's not supposed to go around and around. It's supposed to transport her from one place to another."

"You know what I mean, Selina. There's all this wonderful . . . movement, in all directions. It's extraordinary, Jake. A real accomplishment."

Jake felt himself blush with pride. He was tempted to show them how the wings worked, but the silk panels had yet to be installed, so the superstructure would still be visible. Without the softscape in place it would come off more like a pterodactyl than a monarch butterfly. He showed them Amos's sketch instead.

"This is how it'll look," he said, offering the blueprint to Selina. "It's all about—you know—transformation."

"What's that writing on the front?" asked Selina.

Marguerite tilted her reading glasses and read aloud: " 'Anna Madrigal—World's Oldest Transgender Activist.' "

"That's lovely," she said.

"Really?" grumbled Selina. "What if it said, 'Marguerite McGillicuddy—World's Oldest Math Teacher.' Would you want to ride around town in that?"

Marguerite cocked her head in silent concession to Selina, then turned back to Jake. "You might want to go with something like . . . 'Transgender Pioneer Anna Madrigal.' "

"Sure," he said. "Cool. Fine." At this point there was everything to gain by compromise. He was just glad they had moved away from safety issues and onto more mundane considerations. It was starting to feel like a done deal. He signaled for the guys to come down, since they were following this exchange too intently.

"Does she know about this?" asked Marguerite.

"Not yet," he said.

"Why not?" asked Selina.

Jake explained that first he had to be sure he could create something worthy of Anna's iconic stature in the LGBT community. He wanted every last piece in place, he said, before unveiling the finished product. And naturally that meant the support and approval of Selina and Marguerite, Anna's most trusted confidantes in the community and, needless to say, icons in their own right. He had his tongue so far up their asses, it was a wonder he could talk at all.

"How do you know she would even do it?" asked Selina.

Jake shrugged. "We're honoring her. Don't people *like* to go places where they're being honored?"

"The Hyatt Regency, maybe. Not Black Dog City."

"Rock," said Jake.

"What?"

"Black *Rock* City. It's named for the desert."

"It's in a desert?"

Jake shrugged. "An alkali flat, actually."

Marguerite gazed hopefully at Jake. "Is that better than a desert?"

Jake decided not to answer that directly. "I'm gonna rent an SUV with AC. We can come late and leave early and . . . you know, totally avoid the crowds. We'll have a great time, I'll be with her every minute, she'll feel the love . . . we'll have a photo op and get the hell out of Dodge the next day. Easy peasy Japanesy."

It was just a stupid expression his mom used all the time back in Tulsa, but it tumbled out of him as if he'd coined the phrase himself. Selina made a face like he'd just spilled a glass of Two-Buck Chuck on her nice white couch.

"What?" he said. "You're Korean. Gimme a break." He looked to Marguerite for support. "Doesn't this seem cool to you?"

Marguerite took her time answering, probably because she had to keep peace in the flat. She and Selina were not a *couple* couple, but they had shared that space for years, so they squabbled about everything in private. Jake had lived there with them, in fact, until he escaped downstairs into the low-stress Eden of Anna's flat.

"It *does* seem very cool," Marguerite replied. "But there are other considerations. Cool isn't always enough, Jake."

Oh great, he thought, now the good cop was turning on him. "Why are you making me sound like some sort of flake? I may not be as old as you two—"

"*Easy*," warned Selina.

"—but I am middle-aged, and—"

"You are *not* middle-aged," gasped Marguerite, sounding like a maiden aunt who suddenly wondered where the time had gone.

"I will be," said Jake. "In a few years."

Selina gripped Marguerite's arm in an act of sisterly consolation. "It's so unfair, isn't it? Age is so much kinder to the rougher sex."

Marguerite wrenched her arm free and returned to the subject, addressing Jake in an even tone: "I know how much you want to celebrate Anna's life, and I think that's just beautiful—but she's very frail now. No one knows that better than you, Jake. There are blinding dust storms at this place and cruel, debilitating heat—"

"It's not that bad," said Jake.

"Yes, it is. I've been on YouTube. Don't bullshit me, Jake."

The Clint Eastwood approach was not typical of Marguerite, so it knocked Jake back for a moment. He imagined her unleashing that tone on her students at the Harvey Milk Academy, having judiciously saved it for just the right moment.

"And here's what you must know," Marguerite went on. "If you ask Anna to do this, she will do it. There's no doubt about that. She will say yes, because she won't want to disappoint you. We know what she's like—all three of us—and it's why we love her like we do. So here's what you have to ask yourself, Jake—"

Do you feel lucky, punk? Well, do ya?

She didn't say that, of course, but it's what she meant. Did he want to take sole responsibility if Anna died for an avoidable reason? The answer was no fucking way, which was why he'd hoped for a different response from the Ladies Upstairs, and why he felt, at this very moment, both pissed off and relieved.

What had he been thinking? It had been almost eight years—eight years!—since he and Marguerite and Selina sat by Anna's bedside after she suffered that stroke. She had been in a coma, and they had not expected her to come back.

"The good news," said Selina, with uncharacteristic chirpiness, "is that none of this"—she made a sweeping gesture at the art car—"has to go to waste. You can still go to Burning Rock with your friends. It can still be a lovely tribute to Anna. You can ride up there on the top and—I don't know . . . carry a big picture of her."

Marguerite's face lit up. "I can give you that shot of her in the garden."

Jake shrugged. "Sure."

"And then," said Selina, building steam, "you can tape the whole thing and share it with her when you get home. Think how much she would love that!"

Jake felt something akin to mourning as he stared down at his battle-scarred work boots. He had not planned on giving Anna a tape; he had planned on giving her an Adventure, like Richard Halliburton himself, swimming the Panama Canal or crossing the Alps on an elephant. Then, in a flash of insight, he remembered Anna's scorn for the way Halliburton had died: lost at sea in a typhoon on some hokey-ass Chinese junk. "He was just being *vivid*" was how she had put it, and the same could be said of Jake's pedal-driven butterfly if it were to collide, say, with a blissed-out biker in a K-hole or a giant fire-belching mechanical octopus.

He was still young enough to take that chance for himself, but too old, he realized, to take it for Anna. That sucked. It really did.

He was glad about one thing: that he had told no one but Amos and the other people at Trans Bay about his dream of taking Anna to Burning Man. If he had blabbed to Michael or Ben or Shawna—all of whom were going—the postmortem would have been endless. They would have felt the need to commiserate, even if they'd always secretly thought it was a stupid idea. And Jake would have been obliged to trot out his reasoning (stupid as it might have been) for the umpteenth time. This way, at least, the dream could evaporate without further scrutiny or justification.

Jake felt for sure that Michael would bring up Burning Man when they met at a gardening job that afternoon. Burning Man was only six days away. But Michael was strangely silent, almost sullen, as they pruned the big podocarp hedge at a house on Belmont. Ever the greenie, Michael habitually shunned the use of gas power for hedge-clipping, but today his fierce little handmade snips seemed less about ecology than horticultural torture—death by a thousand cuts.

Something was clearly bugging him.

"Sorry I was late, boss," Jake offered at last. (They'd been partners in this business for years now, but Jake kept the term out of simple affection, and because there was something inherently male, he believed, about one guy calling another guy "boss.") "I had some friends I had to see in the East Bay."

"Please," said Michael. "You work a helluva lot harder than I do."

Jake shrugged. "You're older."

"And one of these days I'm not gonna show up at all."

"I know."

They had discussed Michael's retirement on several occasions, and you could easily read it between the lines of every grunt Michael uttered while going about his work. He was several years past sixty now, with a bum shoulder, terrible allergies, and neuropathy brought on by his HIV meds. He could not do this forever.

"I'm telling you," said Jake. "You should start selling your weed to the clubs. That shit is kick-ass. Amos and I got so fucked up at the Schmekel concert."

"Okay . . . I give up . . . Schmekel?"

"All-transman, all-Jewish band. Sort of punk, folky, satirical—you know."

"Sounds fun."

"Yeah, except that Amos is a Jew, and loves all that cultural Let My People Go shit almost as much as he loves transmen."

"So?"

"So . . . there's a hot guy in the band . . . he's got this Jason Biggsy nerdy horn-rimmed thing going, and Amos is, like, practically coming on his pecs—like he can't wait to take him home to Mama and eat shiksa balls at Passover."

Michael smiled. "Matzoh."

"What?"

"Matzoh balls. Shiksas are gentile girls."

"See? Totally fucked already. Jewish trumps everything. Even not having a dick."

Michael laughed and stopped snipping for a moment. "And this guy in the band is from here?"

"No. Brooklyn."

"Amos adores you, you idiot."

Jake sort of knew that, but verification was appreciated. Having endured three shitty relationships with bio guys, he had all but thrown in the towel over penises. There was plenty of butch out there, after all, and no shortage of toys. A guy could always do without if it meant not having to deal with fucked-up fetishists or bored married gay dudes looking for a three-time thrill. But when he saw Amos Karpel on Buck Angel Dating, he decided (on the strength of his kind dark eyes and sleekly muscled arms and a genius quote from Patti Smith) not to hold his dick against him.

They had been dating for three months. Not long enough for Jake to have expectations of anything permanent, but long enough to worry about whether he was hip and smart and, yes, Jewish enough for Amos.

Oklahoma dragged along behind him like a ball and chain.

When Jake came home that night, Anna was in the parlor eating delivery Thai with Brian and his new wife. Jake had met Wren several days earlier and had liked her—he had told Brian as much—but tonight he felt like hitting the sack with Amos on the cell. He was glad that Anna had company, though. It would make this easier.

"By the way," he said as casually as possible, sitting down on the arm of Anna's chair, "I'll be away for a few days, so Selina has offered to sleep over while I'm gone. Hope that's gonna be okay?"

"Of course, dear. But Selina won't be necessary."

Jake touched her back lightly, feeling the sharp parenthesis of her shoulder blade beneath the smooth satin of her kimono. "She really doesn't mind," he told her. "I think she sort of misses you, in fact."

"It's not that, dear. I just won't be here."

"Oh."

"Brian and Wren are absconding with me."

Jake slapped a smile on his face and turned to Brian. "No shit? Where to?" Despite his best effort, he could already feel the jealousy burning in his cheeks.

Brian looked uncomfortable. "Just a little joy ride in the buggy."

Wren glanced at her husband, then back at Anna.

"To Winnemucca," Anna said at last, almost as if it were a confession.

9

Curlicues

A customer at the Blue Moon had left behind a fancy leather valise that, after a decent interval, Margaret gave to Andy. He kept it in his room, knowing that its sophisticated air would have invited ridicule at school. He used it to store treasures (a Barlow knife, some arrowheads, a large ivory brooch he had once told Mama was part of his "pirate costume"). Andy loved that valise—loved the buttery French sound of it: my *valise*—so he despaired at the thought that one day some big-city hotshot might return for another Dambuilder's Delight with Margaret and, in a moment of clarity, remember exactly where he'd left his most prized possession.

The valise was the perfect size for *Richard Halliburton's Book of Marvels.* Andy would have felt foolish walking into the Martin Hotel with that bruiser of a book under his arm, and a paper bag would have made him look like an Okie, but the valise, he thought, was just the ticket. It looked sporty in his hand as he gave himself a once-over in the closet-door mirror. He had broken out his best slacks and a sky-blue gingham shirt with cowboy stitching on the pockets. Feeling a sting in his nostrils, he wondered if he might have slapped on too much bay rum.

Mama settled that issue down in the driveway.

"Lord, son, you smell like a cathouse!"

Mortified, he touched his tainted cheek. Mama had made that joke with him more than once—not out of meanness, he reckoned, but because it showed she wasn't ashamed of the life she was leading. "Should I go wash my face?" he asked.

"Nah. You're fine. It'll die down by the time you get to town."

He opened the door of the truck and climbed onto the running board. "You look right spiffy, son." She was beaming up at him, happy as a lark because he had lied to her—well, sort of lied to her—about why he needed the truck. He had told her he was meeting friends for supper at the Martin (friends plural, since only one would have aroused suspicion), and she had asked if "that nice Watson girl" would be among them.

His answer had been a shrug and a rogue's smile, but that had been enough for Mama. The mere *hope* of Gloria Watson was worthy of transportation.

Once he was behind the wheel, she barked instructions: "Don't drive 'er too fast. The hubcaps come off when you hit the potholes. And don't let the sheriff see you, for pity's sake. And park her around back, so folks can't see it, or they'll think I'm pickin' up a pussyhound at the train station. You don't need that kinda talk."

He knew all that already.

"And don't kiss 'er till it's time to say good night."

She wasn't talking about the truck anymore. "C'mon, Mama."

"Otherwise she'll think you think she's loose." She slapped the side of the truck as if it were a poky horse being released into a corral. "Go on now. Git!"

A dusty pink twilight had settled over Winnemucca by the time Andy arrived at the Martin. He had parked near Pioneer Park and crossed the sluggish river on foot, leaving plenty of room between him and the telltale truck. He had enjoyed the walk: the blue-shadowed evening, the pendulum swing of the valise (as devil-may-care as Fred Astaire himself), though he refrained from swinging it when anyone was looking. Swinging a valise was probably just as bad as twirling.

Eight or ten people had gathered on the porch of the hotel. Some of them were waiting to be seated. Others, beer bottles in hand, had abandoned their meals to watch a long, rusty necklace of boxcars clattering through town. It was part of the nightly show at the Martin. Andy recognized several valued customers of the Blue Moon, but he knew from experience not to greet them. Not in town. Not with their wives around. He had learned that lesson—and how—when he was only seven.

Inside the dining room, the two common tables were riotous with chiming silverware and chatter—gossip about everything and nothing: fly strike, the church supper, Mr. Hoover's gold speculation in Jungo. Andy stood against the pressed-tin wall, the valise held tight against his leg, waiting for a glimpse of the Basque boy. The servers were both girls tonight: a tall, horsey redhead from Sparks and Lasko's sister Hegazti, who overcame her crippling name with an uncanny gift for balancing huge platters of food on both slabs of her substantial arms. The all-but-edible aroma of crusty lamb and roast potatoes reminded Andy that an actual supper lay ahead.

In his fever of preparation he'd almost forgotten about that.

A shiny cream-painted door swooped open and produced Lasko like a magic trick. He'd obviously been washing dishes, since his shirtsleeves were scootched up, and his swarthy arm still bore flecks of soapsuds, like sea foam on a rock. He acknowledged Andy with a wink and lopsided grin, motioning for him to enter. Andy squeezed through the crowded room, suddenly feeling like a privileged character, even though, of course, he was just being admitted to a kitchen.

"You sellin' Bibles or something?" Lasko encircled Andy's shoulder with his arm, buddy-buddy as can be, like a ballplayer leading another one off the field.

Andy didn't understand. "Why?"

"That," said Lasko, nodding toward the valise.

"Oh . . . that's the book."

"What book?"

"The *Book of Marvels*. The one I showed in class?"

"Oh yeah . . . sure thing."

"You said you wanted to borrow it."

Lasko finally caught his drift. "Yup, sure did. Thanks, Andy."

This was a moment both marvelous and confounding. Lasko had spoken Andy's name for the very first time, and he'd done so as if they'd known each other forever. But now the Halliburton book seemed like little more than a prop, a handy excuse for their meeting. What was going on here? Andy tried not to read anything into it; tried and failed completely. His heart had a way of prancing ahead of him.

"Sit down," said Lasko. "I'll get us some grub." He pointed beyond the sink to a scarred green card table and a couple of metal folding chairs. It was already set for dinner. "It's better there. The old man don't like company for supper."

Andy wasn't sure what this meant until Lasko's eyes led him to a larger table, where Lasko's father sat sucking on a gravy-coated rib. He looked something like Lasko, but thicker of frame and darker-skinned, the only *mexicano* in this swarming *basco* beehive. He did not once look up from his glistening pile of bones, even when he muttered "No mas" at his daughter as she staggered through the kitchen with her platter-juggling act. The man struck Andy as sullen, dangerously unhappy.

"He don't mind if we're here," said Lasko, sensing Andy's concern.

"You sure? Cuz I don't mind if—"

"He can go to blazes," Lasko muttered under his breath. "I work two jobs. I can have friends. You want ribs or lamb?"

"Uh . . . lamb, please." It was "world-famous," after all. "Is your mother cooking tonight?"

"Nah, she's at St. Paul's polishing candlesticks. She does it every month. Creamed spinach and bread rolls?"

"You bet."

Lasko rose and conveyed the order to the redheaded girl as she filled a platter by the stove. There was something about the way he murmured into her ear, touching her arm ever so slightly, that made Andy wonder about them.

"Is she your girlfriend?" he asked as soon as the girl had left them alone with their massive dinners.

Lasko made a face. "Why would you think that?"

"I dunno. You were so nice to her."

Lasko stabbed a stub of roast potato with his fork. "You get a lot more food that way." He winked at Andy and proceeded to chew vigorously. "I wanna show you something when we're done, but you can't make a big hoo-ha, okay? Just act natural in front of customers. I don't wanna rile the old man."

That was all the incentive Andy needed. The nature of his challenge remained vague, however, until they had polished off their plates and headed back into the boisterous dining room, where Lasko stood next to the hat hooks and cast his eyes suggestively toward the wall. It was an exaggerated gesture that anyone watching would surely have noticed. He would make a terrible spy, Andy thought.

"What?" he whispered. "The hats?"

"The wall, ignoramus."

The wall was a yellowish green dulled by years of grease, the same pressed tin that covered all four walls of the dining room. The pattern was the standard swirl of flowers and flourishes, all but erased in places by layers of paint. Nothing about the wall struck Andy as remotely worthy of making a big hoo-ha.

"It looks old," he offered, trying to make a stab at it.

"Pseesnpukrs," Lasko mumbled. (Or at least that's what Andy heard.)

"What?"

"*Pseesnpukrs.*"

"Sorry, I still don't—"

"C'mon!" Lasko grabbed his tweed cap off a hook and headed for the door. Andy followed him into the silky night, still toting the valise and feeling chastened and simple-minded. Lasko blazed a trail along the railroad tracks, where a weedy swath of gravel and broken glass finally gave him the privacy he needed.

"Pussies and peckers," he blurted. "Didn't you see them? They're everywhere."

"On the wall?"

"Yessiree! All them little curlicues are nothin' but sex organs. Some of 'em are pussies and peckers at the same time. Whatchacallit? . . . hermapherdike."

Andy frowned. "Not on purpose, though? The pattern, I mean?"

"Hell yeah, buddy. Fifty years ago that place was a whorehouse!"

The thundering silence that followed had to be filled by someone, so Lasko obligingly did it. "No offense. I just think it's a hoot that my mama and Father Garamendi and that snooty Mrs. Snow all sit there and never even see it."

"Yeah," said Andy without much conviction, since he himself had sat there and never even seen it.

"You have to be lookin' for it," Lasko added generously.

"Guess so," said Andy.

Lasko picked up a piece of gravel and chucked it down the tracks. "I don't care about your mama or the Blue Moon or nothin'. No matter what anybody says. I figure we got more in common than most people in this hellhole. Hell, you're a lot smarter'n I am. You memorize poetry and shit. You read books."

I not only read them, thought Andy, I carry them down the railroad tracks in a heavy valise for no earthly reason in the dead of night.

Lasko was picking up speed now, building toward something with every breath. "Shake a leg, Andy! Here's a place we can sit." The place was a rough cube of concrete, set back from the tracks and prickly with rusty metal. It was barely big enough to hold them both, but they managed somehow, feet dangling and trousers touching perilously. Lasko fished a match and a cigarette from his shirt pocket.

"Want one?"

Andy shook his head. He had tried that once and found it unpleasant.

"It's a Camel."

"That's okay."

Lasko struck the match against the concrete, lit the cigarette, and took a long drag, staring into space with shiny black marble eyes. Down the railroad tracks red and green lights were blinking like lost pieces of Christmas.

"How does that poem go, anyway?"

There was only one poem that Andy knew by heart: Tennyson's "Lotos-Eaters." He had recited a portion of it in Mrs. Peacock's English class to a sea of listless faces, unaware that he had caught the fancy of anyone, much less Lasko.

"I don't know it all," he said.

"Just do what you know." The tip of Lasko's cigarette went bright orange in anticipation.

Andy thought a bit. "Um . . . okay." He straightened his spine for the recitation. "Eating the lotos day by day, to watch the crisping ripples on the beach, and tender curving lines of creamy spray, to lend our hearts and spirits wholly to the influence of mild-minded melancholy, to muse and brood and live again in memory with those old faces of our infancy."

He stopped, embarrassed, unsure how much he could remember. Lasko was still gazing ahead, his face wreathed in smoke. His leg was still pressed against Andy's, warm as a radiator and just as solid. "Have you ever been to a beach?"

Andy said he had never even seen an ocean.

"Me neither. They have beaches in Frisco, but it's too cold to swim in the ocean, so they all go to this big swimming pool. Indoors with big glass windows and stuffed bears and a penny arcade. They have a big waterwheel up above it."

"What do you mean?"

"Like at a sawmill, you know?" Lasko turned to Andy, his face so close that Andy could feel the breeze of his tobaccoey breath. "Only you jump into it, and it tumbles you round and round and dumps you into the pool, one on top of the other."

"Wow," murmured Andy, ostensibly about the mechanism, but mostly at the thought of being tumbled round and round and dumped on top of Lasko. "Really nifty," he added, impersonating the hale-fellow tone of the Hardy Boys.

"I figured you for the adventurous type," said Lasko. "Soon as you brought that book to school." He looked down at the valise, waiting at their feet like a puppy craving attention. "I can pull this off, Andy, but I need a buddy to help me."

"Pull what off?"

"My escape to Frisco."

Andy envisioned that rattletrap truck bouncing over the Sierra, dropping hubcaps at every treacherous turn. "That's a long trip, Lasko. My mama won't let me drive that far."

"We ain't talkin' to your mama." He shook Andy's knee conspiratorially. "Or my mama neither. Besides, you don't need to drive me. I just need you to help me for one day. Right here in town. Easy as pie. *You can be my alibi.*"

Those five words, with their presumption of intimacy, seduced Andy so completely that they might have been imprinted on a candy Valentine heart.

"Do you have your own car?" he asked.

"I got more than that," said Lasko. "I got a dozen cars, and they're all air-conditioned."

Andy gaped at him. "The Rexall Train?"

"See?" said Lasko. "Look how smart you are!"

10
Sneaker Wave

"Wrong Diana," said Ben as a smile exposed the gap between his teeth.

They were standing on the brink of the continent at the new visitor center next to the Cliff House. Michael had already admired its low profile, the clever way its timber and raw concrete echoed the ruins of the Sutro Baths down below. The swimming pavilion had once been as glassy-eyed and cavernous as a Paris railway station, but a suspicious fire had gutted it in 1966 (over a decade before Michael's arrival in San Francisco) leaving only this footprint of a temple, a sea-stained Mondrian. Harold and Maude had famously frolicked among these ruins, and Michael himself had often reflected on them, back in the day, when exploring the nearby pagan shrubbery.

This was their Sunday expedition. Couples could get stuck in ruts if they weren't diligent, so Michael and Ben had resolved to seek out a different venue every week. In recent months that had meant the Point Isabel dog park, the Disney Family Museum in the Presidio, the Kabuki Theater (for movies with margaritas and turkey salad sandwiches), and the Hunky Jesus Contest in Dolores Park (a repeat, admittedly from last year, though there was always something original). Michael had heard raves from the poppers guy at Does Your Father Know about a statue of Diana recently erected at the new visitor center, so he had proposed a visit, never once considering that it might have been Diana the Huntress and not the Princess of Wales who had been depicted. Ben had found the mix-up amusing.

"Why would you even think it was *that* Diana?"

There was no way out of this but a pokerfaced gag. "Because she is loved by our people."

"Gay people?"

"Yes," he replied with exaggerated dignity. "And anyone who might enjoy her company while gazing upon the Pacific."

The truth was that people barely talked about the sad Spencer girl anymore. She was yesterday's tabloid, a one-off episode on the History Channel. There was a new princess now, a pretty non-troublesome Disney brunette who seemed to have been special-ordered by the palace for smooth operation. Michael felt old and silly.

Ben, sweetly, let him off the hook with a sudden change of subject. "So why Winnemucca?"

Michael grinned. "That should be the slogan for tourists."

"And they're driving there in Brian's Winnebago?"

"That's what he said." Michael turned up the collar of his peacoat against the tiger bite of a blue summer day. "They're spending the first night in Tahoe. Part of it's about spending time with Wren. The rest of it—whothefuckknows?"

"Have you ever been to Winnemucca?"

"No, as a matter of fact. Have you?"

"Once. A long time ago. It's a strip of motels and casinos and fast food places. It can't come close to whatever Anna remembers."

"I know," said Michael. "I've Googled it. They still have brothels, but—oh, it's tragic, you don't wanna know. It's not about tourism for Anna, I can tell you that. Brian said she said something about 'unfinished business.' "

"When was she last there?"

"Nineteen thirty-six, as near as I can figure."

Ben whistled.

"I know," said Michael. "What could possibly be unfinished? Everybody must be dead. The Blue Moon is long gone."

"But Mona went there, of course. Back in the seventies."

It was wonderful to hear Ben speak of Mona as if he had actually known her. Michael's old roommate at Barbary Lane had died of cancer in the Cotswolds well before Ben entered Michael's life, but she had already become a substantial deposit in Ben's memory bank. Michael had heard him regale strangers at parties about Mona at the nude beach, Mona going ballistic at the ad agency, Mona chasing women on the island of Lesbos, as if Ben himself had been witness to those moments. It was one of the joys of being married to him. The line between the past and the present, as Edie Beale once called it, was penetrable when Ben was around to listen.

"She not only *went* to the whorehouse," Michael said, giving it the drama it deserved, "she worked as a fucking receptionist. She was the reason Anna saw her mother again. Mona, the last of the big-time hippies, this unregenerate gypsy, was the glue of the three generations. That ended up being her purpose—you know."

"I do know," said Ben.

Michael sighed and gazed at the gulls loitering above the ruins, their cries as random and unmelodic as creaky hinges. "You know all my stories now," he said. "It's bound to get tedious."

"I wish I'd known *her*," Ben replied, sidestepping the question so adroitly that it offered the gentlest imaginable honest answer.

"So we're all heading to Nevada this week," said Michael, ticking them off on his fingers. "Us . . . Jake and Amos . . . Brian and Wren . . . Anna. Can you believe that? It's kinda weird. It's like *Happy Days* goes to Hawaii."

Ben smiled. "Winnemucca's a far cry from Burning Man."

Michael mumbled in the affirmative.

"They're in the same part of the state, but you get to them on completely different highways from different directions. There's a wilderness between them." A crazed pearly light in Ben's eyes suggested nothing so much as a forest ranger who has just been mobilized for a wildfire. He was so ready for all this hardship. "I found the tent," he said. "It was in the garden house under a piece of plywood. Pretty good shape, looks like. And there's a big sturdy tarp we can use as a windbreak."

"That's good," Michael said.

"Is Shawna taken care of?"

He felt the tiniest twitch below his right eye. "In what way?"

"You know—tentwise."

Michael tried to sound nonchalant. "I doubt we'll see her again once we're there. She's bunking in three camps, near as I can make out. And access to a daybed at the Ashram Galactica—whatever that is—god help us all. Has she called you yet?"

"No," said Ben.

"She's going to. But don't tell her I told you, because she wanted to tell you first, but I don't want you to be put on the spot—and you will be, believe me—because it's very sweet, it's just as sweet as it can be, but it's also very embarrassing and . . . deeply, deeply icky. I just wanted you to be prepared."

Ben regarded him, slack-mouthed. "What on earth are you—"

"She wants your sperm when we're at Burning Man." Michael threw up his hands, relinquishing the concept to the winds. "She wants to get pregnant there. She loves you and admires you and thinks your sperm would be most excellent. She doesn't expect you to be the father, just the donor. That's pretty much it, except the spiritual angle, which I'll leave to her. Oh, yeah, and it's fine with her if I'm around during the sperm extraction process. In fact, it would be great. Even lovelier."

Ben made a disbelieving face. "She did not say 'sperm extraction process.' "

"Not in so many words, but . . . c'mon, honey, this has gotta be creeping you out."

His husband shrugged. "It's a little . . . too close for comfort, yeah. I'll give you that. With all of us in the same tent."

"Not in the *same tent*! Ugh, no. Is that what you thought? Another tent, for God's sake. At another camp. With a bicycle ride in between. And her friend Sharon from Zynga. And a big fertility theme party with Tibetan prayer bells and Aimee Mann's second album while she lies perfectly still for half an hour with legs thrown over her head. Why are we even talking about this?"

"Why you acting so horrified? People do this all the time."

"You *want* to do this?"

"I didn't say that. I just can't figure why you sound like somebody's Aunt Gladys."

"Well, exactly—I *am* her Aunt Gladys. You hit the nail on the head. I practically became her second father after Mary Ann left, and it just feels weird to me. I can't help it. It's too personal or something. It's almost like . . . . incest."

The word came out like a rattlesnake's hiss, prompting a short blond woman standing nearby to turn and glare daggers at them.

"It takes way too much explaining," Michael told her with a shooing motion. "Look at the scenery, please."

"In the first place," said Ben, leaning closer and lowering his voice significantly, "it's not you she's asking, it's me—"

"And it's a lovely compliment, sweetheart, it really is."

"In the second place, I've never known Shawna as anything but an adult. I'm not related to her either. Neither are you, for that matter. Nobody's related to anybody here. And Shawna is almost thirty years old. Chillax, Michael."

"*Chillax?* You don't say Chillax."

"I'm saying it now. Because you're acting like you're twelve and hormonal."

If only he knew, thought Michael. Sixty-two was a *lot* like twelve and hormonal. Teenagers rage against the end of childhood, old people against the end of everything. Instability is a permanent condition that adapts with the times.

"There's such a thing as emotional incest," Michael said, in lieu of exposing his petty fears, the hard truth of what he was feeling. To admit that, here and now, would have been humiliating. Not to mention unattractive.

"It's not incest," said Ben. "It's not even close."

"It's Soon-Yi incest."

"Oh, please." Ben snorted. "Soon-Yi incest."

"Well—"

"Woody Allen was *fucking* Soon-Yi. This is a procedure, Michael, nothing more. And again, it's not *you* she's asking, it's me." Ben seemed to ponder the ramifications of that. "Did you tell her how you feel about this?"

"Of course not. I told her to talk to you."

"But she knows. You can't hide shit. You must've hurt her feelings."

"I don't think that's true at all."

"So why hasn't she called me?"

"I couldn't tell you that. I'm trying to stay out of this."

"Oh, and a great job you're doing, too."

It wasn't like Ben to clock him so snidely. Michael was on the verge of defending himself when he saw the never-disguisable hurt in his husband's eyes. And he knew instantly that he was not the person who had put it there.

"Oh, listen, honey, the only reason she came to me first was that she and I have known each other for so long—"

"—and you're the official keeper of my sperm."

Michael regarded him, hand on hip, incredulous-ghetto-chick style. "Shut up, okay? The only reason she came to me first is that she wanted me to know that she would have asked me first if I hadn't been HIV-positive."

Ben took that in for a moment. "Before me, you mean?"

"Well, not before you, but . . . in addition to."

"You said first. You said she would have asked you first."

Michael blinked into the wind. "She was being *nice*, Ben. Trying not to hurt my feelings. She wanted this to be about all of us, and she felt awkward about it. Understandably, if you ask me. She's already got another guy lined up, and she knows we have no interest in babies, but she wanted to run it past us anyway. Just in case."

"And she couldn't have said all that to me?"

"I suppose she could have. But she didn't. She confided in me the way she always has, and I've fucked it up in my usual asshole codependent way."

Ben gave him a heavy-lidded look that said, *No argument here.* "She can read you like a book, Michael. She must know how you feel about it, so that's the end of that. My guess is, she's hurt and mortified. I'm not expecting a phone call."

Michael hesitated then asked: "Do you want one?"

"I do now, yes."

"Really?" Michael drew back like he'd been slapped.

"Yes. So I can at least tell her I was honored to be asked, and I'm not as repelled by the invitation as you seem to be."

"Fine," said Michael. "Do you want me to call her?"

"No. Just leave it alone. If she doesn't call, I'll talk to her when we're on the road."

"Not when we're all in the car?"

"No. When you're out taking a leak or something."

"No problem. Do you feel like breakfast?"

"Louis'?" Ben had cast his eyes at the newly reopened diner on the highway.

"Pancakes," said Michael. "Pancakes and apple-wood-smoked bacon."

And thus the storm appeared to pass.

Ben had cabinetry to finish for a client in Pacific Heights, so after breakfast he dropped Michael at the house and left for his workshop on Norfolk Street. Their Sunday excursion felt truncated to Michael, though not in a perilous way. They were nice to each other during the drive, and they both knew that a check from a client would be useful right now. It made sense for Ben to finish this job before they left for

Burning Man. The mortgage on their mountain property in Pinyon City (now on the market at a savagely
reduced price) was about to balloon like a hemorrhoid.
Foreclosure would soon be upon them without serious
groveling to the bank.

Social security would help, eventually, but that
was still three years away, and Ben, though legally
Michael's husband in California, would not be eligible
for the check after Michael died. Assuming, of course,
that social security was even around in three years, that
Congress hadn't gutted the system to bail out a bank.
It was easy enough to rail against the 1 percent, but
the truth was that Michael and Ben had become their
willing handmaidens in these New Hard Times. Their
clients had once come from all over—from people like
them, artists and office workers—but now only the
rich could afford tended gardens and custom furniture.
It was the 1 percent or nobody.

There was comfort in knowing that most of their
friends were in the same leaky boat. They were count-
ing their blessings, waiting for a sneaker wave that
would take them to shore. They had moved to the
North Bay or the Excelsior. They had left Whole
Foods for Trader Joe's or Costco. They had rationed
out their restaurant meals and curtailed most impulses
involving clothes or condiments. Their cars had gone

third-world, because they had let go of such vanity, and because it was depressing to send a many-times-dented Prius through a carwash.

Ben and Michael had a few well-off friends: executives at Twitter and Google they had met among the poor at Lazy Bear and Litquake; an artisanal chocolatier who had sold his brand to a conglomerate; a handful of doctors and lawyers; DeDe and D'orothea Halcyon-Wilson, with their bottomless family money; Michael's old friend Mary Ann Singleton, who had divorced well in the east and come west again to find her bohemianism in Woodside with a reconstituted maiden name. But Ben and Michael saw less of these people now—there was no denying that. Something lurked in the chasm between their incomes, something less about envy or snobbery than deep embarrassment from both directions. It was just easier to stay away.

Of all Michael's close friends, Brian seemed the least concerned about poverty. He was the oldest of the bunch and had lived in an RV for the past eight years, but he was newly married to a woman he had known for two weeks in the late 1980s, and their bliss seemed simple and complete. They were moving to a small adobe house in New Mexico that had belonged to Wren's late aunt. Their plan was to make lamps and key chains out of recycled license plates. There was a market for that in Madrid, Wren explained, which was not pronounced like the city in Spain.

"The accent is on the Mad," she added with a boisterous laugh. She was sprawled on the sofa at Michael and Ben's like an eighteenth-century courtesan, steely-tressed now but as lush and striking at fifty as she had been half a lifetime earlier. "It was a coal mining town, nearly a ghost town, actually, until the hippies came along. It's a little touristy in the summer, but it's still funky and falling-down in places, and it's beautiful there in the hills. John Travolta made a movie in Madrid a few years back. There wasn't a masseur for miles around who was safe."

Michael and Brian chuckled in unison. Brian was clearly doting on her.

"Seriously," said Wren, "you and Ben should come visit."

"We will," said Michael.

"We'll still have the RV. You can stay there."

"It's a deal." Michael wished Ben would hurry up and get home to meet this still-glamorous witness to his vanished past. The mention of Brian's RV, however, threw him back into the immediate future. "I'm glad you're spending time with Anna," he said. "I'm sure Brian is, too."

"Oh, man," Wren exclaimed, "she is such a fucking joy. We spent the whole morning with her at her flat, getting ready for the trip. I'm just jealous you've had all these years with her. Do you think we're making a mistake, Michael?"

This sudden shift of tone brought a quick glance from Brian.

"We're not making a mistake," he said quietly. "This was your idea, Wren. Don't start getting cold feet."

"She's so frail, though, pumpkin."

"She may be, but this is important to her. It's obviously on her bucket list, and we're not gonna let her down. She won't have to get out of bed if she doesn't feel like it. We can do this, Wren. We're probably the only people on earth who can."

Wren undercut Brian's melodrama by lifting her hand in a stage whisper to Michael. "Batman here means the Winnebago. We're offering door-to-door service."

"To *what*, though?"

"Not a what, a who. Someone named Oliver Sudden."

"Who the hell is Oliver Sudden?"

It was Brian's turn to answer. "Apparently he worked at her mother's brothel."

"No way. He'd have to be a hundred-and-fucking-five."

Brian shrugged. "One would think."

"She's jerking your chain, Brian." Michael laughed as the light dawned. "It's an old vaudeville joke. All of a sudden. Oliver Sudden my heart sings. There's a Sister of Perpetual Indulgence right now who calls herself Sister Olive O'Sudden."

"No kidding." With the cocksure leisure of a cowboy pulling a pistol from his boot, Brian unbuttoned his shirt pocket, produced a square of folded paper, and handed it to Michael. "Wonder how she was able to Google him?"

Michael unwrapped the paper and studied the evidence in Times Roman: Oliver Sudden, 2261 Sandstone Drive, Winnemucca NV 87678.

"Well, what do you know?"

"Not much," said Brian. "If we're talking about you."

Michael ignored the bro-to-bro teasing. The printout was a city roster of some sort, public utilities maybe, a list of names and addresses, the scantiest of online profiles. He handed the paper back to Brian. "Anna Googles?" he said.

"Apparently. When we're not looking." A grin rippled across Brian's face. To Michael he had always looked a little like Jeff Bridges, and even more so now that he was getting old. It allowed you to forgive him many things.

"And c'mon," Brian added. "Is Anna Madrigal really known for jerking chains?"

Michael had to admit that she wasn't.

Brian threw his hands up, accepting victory before an invisible jury. He had once been a lawyer, and sometimes it showed.

Wren rolled her eyes at Michael, then shook Brian's knee in reprimand. "Don't be insufferable," she told him, but she made it sound like a love song.

THE DAYS OF ANNA MADRIGAL · 141

"And c'mon," Brian added. "It's Anna Madrigal
really known for jerking chains."

Michael had to admit that she wasn't.

Brian threw his hands up, accepting victory before
an invisible jury. He had once been a lawyer, and some—

11
Complicated Machinery

Shawna didn't feel like cooking the night before the trip to Burning Man, so she asked Sharon to meet her downstairs at Another Monkey. The place was sort of elegant for a Thai restaurant: Buddhas under pin spots, copper piping as a design element, a unisex restroom with shallow sinks and translucent toilet stalls. Back in days of yore this had been one of those deafening dot-commer places with a one-word name (Revelations or Colander or whatever), but it was less pretentious now. Shawna would sometimes order pad thai at the register and take it home on the elevator. They might have done that tonight, if not for Sharon. Shawna had taken Sharon home once, and Sharon had flown with it, texting about soul mates before Shawna had time to wash the strap-on. Sharon did not need encouragement.

"The grilled beef salad is good," said Shawna. "I've had that several times."

Sharon closed the menu shut with a winsome smile. "Good enough for me, then." She leaned forward on her elbows, brushing aside a vagrant strand of pale brown hair. "I've gotta tell you, Shawn. I am so excited about this."

Shawna hated that Sharon was calling her Shawn now—not because it masculinized her name but because it claimed a lover's right to abbreviation.

"Excited about what? Oh, your first time at Burning Man. That's gotta be big."

"No." Sharon's eyes darted around the room as if she were about to place an order for crack. "The first time I ever helped someone get pregnant. It's like being a midwife or something. Except with a turkey baster instead of forceps."

"A bicycle."

"What?"

"I need you for the bicycle, Sharon. I've got the turkey baster covered."

"Oh." Sharon's face fell. "Who's doing that?"

"I am." Shawna gave her a sly but gentle smile. "It's complicated machinery, but I think I can handle it."

It took Sharon a moment to recover, but she managed. "Oh . . . well, sure . . . I just assumed since I'd be transporting it—you know . . ." She bludgeoned the rest of that thought by reaching for the Zynga tote bag she'd left on the floor by her chair. "This is for you. I made it myself. I hope you don't already have one."

Shawna could feel the burn of Sharon's expectant gaze as she removed the contents of the bag: a small blue shawl covered with yellow squiggles and circles. At least, that's what they looked like. She could think of nothing to say.

"It's a fanny blanket," said Sharon. "You put it over your fanny while your legs are over your head. You're less exposed during the impregnation, but . . . you're still comfortable and it's . . . you know . . . celebratory."

"It certainly is. Wow. This is . . . amazing."

Fuck me, thought Shawna. She thinks we're having a baby together, so she's made me a twat cozy. The lesson here was an old one: do not accept favors from lovesick one-night stands if you're not prepared for them to crank up the U-Haul.

"See?" said Sharon, pointing to the squiggles and circles. "Those are little sperms and eggs."

"So they are." Shawna hated herself for joining that asinine Conscious Dance workshop, and for getting so gabby afterward with Sharon. But how could she have known that her unilateral pregnancy plans would get Sharon so hot? Or that Sharon, having already scored a ticket to Burning Man, would soon be inescapable?

Sharon swiped at her hair again. "I know it's kinda silly."

"Not at all. It's a nice thing for a friend to do."

The f-word was strategic, and it left an excruciating silence between them. Finally Sharon said, "Have you spoken to that guy yet? The furniture maker?"

Shawna decided it would help Sharon to know that everyone gets rejected. And it would certainly help Shawna to unload this humiliation on a nonintimate, someone who wasn't part of her logical family. "I spoke to his husband," she said.

"And?" Sharon gazed at her, all goggle-eyed and earnest—Amanda Seyfried in the Grecian moonlight— as if Shawna had just announced her first belly thump.

"I think I grossed him out."

"You're kidding?"

"No."

"What a dick!"

Don't attack him, thought Shawna, just so you can be on my side. "He's not a dick, Sharon. He's someone I've known all my life. He's like an uncle, only not my dad's brother. I think he's squeamish about his little girl."

Sharon frowned. "It's not like he has to be there. And you're gonna get pregnant one way or the other. That doesn't feel like the real reason to me."

Shawna hated her for saying this, because she was feeling the same thing.

"Anyway," said Sharon, "why not just go directly to the carpenter?"

"Furniture maker. Because I'm sure he's spoken to Michael . . . his husband, and he hasn't called me yet. It's gotta mean he feels the same way. Maybe they both think I'll make a shitty mother and can't bring themselves to tell me."

"I think you're better off with Caleb," said Sharon. "I saw him this morning, and he was so excited about it."

Shawna's stomach knotted. "You know Caleb outside the dance workshop?"

"Sure. He works at Zynga too. In accounting."

"He understands we're not coparenting, right?"

"Absolutely. He says he just wants to give back to the earth. Isn't that a sweet way of putting it? We were coordinating things at Starbucks this morning."

This was bad news, since Shawna had already considered eliminating the bicycle—and thus the middleman—altogether. With the use of a festive partition Caleb could have given back to the earth in Shawna's tent, thereby removing the need for Sharon, panting heroically over that grotesque taint warmer. Now there were two Zynga geeks, two pawns of a corporate empire, conspiring to play FarmVille in Shawna's uterus. It might have been doable if not for the crazed gleam in Sharon's eye. Unreciprocated love was the deal-breaker here.

There had to be someone other than Caleb. Someone Shawna knew and trusted who was not in cahoots with Sharon.

Stay loose, she told herself. Stay loose, and he will come.

So to speak.

For the rest of dinner, Shawna steered the conversation away from the big insemination. They talked about the practice of gifting, the Burning of Wall Street installation, the fucked-up new ticketing system that had decimated some of the camps and was now demanding online orders so precisely timed and hideously prolonged that you could have been on the line at the fucking DMV. Sharon, of course, was still auditioning for the role of desert wife, offering Shawna the use of her CamelBak, her daytime goggles, her iridescent green harem pants that would look, she insisted, totally sick on Shawna.

They parted outside the restaurant. Shawna made a show of heading upstairs to her condo (since she'd claimed to have packing to do), but she stayed only long enough to pee and wash her face and grab a drag off a doobie. She needed loud music now, and meaningless laughter, and anyone disinclined to knit things for her pussy. She knew she would occasionally need company on this long slog to single motherhood, but she wanted it to be the right company, for the right reason. And she would not beg anyone, not even family, to be part of the process.

This was her doing, her baby. Her own version of sacred.

Sofuckyouunclefuckeryou'reafuckinunclefucker . . .

Maybe she could get them to play that song at Martuni's.

That might help a lot. That and a couple of appletinis.

She would begin the purification process as soon as she was on the road to Black Rock City. No booze, no weed, no gluten, no molly. Seriously.

But tonight she was throwing a bachelor party for her baby-maker.

12
Imagining Amos

They had found a good spot at Martuni's (out of the crush but close to the piano), so Jake staked a claim while Amos went for cocktails. The sight of this guy— *his* guy—wriggling through the crowd warmed Jake with an old contentment. He remembered a time when his name was still Janice and he and Dan Strayhorn had dug army foxholes in Dan's backyard in Tulsa. Dan had treated him like a buddy, had *called* him buddy, in fact—no cracks about girls—as they swung pickaxes on a sweltering summer afternoon. The foxholes were more like shallow graves, but they roofed them with planks and dirt and talked to each other for hours, soldier to soldier, each in his own bunker, through a length of buried garden hose. Reduced to a voice in the loamy darkness, Jake could be exactly the boy he was supposed to be.

Amos was that voice through the hose, that trusting headlong tumble into camaraderie. Jake had always been imagining Amos: someone who would hold him close and treat him as the same rough creature without effort or delusion. Amos, by his own admission, had never imagined anyone like Jake, but it didn't matter. He responded to Jake, admired him. "You're a better man than I," he declared one night after sex, and Jake had almost instantly been moved to silence.

"I'm sorry," Amos blurted. "That was lame."

"No, it wasn't."

"Yeah, it was way too gooey Jewy. I work too hard at being a mensch."

"You didn't mean it?"

"No . . . I meant it."

"Then shut up, dude."

Amos laughed and used his T-shirt to mop the pearly splatter off Jake's chest. "It just sounded so self-consciously liberal. I hate that."

"I liked it," said Jake. "So shut the fuck up."

That's how their valentine had read.

It had worked for both of them.

Someone had commandeered the piano to bang out "I'm Yours." Amos was across the room, holding Manhattans aloft like amber lanterns, but somehow he managed to swap smirks with Jake. The two of them had a running joke about that song, the way Jason Mraz had been every-fucking-where on their first few dates, bouncing out of cars and bars with all that you-done-done-me stuff, all that certainty about love, love, love. You had no choice but to dis it with someone you'd just met, or it would take you down with it. But the very act of dissing it had already made it their song, their reason to catch the other's eye across a crowded room.

Amos handed him the Manhattan. "I think most of it's still there."

Jake took a sip to prove him right. "Thanks, bud."

Amos pulled his chair closer to Jake's. "Isn't that your friend over there? The one who wrote the best-seller?"

"Shawna?"

Sure enough, it was Brian's daughter, looking more like Zooey Deschanel than ever now that she'd let her bangs grow back. She was sitting with a skinny guy whose hair was a dandelion about to explode. Jake hadn't seen him for several years, so it took a while to place that long, blank Nordic face—Otto, the street clown/puppeteer that Shawna had gently dumped when he got too serious.

Realizing that Jake had spotted her, Shawna head-lamped her eyes and twiddled her fingers at him. "Hang on to our seats," he told Amos. "I'll be back."

He made his way to Shawna and kissed her on the cheek.

"Hey, doll."

"You remember Otto, right?"

"Sure, hey!"

"Otto, Jake . . . Jake, Otto." Shawna sounded unusually chipper, hyper almost. "We just bumped into each other. Right here. A few minutes ago. Isn't that wild?"

It didn't strike Jake as especially wild, but he left it unchallenged, laying his hand on Otto's shoulder. "So how's ol' Sonny?"

Otto looked confused. "Who?"

"Your puppet." Jake mimed it with his hands. "The monkey puppet?"

"Oh . . . Sammy."

"Right, sorry . . . Sammy."

"He passed on to Nirvana."

"Wow." Jake spoke the word quietly, respectfully, seeing a cloudiness in Otto's eyes that had to be honored. "How does that happen exactly?"

Otto sighed. "I was broke, so I got a job at Trader Joe's. It was time to get off the street. I couldn't stand to think of Sammy cooped up in the box all the time, so I took him to the Burn last year and . . . we said our good-byes at the temple burn. It was awesome, but—I gotta tell you, man . . . really, really hard."

Jake found this tale far more disturbing than he'd expected. "I guess you couldn't have sold him, huh? Or given him away?"

"You don't do that to your child," said Otto.

You don't incinerate him either, thought Jake, unless you're some old dude in the Bible. And there was something especially disturbing about sacrificing an inanimate object that depended on you for its life.

You just don't do that, dude. You don't take a dog back to the pound because you don't want to feed it anymore.

Shawna was fidgeting with her cocktail napkin, Jake noticed. Something was distracting her, and he was pretty sure it wasn't premeditated puppet-cide. "So," she said in an odd little voice, "we're all heading for the playa this year, looks like."

Jake turned to Otto. "You too, huh?"

"He's on the temple crew," said Shawna. "It's gonna be ah-ma-zing this year. All laser-cut with computers. Can you believe this?" She made a gesture that encompassed the three of them. "The world is so fucking small!"

"Cool. Look . . . I better get back to Amos. Just wanted to say hi."

In truth, he just wanted to get away from Shawna's weird energy. She was sounding like a Heather or something. You'd think he'd just caught her with an embarrassing online hookup, or a secret married lover, instead of an old fuck buddy she had long ago sent packing. It wasn't like her. It made no sense at all.

It unsettled him to find Anna gone when they got back to the flat. It really shouldn't have, of course, since they had watched her leave, blowing kisses and waving from the window of Brian's Winnebago like a homecoming queen on a float. But a couple of stiff drinks and a dark, empty house had set Jake to thinking: How would a lasting absence feel? How could he even prepare for that?

He wanted her back. He wanted her back here right now, lighting candles all over the flat—*real* candles with real flames and tons of wax dripping everywhere—whatever the fuck she needed. He felt an icy panic scrape through his chest like a glacier, a dread so complete that Amos detected it and offered distraction.

"I think somebody wants a word with you."

Jake looked down at the tiny black cat encircling his leg.

"Hey, Notch baby—yeah, I know, where the hell is she?" He lifted the cat gently, letting her drape lifelessly over his hand. (That was the way Notch preferred to travel, having lived too long on the mean streets of the city to submit to anything on her back.) He brought her into the kitchen and set her down next to her food. Marguerite and Selina had obviously been here, since the bowl was already filled with Notch's crunchy senior kitty food. She sniffed it once and politely declined.

"Do you want me to stay over?" asked Amos.

"Sure. Why wouldn't I?"

"I dunno. A whole week of Trans Bay ahead of us. Stinky porta potties. Loud music. You might want some down time."

"You mean *you* might like some down time."

Amos shook his head. "Nope. Not what I said."

"Then stay. I'm fine with it. It's easier with the truck, anyway. They only have to make one stop." And I won't be alone here tonight, he thought. I won't be alone here for the first time maybe ever.

The truck had been loaded that afternoon in Emoryville. The Monarch had been dismantled piece by piece and strapped into place on the flatbed, a shapeless scrap pile of poles and pedals and painted canvas that would, he hoped to God, find its way to wholeness again in the desert. He was feeling as wingless and inert as his creation. So much of his focus had been on Anna (getting her there, keeping her safe, thrilling her with his magical ride) that he had lost a sense of purpose.

"It'll be a triumph," Amos told him that night in bed.

"Oh, yeah?" said Jake, settling into the crook of his arm.

"It's magnificent . . . and it grew out of you and her. Nothing has changed in that respect. And she won't miss anything but the hardship. It'll even have its own Facebook page. Felicia is going to film the fuck out of it." Amos chuckled at this unintentional clustering of *f*'s and repeated the phrase slowly, like an exercise in enunciation. "Felicia is going to Film the Fuck out of it."

Jake couldn't handle being silly right now. "The bitch of it is: Anna's going to the desert anyway. She could just as easily die in that RV as in the art car."

"Nobody's dying," said Amos. "Let it go."

Jake turned and looked at him. "What was that you gave her today? When they were leaving."

"Just a card."

"A card?"

"A bon voyage card. Telling her not to worry. That I'd keep an eye on you."

Jake was silent for a moment. "Really? You did that?"

"She worries about you too."

Another silence.

"I bought us something fun for the playa," Amos said.

"What?"

"Magic underwear."

"*Mormon* magic underwear?"

"Why not? You said it made you hot. Ever since you saw Patrick What's-His-Name wear them in *Angels in America*."

Was that how he'd explained it? He had said so much during the gabfest of their first date, from their initial sniff-out at Hot Cookie to their exhausted predawn entanglement at Amos's apartment in SoMa. It had all been true, if incomplete. He had wanted to share with Amos but not overshare, so he couldn't remember exactly what was on the record. He decided to shift the discussion away from his libido.

"How would you even get a pair of Mormon underwear?"

"You mean how would Amos Karpel get a pair of Mormon underwear?"

"No. Anybody. You can't just buy it, can you? You have to have a note from your pastor or something."

"Orrrr . . ." Amos tiptoed his fingers across the raven tat on Jake's bicep. "You could go to a website in China that makes a brilliant imitation."

"No!"

"Oh yeah, that's what I'm talking about. A fine blend of polyester and cotton, and baggy in all the right places. It's already packed in my duffel bag."

"You're nuts," Jake said with a dismissive chuckle, though this was close to being the sweetest thing he'd ever heard.

"So what's the fantasy here?" asked Amos. "I'm . . . what? A young Mormon missionary? An unusually *swarthy* and well-nosed young Mormon missionary who's come to the city to take away your marriage rights? You sense right away that I'm deeply repressed, so the moment our eyes meet at the front door—"

"Pier 39."

"He's canvassing at Pier 39?"

"It's his day off. He's looking at the sea lions. He's wearing a red jacket and jeans."

A sly grin crept over Amos's face. "This is an awfully specific fantasy."

The game was obviously over. "It wasn't that much of a fantasy," he said ruefully. "More like a fucking train wreck in the end."

"But you saw the magic underwear?" Amos didn't seem especially bothered that this scenario had its roots in real life.

"Oh yeah," said Jake. "Four or five times. We did this therapy thing."

"You're losing me here, bud."

"He had a shrink back in Snowflake—"

"Utah?"

"Arizona. The shrink did this reparative therapy where he held him in his arms like a dad would do. Comfort him and call him son and shit. But with their clothes on. Said it would cure queerness. Fill some deep-seated need."

"I'm sure it did. For the shrink."

"Word."

"So you did this with him, huh? In his magic underwear."

"Yep."

"Right here?"

"Sometimes."

"While he was campaigning for Prop 8?"

"Pretty low, right? Sleeping with the enemy."

"Well . . . cuddling with the enemy."

"That's even worse. The enemy should not be cuddled."

Amos laughed. "Or coddled." He slipped his hand between Jake's legs and pulled him closer. He smelled of Manhattans and hair oil and a good day's work. His fingers found Jake's clit and rolled it idly, speculatively, like a pebble he'd just discovered on the beach. "So now you have this thing for magic underwear."

"Sort of. It could be nice to see them come off some time."

"Damn. They never did?"

"That was the deal. Neither one of us wanted to get naked. He didn't want to go all the way with a fag, and I didn't want him to see my *vagine*."

"He doesn't know what he was missing," said Amos.

13
Abyssinia

The beauty of Lasko's escape plan was that most of it could be discussed openly, even at Eagle Drugs, where Mr. Yee mistook the gleam in Lasko's eye for fierce company loyalty. When Lasko crowed to Andy about the twelve cars on the Rexall Train or the hordes expected in Winnemucca or the efficiency with which this blue-and-white python would slither through all forty-eight states, there was no reason for suspicion. For Mr. Yee, and the rest of the town, the Rexall Train was just a one-day extravaganza, a vision that would evaporate as soon as it left the station.

And so it would for Andy, since Lasko had not requested company on his exodus to Frisco. Andy's job was to board the train an hour before departure and tour the exhibits with Lasko, leaving with the crowd once Lasko had found a good hiding place. He might not even need a hiding place. He'd be wearing a white shirt, he said, with the Rexall emblem stitched on the pocket. He could easily be mistaken for someone official, someone who belonged there. And if anyone asked where he was (Mr. Yee, for instance), Andy was to say that Lasko had gone home sick.

Going home sick from the Rexall Train struck Andy as funny, since each of the cars, according to Lasko, was named for a different Rexall product line intended to improve health or well-being. There was Firstaid (gauze and bandages), Bisma-Rex (antacid powder), Cara Nome (cosmetics), and Kantleek (hot water bottles and enema bags). The last two cars were Joan Manning (chocolates), where the staff would be sleeping, and Puretest (Epsom salts and talcum powder), the private observation car of Mr. Louis Liggett Himself, the grand poobah of United Drugs.

Andy had a cartoonish image of Mr. Louis Liggett Himself throwing Lasko off the train by the scruff of his neck. He saw angry steam coming out of the old man's ears and Lasko flailing like they do in the movies. Then he saw a bloody, gravelly death. He shared this vision with Lasko one afternoon as they walked home from school.

"You don't get it," said Lasko. "I ain't no Okie, and this ain't no boxcar. This is the Rexall Train, and I'm a Rexallite. They don't wanna make a stink while they're sellin' these many fine products. It's a palace in there. They've got a four-piece orchestra. They've got an exhibit that shows how maraschino cherries are made."

Andy was kind of curious about the cherries, having experienced them in Reno at the same time he experienced air-conditioning, but they weren't relevant to this discussion. "Lasko, look, the other Rexallites will know each other. They'll know that you don't belong there as soon as the train starts moving."

"No, they won't," said Lasko, sounding testier than Andy had ever heard him. "Half the people on the train will be Pullman employees. I could be one of them. I could easily be that. Everybody will think I'm with somebody else."

Not if you're wearing a Rexall shirt, thought Andy.

Lasko walked for a while in sulky silence, kicking the rubble along the roadside. "I'm pretty convincing, you know. I can talk people into things."

Andy did know that. He thought of Lasko's hand on his shoulder that day at the drugstore. He thought of the complimentary squirt of cherry syrup and the fancy supper at the Martin Hotel and, later that night, the Mediterranean heat of Lasko's leg against his own.

Lasko's offer of friendship had been mildly suspect from the beginning, but Andy, after consideration, had decided that he didn't care. For better or worse, Lasko was adventure in a red sash and baggy pants—Richard Halliburton on a shoestring. This train caper might be goofy as all get-out, but it was harmless enough, and Andy's role as henchman was so peripheral as to seem unnecessary.

So why had Lasko enlisted his aid? Did he just want a witness to his grand scheme, someone to tell people where he had gone and how he had pulled it off? Was it easier to entrust this secret to the bookworm whose mother ran the brothel than to one of his buddies on the baseball team? Or was there something else on Lasko's mind, a secret longing he could never bring himself to name? No matter, thought Andy. Even if Lasko *had* asked him to run away with him on the train, hide with him god-knows-where until they reached San Francisco, even if he had lured Andy with talk of a magic heathen city, of a giant water-wheel in a giant swimming pool, Andy would have had to say no. He could never do that to Margaret or Mama.

Lasko stopped walking and looked directly at Andy. The slanting afternoon light made his embarrassment golden.

He's not used to begging. That face gets him everything.

"Are you in on this?" asked Lasko.

"I'm in. Just tell me what to do."

"Swell." Lasko thrust out his hand to be shaken.

Andy shook it. "Are you coming back?"

"What's it to you?" asked Lasko.

Andy shrugged and started walking again. "I think that's a natural question for one friend to ask another."

"You don't say," said Lasko.

It was one of those dumb things boys come up with when they don't know what to say, some meaningless tough-guy expression they've learned on the radio.

You don't say, wise guy.

But that was just the sound of it. If Andy had been looking at Lasko, if he had seen those dark eyes dance or the slightest curl of his lip, he might have known what to make of it. He might have even seen it as flirtatious, something overblown and sassy that landed, a little clumsily, halfway between Cary Grant and Mae West.

You don't say.

They walked in silence for a while.

"Are you enjoying the book?" Andy asked at last.

"What?"

"The *Book of Marvels.*"

"Oh . . . yeah . . . it's good."

Andy scuffed a cloud of dust at him. "It's not a book report, Lasko. I'm not your teacher. I don't care if you've read it. I know you've got a lot on your mind."

"Like what?" Lasko looked genuinely curious.

"Well . . . packing, for one."

"Packing?" He made a noise like spitting soda.

Andy found himself grinning. "Well, I guess, under the circumstances . . ."

"You don't pack for an escape."

"No, I guess not."

Lasko hooted and bounced around Andy like a prize-fighter, his fists pumping slowly and steadily, teasing but never quite touching the parts of Andy's body they purported to be demolishing. "Pack for an escape!" He sounded pirate-crazy at that moment, scornful too, but it was hard not to smile in the midst of that whirlwind.

When he finally stopped, Andy said, "You must've made plans for the other end."

"The other end of what?"

"The line, Lasko. Do you know anyone in San Francisco? Are you just gonna get off the train and take a streetcar to the swimming pool?"

"I might. I could."

"You have to have a plan, Lasko."

"No, I don't. Not after this. I don't have to have a plan in the world."

They parted in town, not far from Lasko's house. At least, Lasko said it wasn't far from his house, leading Andy to think that he might be ashamed of the place. Either that or he was just ashamed of Andy, the madam's boy he'd brought to the restaurant kitchen without so much as a how-do-you-do from his Mexican father.

Lasko raised his hand in a parting salute, walking backward for a moment as he uttered for the third or fourth time a snappy new farewell that Andy liked to think had been invented just for him. "Abyssinia!"

"Abyssinia," echoed Andy.

He watched Lasko as he headed down the street past Kossol's Korner. He would walk for while, strutting almost, then stop to spar with someone who wasn't there, some mighty invisible foe that had to be vanquished. Even from a distance his long, balletic shadow was comical and melancholy and completely magnificent.

It was coming on dusk when Andy got back to the Blue Moon. Several unfamiliar cars were parked out front, one of which almost certainly belonged to a customer, since Delphine was in her cabinette yelling "Peckerwood cocksucker!" at the top of her lungs. Mama would not be happy about that. She expected the girls to be ladylike. If there was yelling to be done, Mama would be the one to do it.

Andy stopped outside Delphine's cabinette to make sure she was all right. His answer came when the customer, a stumpy, baldheaded, beet-red man, stumbled out the screen door with his shoes and spats and most of his dusty blue serge suit piled in his arms. Upon seeing Andy, he shook his head in contempt, as if to say, *These women!*, presuming sympathy from a member of his own gender.

"Fucking Cajun cunt," he muttered, then stumbled toward his car, arms still brimming with clothes, stopping only to pee on the cactus painted on Violet's cabinette. They despise women, thought Andy. Why do they even bother?

Margaret, slouched against the porch swing, caught the world-weary look on Andy's face as he headed into the house. "Elegant here tonight, ain't it?"

Andy rolled his eyes. "How do they get so plastered so early?"

Margaret followed him into the house so eagerly that he assumed she'd been waiting for him. "Delphine was raisin' more Cain than he was."

"I know. I heard it." Andy's eyes shot nervously to the corner of the parlor, where Mama's big desk was piled so high with ledgers and *Collier's* magazines that you could never tell for sure if she was there.

"It's okay," said Margaret. "She's in town. And what she don't know won't hurt her."

Andy agreed. At this point Mama needed only the slightest excuse to boot Delphine out of her cabinette. Delphine had lately been giving Mama lip, so Mama had been on the warpath. Margaret had never cared much for Delphine, she said, but she didn't want to see her working the arcade either, doing it on the cheap for Chinamen behind the bowling alley. So that meant keeping Mama in the dark about Delphine's tantrums with customers. Margaret liked keeping Mama in the dark.

"It's in her blood, you know. She can't help it."

For a moment, Andy thought she was talking about Mama.

"They get this rage in 'em down in the swamps."

"Oh . . . Delphine." Andy smiled. He loved how Margaret summed things up so neatly, the way she kept things uncomplicated for herself. "That's a new slip," he said, noticing it for the first time. It was powder blue rayon, lace-trimmed.

Margaret ducked her head as if she'd been complimented at a prom.

"Special customer?" asked Andy.

"Just some Stanford boys. They've been here before, but they've got a new chum with 'em." Margaret plumped the white-blond tresses she had piled on her head for the evening. "Girl's gotta keep up her reputation." The brave vamp tone didn't come naturally to her, so she abandoned it immediately. "They're nice boys, though. Polite as can be on the phone. Listen, lamb, can we chew the fat for a sec?"

"Sure," said Andy, already puzzled.

"In your room, I mean?"

With Mama in town, it was hard to imagine what could possibly require privacy. What crisis would have to wait until the girls were out of earshot? The dress, thought Andy. The chiffon shame in his closet. At Margaret's insistence, he had never worn it outside his room—and only three times inside—but Mama could easily have found it. She'd been known to snoop around sometimes, and there was no way to lock his door from the outside. On two occasions Andy had come home from school to find the orange-blossomy sweetness of Mama's perfume, Je Reviens, inhabiting his room like an overripe tropical garden. It troubled him more than it should have. It didn't help, of course, that the name meant "I'm coming back."

Andy led the way into his room. Margaret followed him closely, a picture of international intrigue as she latched the door behind her.

"What's going on?" he asked.

"Are you in trouble, lamb?"

"What?"

"You know you can ask me for money. You don't have to do this." She sat on the edge of the bed and patted the spot next to her. Andy sat down reluctantly.

"Why would you think I need money?" he asked. He received an allowance from Mama every week when she doled out the cash to the girls. It was nothing to brag about, but it covered lunch money and sodas and movies and such. He knew plenty of kids at Humboldt High who didn't even get lunch, much less allowances.

Margaret was studying him with big cow eyes. "It's not like you, lamb. That's what I don't understand. Help me to understand, all right?"

"Margaret—"

"I went into town today to buy me some special emerald-green thread, and I passed the pawnshop on the way out of Hunsucker's." She laid her hand on her chest and sighed, as if the awful truth had just been finally revealed in full.

"And?" he said.

"They had it for sale in the window, Andy." A tear blazed its way through her caky makeup. "I know it's silly. It didn't belong to me in the first place, but it was a nice piece of luggage—real Italian leather—and I wanted you to have it."

The valise, thought Andy. Lasko hocked it.

The emotions jostling within him—confusion, betrayal, shame, guilt—left very little room for the truth. "What do you mean?" he asked, completely poker-faced.

"You know, Andy. That beautiful valise." She pulled a hankie from her slip and blotted her eyes with delicate precision. "I wanted it to be an heirloom from me."

"Ohhhh." Andy made it look like the light had finally dawned. "So that's what happened. I'm so sorry, Margaret. I really am."

"What do you mean?"

"I took it to school last week. I wanted to show it off. I left it by my chair in the lunchroom when . . . you know, I went to stand in line. When I got back, it was gone. I asked everybody around my table, but nobody said they'd seen it."

"You didn't report it to the principal?"

Andy hesitated, scrambling for a way out. "I thought some of the kids were teasing me. I figured I'd get it back in a day or two. I didn't wanna be a snitch. And I didn't wanna disappoint you. I just hoped you'd forget about it . . . eventually."

"Oh, Andy." She looked so relieved that Andy felt even guiltier.

Why am I protecting Lasko? he thought. I'm the one who was cheated.

"We should tell the sheriff. He can find out who hocked it."

"No!"

"Why not?"

"Because . . ." Because what? "Because the valise didn't belong to us either, Margaret. They'll just think you stole it from that fancy customer."

"The sheriff knows me, Andy. He wouldn't think that." She looked devastated now, as if her reputation with the law had gone with the valise. "Besides, we don't have to mention where it came from. We'll say I bought it for you."

"But . . . you can't. Not with that monogram."

"What monogram? I didn't see no monogram."

"It was little. It was on the inside. I thought it was the company at first."

Lie upon lie in the name of love. Not even love yet, and probably never. Just the highly unlikely and nearly impossible possibility of love.

He knew better, of course. Even then, before it happened, he knew better.

14
Only Tales

The middle of California scrolled past them in a golden blur, steepled with the shrines of Petco and McDonald's, a landscape like anywhere else in America. Or the world, for that matter. Years ago, when Wren had modeled caftans among the ancient ruins of Delphi, she'd been appalled by the long suburban drive out of Athens. A terrain intended for satyrs had abandoned its soul to Toyota dealerships.

She opened the ice chest and pulled out a sweating bottle. "Kombucha?" she asked, displaying it lengthwise for Mrs. Madrigal as Vanna White might do. "This is lavender, but we also have hibiscus here at the Club Winnebago Sacramento."

"What is it, dear?"

"Oh shit, who knows. It just showed up in the stores. It has enzymes or something—live cultures—living breathing things. Definitely an acquired taste. Kind of floral and moldy at the same time."

The old woman widened her eyes. "How much more floral and moldy do I need to be?"

Wren laughed and twisted the cap. "It's good, though. I was surprised. Stops short of sweet and gets somewhere deeper in your taste buds, if that makes any sense." She took a sip, then held it out to Anna, who took it from her and drank.

As near as Wren could tell, she liked it.

"Good?"

"Mmm. I've always fallen for a good snake oil salesman."

Wren wasn't sure how to take that, but she laughed.

"It's all in the pitch, isn't it? Show me some enthusiasm and I'll believe anything you say."

Wren chuckled. "Did you learn that at the Blue Moon?"

"In the vicinity." Mrs. Madrigal handed the bottle back to Wren with a tight little smile. "I'm afraid that's a taste I won't have sufficient time to acquire."

"Give her a Coke! I think there's one in there!" This was Brian, yelling from the driver's seat. He liked getting lost in what he called "the Zen of the road," but every now and then he'd pipe up, letting them know he was still there.

"No, dear," said Anna. "I'm perfectly fine."

Wren tucked the bottle back into the ice chest. "Would you like to stretch out? The bunk is right there. We've got at least two more hours until Tahoe."

"No, thank you. I'm very comfy. I love watching the world go by. I haven't done it much lately. It's a treat."

"Am I talking too much?"

"Not at all."

"I wanna know about your life," Wren said flatly. "How you . . . made it the way it was supposed to be."

"My reassignment, you mean?"

"In part, yeah. You must've been one of the first?"

"Oh, no. There were people in the thirties. Dr. Hirschfeld in Berlin had several patients, one of whom died after surgery. The one I knew about, of course, was Christine Jorgensen in the early fifties. Everyone knows about her."

Anna was clearly waiting for an acknowledgment that Wren was unable to provide. "Sorry, that was—"

"Before your time. Of course. She'd been George Jorgensen of the Bronx. In the army like me . . . and she went to Denmark for the hormones and surgery. That's how I got the idea, though that was tricky business a decade later. The Danish hated the publicity around Christine, so they banned the procedure. I had to find a doctor on the sly in Copenhagen." Anna rearranged her hands in her lap with imperial dignity. "Christine was very brave. Heroic, really."

"Having the surgery, you mean?"

"No—well, yes, it was still risky—but I meant back home. The whole sideshow, the cheap jokes. All that 'GI Becomes Glamour Girl' nonsense. She took it with remarkable grace and candor. There were reporters waiting for her at the airport, so she wore sunglasses and a mink and stepped off the plane like a movie star. She owned her truth. It was how she kept the world from hurting her."

Exactly what I did with fat, thought Wren, recalling her life in the world of Big and Beautiful. Tell the joke on yourself first, and others won't get the chance.

"She must have felt so impatient with people," Anna added with a sigh. "Even her doctor didn't understand who she was. He saw himself as performing a humane act for a homosexual. Castrating him for his own good. And the good of society."

"What do you mean?"

Anna shrugged. "So he couldn't act on his unnatural attraction to men."

"Oh, for God's sake!"

"That's the way it was," said Anna.

"Did you feel like a girl when you were a little boy?"

"Oh yes. Always."

"And you were attracted to boys?"

"Yes—but probably not in the way that you were."

"How so?"

The old woman's eyes moved to the parchment-colored hills as she composed her answer. "I was drawn to them romantically. I felt as if I *belonged* with them romantically, but I knew I had the wrong equipment for it, so . . . it scared the hell out of me—repulsed me, in fact, if they even . . ." Her voice trailed off.

Wren, feeling bold, finished for her. "If they came on to you."

"Yes. For sex, mind you. Flirting was fine—lovely in fact—as long as it went nowhere, but . . ."

"When push came to shove . . ."

Anna smiled at her. "Yes. Unthinkable. Utterly. I would have felt like someone deformed."

"Did that happen often?"

"What?"

"A boy coming on to you? Aggressively, I mean."

"You ladies doing all right back there?" Brian asked, yelling over his shoulder again. Wren wondered how much of their girl talk he had heard, and if he thought she was overstepping her bounds with Mrs. Madrigal. Then she dismissed the thought as ridiculous. What bounds could you possibly overstep with this amazing person? In her own way, she had long ago stepped off the airplane like a movie star. At ninety-two she surely had no secrets left to tell. Only tales.

"We're fine, pumpkin," she told her husband before turning to Anna. "Aren't we?"

"Of course," said Anna, looking out the window again.

When they arrived at Tahoe, it was already twilight under the tall trees. While Brian handled the hookup, Wren got Anna settled in a camp chair, so she could look out over a patch of sand at the darkening cobalt glass of the lake. This was one of Brian's favorite places, and Wren could see why. Camp Richardson was a throwback to the 1920s, a rustic resort with Monopoly-board cabins named after the touring cars that once shuttled tourists between here and Placerville: Chevy, Buick, Pierce-Arrow. But the wondrous machines that had brought people to the wild seemed less so now that there was a perpetual traffic jam encircling the lake.

Wren set up a camp chair next to Anna's and collapsed into it. Anna turned and smiled at her, then returned her gaze to the lake.

"I'm as old as this place," she said. "Maybe a little older."

Wren wasn't sure how to respond, so they let an easy silence fall.

Finally Anna said, "I'm glad you're with him."

"So am I."

"His first wife wasn't meant to be married. Some people aren't, you know. Very sweet, but . . . I knew from the day I met her." A breeze tousled a wisp of Anna's hair, so she corrected it. "Brian was always gallivanting around, mind you, but I knew he was heading for this. Always."

Wren raked her fingers through the cool sand next to her chair. "I was a major gallivanter, too. Maybe that's why it works so well."

"Quite possibly."

Another silence.

"I wish you weren't going away," said Anna, adding after a moment, "I wish *I* weren't."

Wren reached across and took her hand. Twigs swathed in cool silk.

"Thank you for not contesting that," said Anna. "It gets tiresome being told you're immortal."

Wren chuckled. "I'll bet."

"Help me up, dear. Just for a second. While we still have the light."

Wren helped the old woman to her feet. "Do we have a mission in mind?"

"Oh yes." Anna pointed a shaky finger at the blue-shadowed beach in front of them. "Just from here to there will be fine."

Wren took her arm and began to walk. "Wait," said Anna, holding back, rubbing one Chinese slippered foot against the other in a way that puzzled Wren.

"Goddammit. Help me get them off, would you, dear?"

"Do you have a stone or—"

"I just want them off."

She wants to go barefoot, thought Wren. "Steady yourself on my shoulder," she said as she knelt and removed Anna's slippers one at a time, following up with the socks. Even in the rapidly fading light the seashell-pink varnish on Anna's toes was unmissable. "Nice color," said Wren. "I like a girl who paints her toenails."

"Done it most of my life. Or had it done."

"Even back at the Blue Moon?"

"Oh yes. My friend Margaret did it. One of the ladies."

"Who does it now?" Wren began to lead Anna slowly through the sand.

"Who do you think?"

"Jake?"

Anna chuckled. "Helps to keep his lady side alive."

"And that's a good thing?"

"Mmm. For all of us, dear. Both sides are necessary."

"So how did you keep your man side alive?"

Anna stopped walking for a moment to wriggle her toes in the sand. "Ohhh, that feels lovely. The earth knows exactly how to hold us if we just let it."

Wren wondered if she'd finally asked the wrong question, but Anna eventually replied: "Your husband."

"Sorry?"

"How I kept my man side alive. He was my buddy at Barbary Lane. We had some fine man-to-man talks. The way men can do sometimes."

And it made him a better man, thought Wren.

It made him exactly the kind of open, unthreatened, and sexually confident man that she was able to live with.

In this case, for a lifetime. Whatever that means for the two of us.

They ate dinner together—a big paella for three—on the porch of the lakefront restaurant at Camp Richardson. There was sangria too, several pitchers, and a waiter who thought it was cute to call Anna "young lady" with every refill.

"Condescending asshole," Wren muttered, as soon as he was out of earshot.

Anna took a sip of her sangria. "I don't mind, dear. He thinks he's being charming."

"That's very gracious of you, but, if he talked to *me* like a six-year-old, I'd personally hand him his nuts on a platter."

Brian and Anna both laughed. "I doubt Anna would be bothered by 'young lady,' " said Brian. "She built the word 'girl' into her name."

Wren didn't have a clue as to what he meant.

"Her name is an anagram," Brian announced with a note of triumph in his voice. "Anna Madrigal is an anagram for 'a man and a girl.' "

"No shit?" She looked to the old woman for confirmation.

Anna just shrugged. "The letters do spell that out."

"She tortured me with it for weeks," said Brian. "In those days you couldn't figure it out on a computer."

Wren fished an orange slice out of her sangria and popped it into her mouth. "So you picked your name because it was an anagram for—"

"Actually, no. The anagram came later. I mean, I realized it later. Everyone's name is an anagram for something. Almost everyone's."

"Large wounds," said Wren.

"Pardon me, dear?"

"Wren Douglas is an anagram for 'large wounds.' " She lowered her eyelids at Anna. "Can you imagine how much *that* played hell with a fat teenager?"

They shared a merry moment of bonding until Brian interrupted it. "Wait a minute," he said to Anna. "You told me you chose your name for the anagram."

The old woman shook her head slowly. "I told you it *was* an anagram. There's a big difference."

Brian's face turned pouty. "So you were just blowing smoke up my ass."

Anna smiled dimly. "You may have been inhaling, dear, but I wasn't blowing."

That got a snorty laugh from Wren, who filed it away for future use.

Her husband, however, seemed determined to carry through with his indignation. "Okay, then where did Anna Madrigal come from?"

"Winnemucca," said Anna, as if the answer were patently obvious. "In more ways than one."

It occurred to Wren, not for the first time, that Mrs. Madrigal enjoyed a good conundrum. Even at this age, with all her cards seemingly on the table, she liked being a woman of mystery. Wren remembered the Google printout in Brian's shirt pocket and how the old woman had presented it to Brian without explanation.

"Tell me," said Wren. "Would this have anything to do with Oliver Sudden?"

Anna smiled over the rim of her sangria glass. "If I knew the answer to *that*, my dear, I wouldn't have asked for a ride."

15

Matter Out of Place

I t began as a hidden processional on the freeway. The odd car with hieroglyphics of the Man taped on the back window, an RV adorned with clunker bicycles, the occasional flatbed truck, its tarp bulging scrotally with carnival parts. For the first few hours, these encounters were random enough that you could enjoy a secret communion with the other pilgrims in the bland mainstream of traffic.

But once the freeway was gone, and the highway had become a country road, the funnel into Black Rock City narrowed to nothing and a new sort of communion began. They were stopped now, completely, thousands of engines silenced in the midst of a hazy gray desert. One by one people emerged from their metal shells to assess the situation and pee by the roadside.

Michael thought of a train stalled on the tracks. Any moment now, the bandits would board them and begin to plunder.

"Let's get out," said Ben. "We're gonna be here for a while."

With no further urging, Shawna leaped out of the back seat and onto the trailer, where she pointed ecstatically to the horizon. "Omigod, guys, look!"

Ben and Michael followed her onto the lumpy hillock of camping equipment and boxed water bottles, Michael faltering in the process. Ben grabbed his hand and steadied him, an act that was simultaneously endearing and humiliating.

"I'm fine," said Michael. "Thanks, sweetie."

Great. Flunking the physical already.

"What are we looking at?" asked Ben.

"Our peeps," said Shawna.

There, in the distance, the line of traffic made a single glittering brushstroke across the landscape, encircling everything like a noose.

"Shit," murmured Michael.

Shawn mistook his horror for amazement. "Is that not awesome?" Her own tone suggested someone who'd just beheld a queue of disabled believers at Lourdes.

"And that's not even the end of the line," Ben told her. "That's just the part we can see."

Michael groaned. "Dare we ask where the beginning is?"

The three of them turned in unison. What they saw, first thing, was a fortyish guy in a sarong making an effusive bow to the sunset from the top of his Cruise America RV. He was also blowing bubbles (a little frenetically, Michael thought), as if to say that his bliss was *on*, motherfuckers, gridlock or no gridlock.

"Woohoo," he called upon spotting the threesome on the trailer. He wasn't exactly greeting them, just demonstrating his ability to make that annoying sound.

Michael woohooed back, perhaps ineffectually.

Shawna giggled, gazing up at him. "You need to work on that." She looked radiant in this light, already halfway to pagan princess. While he, in Bermudas and XL baggy tee, still undoubtedly looked like Granddad at Disneyland.

"I have to build up to it," he told her. "I can't just woohoo from a cold start. I've never been like that."

Shawna held onto his arm. "I know, Uncle Mouse."

He wondered if this old nickname had been summoned for nefarious purposes. They had not discussed the sperm thing (as Michael had come to think of it) since Shawna first broached the topic. He assumed that Ben had spoken with her, bowing out gracefully, but he didn't know for sure. He hadn't asked. He wanted Ben to know that he, Michael, could leave the subject alone, keep his nose out of things.

"He's got the right idea," said Shawna.

Michael was rattled. "What?"

"The guy in the sarong. We could be here for hours. We have to let go of our traveling mentality and Be Here Now."

"She's right," said Ben, taking Michael's other arm.

He sighed. "You can't Be Here Now if you haven't gotten there yet."

That would have been a lot funnier if it hadn't become the theme of the day. The line of vehicles stopped and started and stopped again until they finally arrived in Gerlach, a charmingly mutant village that might have been too much like *The Hills Have Eyes* had the locals not been hawking glow sticks to Burners off their front porches. By the time they passed through town, night had fallen, bringing with it a dust storm of Old Testament proportions. Ben, as usual, thrived on the challenge, remaining cool-headed in the face of calamity. While the wipers carved adobe arches on the windshield, he drove with the focus of a tank commander, squinting into the whirlwind that repeatedly erased the taillights ahead of them. Those lights, Michael reminded himself grimly, could well be attached to Mr. Woohoo himself, who, having prematurely snorted huge amounts of K three hours earlier in a porta potty in Nixon, was now on the verge of passing out at the wheel.

"This is a fucking nightmare."

"You're not being helpful," Shawna observed from the back seat.

"You're right." He turned penitently to his husband. "What do you need, honey? Some water? A Clif Bar? A blow job?"

Ben smiled wearily. "My neck is really tight."

"I'm on it," Shawna told him.

And she was, instantly, digging into his shoulders with her strong little hands.

Ben gave an involuntary moan. "We should be reaching the checkpoints soon."

Michael did not like the sound of that. "What are they checking us for?"

"Tickets, mostly," said Ben. "Stowaways. Feathers. Stuff like that."

"*Feathers?*"

"It's the worst kind of MOOP," said Shawna. "It's completely irretrievable. They won't let you bring feathers in at all."

Michael already knew about MOOP—Matter Out of Place—Burning Man's version of litter, only stricter than litter, since it included things like apple cores and dishwater, anything that might alter the delicate ecology of an irreversibly lifeless alkali flat. It figured that a place without birds would not look kindly upon feathers.

"Damn," said Michael. "Good thing I hid my boa up my ass."

Ben grinned. "Never mind that. Where's your ticket?"

"I have it," said Michael somewhat defensively. "It's in my bag."

"Which is where?"

"Shit, shit, shit!"

"In the trailer, right?"

They had been stopped for a moment, so Michael knew what he had to do. "I'll get it," he said. "Just don't leave me. I'll never find the car again."

"Wear your goggles," said Ben.

"Shit."

"They're in the bag too?"

"Don't lecture me," said Michael. "Not now."

"What did I say? Did I say anything?"

"Hang on," said Shawna, fumbling in the back until she produced a filmy blue-and-green scarf and handed it to Michael.

"I won't be able to see," he said.

"Just over your mouth and nose, dude. And keep your head down."

He opened the door and plunged into the tempest of grit. It was called a whiteout, but under the headlight beams, the stinging air was a hybrid of mustard and taupe, a noxious gas on another planet. Leaning into it, scarf pressed to his face, he made his way to the trailer, where he fumbled through a web of bungee cords until he found the bag. The traffic, to his alarm, had already begun to move again, so he stumbled back to the door, expecting chastisement from an orchestra of angry car horns. But people weren't honking at all. *They were not honking*.

He opened the door, scrambled into the seat, slammed the door.

"Got it?" asked Ben.

"Got it." He dug the ticket out of his bag and held it up as belated proof of his competency. It was as intricate as currency, almost as large, an extravagance of design worthy of admission to Willy Wonka's chocolate factory.

He handed the scarf back to Shawna. She dusted the side of his head with it. "You're gonna get a lot blonder before this is over."

"It's a look," said Michael.

Shawna had lobbied for years to "do something fun" with her old queer uncle's hair, but he had steadfastly refused, claiming, now that he was gray, to be "one of God's blonds." He had never seen anyone his age with pleasingly dyed hair.

The dust, however, when examined in the mirror, did do something interesting—a lighter, duller, more powdery effect that bordered on *Les Liaisons dangereuses*.

He already wanted a shower.

At the checkpoint they were greeted by a lanky kid in dreads and buckskin who leaned into the Outback with a flashlight. He was completely furred with dust like a mannequin in an attic, or maybe an astronaut blighted with an alien fungus, but he still managed to exude proficiency and good cheer. "Welcome home, folks!"

"Thanks!" said Ben.

"How many you got?"

Ben held up the tickets. "Three. One in the back."

"And no feathers," Michael added.

"What?"

"I am without feathers. Feather-free."

Ben shot him a look. "Let the guy do his job, honey."

"It's cool," said the guy. "Is he a Burgin?"

"Is he ever," said Shawna.

"A *what*?" asked Michael.

"A Burning Man virgin," Ben explained, without turning back to Michael.

They were talking about him as if he weren't there, or at least as if they didn't care. It was oddly reminiscent of childhood road trips in Florida with his family. *Is this the little feller's first time at Parrot Jungle?*

"Do I sound Burginal?" Michael asked the guy.

"A little." Perfect white teeth flashed from the concrete-colored face. "Don't sweat it. You'll get into it quicker than you think. My dad did."

"Your dad's a lot younger than I am."

"I doubt that," said the guy cheerfully. "He's pretty old."

"Oh good," said Michael, deadpanning.

"Take it real slow." The guy was talking to Ben again, grown-up to grown-up.

From there, they were divided into separate lanes, the boundaries of which were almost impossible to read in the whiteout. Place de la Concorde, thought Michael, though a lot slower, of course, and some of the vehicles were as big as houses. They *were* houses, lumbering out of the dust like weary elephants, their hides absorbing the paleness of the land, their Rent Me ads pasteled into submission.

"You think there'll be greeters?" Shawna asked Ben.

Michael was thinking, Is there a maître d' at a tsunami?

"I doubt it," said Ben. "The guy back there said 'Welcome home,' so maybe they're doubling up in the whiteout."

Shawna touched Michael's shoulder. "Normally there are people who greet you and say 'Welcome home' and get all the Burgins to roll in the dust."

"Forget that shit," he said.

"You have to give in to it, Michael."

"I don't have to give in to anything. I have nothing against getting dirty under controlled circumstances—"

"Not the ritual. The dust itself. You have to make peace with it sooner or later. You have to . . . let the barnacle form."

"Seriously, Shawna, if you tell 'em I'm a Burgin . . . I have to let the barnacle form? What sort of fucked-up shit is that?"

She giggled. "Okay, then . . . a pearl can't be a pearl without a grain of sand."

"*Grain?* You want grains?" He tousled his hair briskly. "I've been out in that shit, sister. Don't talk to me about grains."

"Okay," said Shawna, going comically hangdog the way she had done as a child. "There's gonna be one really disappointed hippie chick in a Raggedy Ann wig . . . with big baby-doll shoes . . . . and a landing strip the exact same color as the wig."

"Now you're just trying to scare me," said Michael.

Their tank commander chuckled. "It's a moot point, anyway. I think we're there."

"There" in this instance could have meant a physical arrival or a simple lifting of the dust, a magician's trick that left them on a vast darkling plain dotted with phantasmagorical color. It was probably both things, of course, but regardless of the alchemy, they found themselves, suddenly, on the outskirts of a Fellini carnival on Mars.

"We need to look for street signs," said Ben.

"What's our address?" asked Shawna.

Michael knew the answer to that—"Eight o'clock and Edelweiss"—so all eyes were instantly upon him, widened in exaggerated amazement.

"What?" said Michael. "I wanted to know where we live in case I get lost."

"But you remembered," said Shawna. "Nice job."

Michael accepted the compliment, though he knew he could not have done it without the aid of Julie Andrews and the von Trapp children.

He remembered, too, that the streets formed concentric circles around the playa (an open space for art installations), and that the whole place was two miles wide. *Two fucking miles.* Like the Great Wall of China, this psychedelic gypsy camp could be seen from space: a crescent moon blazing gold in a valley of nothingness.

But even satellite photos had not prepared Michael for the immensity of the place. As they drove down one of the streets, past block after block of dust-fuzzed tents and shade structures jutting like bat wings into the sky, the night rang with the sound of sledgehammers on rebar. It was early days, Ben pointed out, so the full effect had yet to be realized; it was still a coloring book waiting for clever children and their crayons. But one by one, between patches of vacant darkness, the camps were emerging, a conspiracy of colored lights and towers and streaming banners, an ephemeral city rising to its feet.

It *could* be another planet, thought Michael, if not for the familiar moon lolling on the dark shoulder of the mountains.

Ben reached over and held his leg. "It's gonna be blue while we're here," he said.

"What's gonna be blue?"

"The moon, honey. We're having a full-fledged blue moon. You know what that is, right?"

Michael did not know, actually.

"I'm familiar with the whorehouse," he said.

16
Wisteria Toes

The Stanford boys were getting rowdier downstairs, howling Margaret's name in the parlor as if it were a football fight song. To Andy, something in their tone sounded cruel, something beyond the usual coarseness of men toward the girls at the Blue Moon. He wondered if Margaret's age had made her the butt of mean jokes they shared with each other. If so, he hoped she didn't know it.

He had put on the dress tonight, so the bedroom door was latched. A warm, fickle breeze from the window found the chiffon and made it flirt with his legs. His toenails, as of this afternoon, were painted a shade of wisteria Margaret had chosen to match the dress. He walked slowly across the room, pivoting on his toes like an English lady going barefoot on the lawn of her country estate. Summery, he thought. That's how I feel. He had heard Loretta Young use that word once in a movie and had always wanted to use it himself. *My, don't you look summery tonight.*

He extended his leg and gazed down at the perfect nail polish, the curve of his calf under the wispy fabric. It was hard to imagine how this could be improved upon. Below the knees, thanks to Margaret, he was all he was ever meant to be.

A noise at the door made him stiffen in alarm. It was not a knock either but a thwarted invasion, which could only mean Mama herself was shaking the door against its hardware-store latch. She did it, as usual, more out of pique than in hope of entry, but Andy, in his rising panic, could almost feel the screws flying out.

"I'm not decent, Mama."

"Well, why the hell ain't you?"

"I'm just . . . . changing clothes."

"Ain't nothin' I ain't seen before!"

Andy kept quiet. *Oh, the things you haven't seen before.*

"Better not be diddlin' yourself. You gotta save that for somebody nice."

"Mama, please—"

"I left 'em by the kitchen door."

He was too shaken to think straight. "What?"

"You said you wanted the truck tonight."

"Yes, ma'am. Thank you." He had dropped Gloria Watson's name at supper, so Mama, going all whirly-eyed at the mere thought of Gloria's dowry, had offered transportation. She probably wouldn't mind one bit if Andy were to knock Gloria up. Mama had once remarked, in all seriousness, that shotgun weddings paid just as well as the other kind. Not that there was a chance of Andy knocking *anyone* up.

"Where are you takin' her?"

"I have to get dressed, Mama. I'm late."

Both things were true; tonight was Lasko's night at the Martin, and he got off work at nine. It wasn't the ideal solution to the problem, but Andy had been left with no other choice. Lasko hadn't shown up at school for several days, and Andy's low-key detective work at Eagle Drugs had produced only a cryptic explanation from Mr. Yee: "He got the day off. He's not feeling so good."

Andy hoped that what Lasko was feeling was remorse for having hocked the valise. If not remorse, at least embarrassment over the betrayal of their friend-ship. Or, barring that, some degree of fear that Andy might actually stand up for himself. A theft was a theft, even when it involved a valise left at a brothel that a hooker had entrusted to a boy who had lent it—just lent it, mind you—to another boy. The law might like to know about this, Andy figured. There could be serious consequences.

It was strange to feel such unbridled hurt and anger. As a rule, he tried not to indulge in those emotions, knowing how easily they could overwhelm him. Hurt and anger were to be expected by a boy like him, living where he lived, knowing what he knew about himself. But Lasko's action was beyond the pale. It implied that Andy was completely unworthy of respect, exempt from the ordinary rules of society.

It implied that Andy had no choice but to keep his mouth shut.

He waited in the shadows outside the Martin while the dinner crowd dispersed. He had already decided that confronting Lasko in the restaurant (or worse yet, in the kitchen) would be foolish. Lasko's father could be there, for one thing, or any number of relatives who didn't know Andy from Adam and would surely unite against a stranger with an accusation. It was better to talk to Lasko where no one else could hear them. Better to wait until he was walking home.

Ten minutes passed. Twenty. Andy studied the stragglers left on the porch, the kitchen help spilling joylessly out of the back, but Lasko was nowhere to be seen. The only person he recognized was Lasko's sister Hegazti, the shy, big-armed girl so adept at balancing plates. He considered questioning her about Lasko, but decided instead to tail her, since that would probably yield more information.

She was heading away from the tracks along the alley behind Bridge Street. No one else was going that way, so Andy, wary of looking ominous, waited until Hegazti had turned onto another street before sprinting to catch up with her. When he saw her, she was turning again, this time into a vacant lot bristling with spindly weeds and auto parts. There was a house on the far side, next to which a flaking wall bore the ghostly remains of a word—LOTHING—which marked the back of a haberdashery that had gone bust when Andy was still a youngster. A naked lightbulb on the landing caught Hegazti's red blouse and made it ignite in the darkness.

She was talking to someone in the shadows. Her voice was gentle, placating. Andy could not make out anything, so he moved closer.

" . . . I made it specially for you."

"No! I don't want it!" His voice was slurred, but it was Lasko.

"It's cream-filled."

"No me molestes!"

"Cabron!"

The red blouse extinguished itself. Andy heard a door slam. He walked as casually as possible past the house, implying that he was on the way home himself. Hegazti was inside now, her big arms all but blocking the view into a brightly lit kitchen. She was talking loudly to another woman, Lasko's mother presumably, but she was speaking Basque now, not Spanish. Andy could not understand a word of it, but her agitation made it clear that she had been the one who slammed the door.

So where had Lasko been?

Andy peered across the weedy lot, where a garage was leaning drunkenly against an amputated cotton-wood. Its splintered walls had been patched with a Coca-Cola sign as big as a bushel basket. A corona of light, too faint to be electric, was seeping around the edges of the sign. Someone is in there now, he thought.

He moved closer, already weighing and discarding his words for what lay ahead. He had come here in the name of his self-respect, his honor, and it was too late to back out now. He stopped at the garage door and addressed it quietly.

"Lasko?"

Nothing.

"It's Andy Ramsey. I'd like my book back, please."

Still no response, just the sound of clumsy movement inside. Andy commanded himself to breathe.

"I won't make trouble, Lasko. I just want the book back."

The door creaked open. Lasko appeared in silhouette against the erratic flicker of a kerosene lamp. He was swaying slightly in a soiled undershirt and baggy trousers, and even from a distance, Andy could smell the *basco* wine on his breath.

"I haven't finished reading it," Lasko said.

"I don't care. I want it back. I know what happened to the valise."

"No, you don't."

"I saw it, Lasko. I even know how much you got for it."

Lasko's eyes darted nervously toward the house. "Pipe down, okay? I'll get you the book." He beckoned Andy with a sloppy sweep of his arm.

Andy hesitated, peering into the garage. "Is this where you live?"

"It's sorta my clubhouse."

Andy knew that was a lie. He could see a swayback bed against one wall, a table with a washbasin and a toothbrush, a nice shirt for school hanging off a nail on the wall. It looked, unmistakably, like a place to which someone had been banished. This was Lasko's

Elba, and he was ashamed of it, a fact that somehow, to Andy, made him much more sympathetic, if not an ounce more trustworthy.

He entered the lamplit cavern. Lasko tugged the door shut behind them. "Take a load off," he said. Andy hesitated, wondering if his righteous indignation could survive sitting down. Finally he sank to the edge of the bed, since there was nowhere else to sit. Lasko pulled the *Book of Marvels* from a shelf above the bed and handed it to Andy. "I'm sorry," he said soberly, the way drunks do. "I enjoyed it greatly." He sat on the other end of the bed, head down, hands dangling between his legs, a whipped puppy. His dejection seemed so real that Andy's ire dwindled.

"It's not the book, Lasko, and you know it. That valise wasn't yours to hock. It was a gift to me from someone who was hurt because she thought I was the one who had hocked it. I had to lie to her about where I had lost it. If you needed money for Frisco . . . for the swimming pool or something . . . I would have been happy to . . . well, I might have been able . . . but this way I can't trust you at all. I'd like to be your friend, but why should I even help you anymore? Tell me that, Lasko. How do I know you won't stick up a bank before you get on the Rexall Train?"

And that, Andy realized, was a question he had never imagined asking anyone. The sheer novelty of it was exhilarating—not to mention the chance to sound like a spunky dame in a radio play. Lasko, however, was not in the least impressed, showing no sign of penitence whatsoever. His eyes were still fixed on the greasy packed earth beneath his feet. "I didn't hock that valise," he said gruffly.

Andy groaned. He was tired of being a lady about this.

"I didn't," said Lasko.

"Don't play me for a fool, Lasko. I went to the pawn-shop. I looked at the tag myself. It said 'Madrigal' plain as day."

Lasko shrugged morosely. "There's more than one Madrigal around here."

Scowling, Andy raised his voice. "*Who?* Hegazti?"

"Shhhh." Lasko pressed a finger to his cushiony lips, then whispered a single word: "Papi."

"Your father hocked my valise?" Andy pictured the sourpuss in the restaurant kitchen, the coarser, older version of Lasko who had barked orders to Hegazti and never acknowledged Andy's presence. "What right did he have to do that?"

Lasko started to speak but stopped himself.

"Lasko?"

"He said he didn't want no *puta* suitcase in his house."

Puta. Whore. One Spanish word Andy knew well.

"But how did he know about Margaret?" Andy had never told Lasko where the valise had come from. They'd never talked about the valise at all.

"Who's Margaret?" asked Lasko.

Oh, thought Andy. He *doesn't* know. The old man had simply seen Andy with the valise at the Martin, and that had made it *puta* by association.

"It doesn't matter," said Andy. "Just someone I know at the Blue Moon. Forget it."

A long, draining silence followed. Then Andy said, "My mother runs a legitimate business, you know."

Lasko grunted yes. "My old man goes there sometimes."

No surprise there. Half the town did. "But he doesn't approve of me." It wasn't a question, just a stark statement of fact.

"Nope," said Lasko with a wicked smile, waiting a moment before reaching over to sock Andy's arm with the utmost gentleness. His drawn-out sparring match had finally made contact. "He thinks you're a bad influence."

"So he stole my valise."

"Yep."

"And he makes you live out here?"

Lasko nodded. "Till I've learned to be a man, he says."

Another long silence while Andy wondered what exactly that meant.

"Are you scared of him?"

Lasko hesitated, then pulled a Carnation Milk box from under the bed. There was a small pistol inside, swaddled in kitchen rags and dull with dust. To Andy's relief Lasko didn't pick it up, just pushed the box back under the bed.

"You wouldn't use that, would you?"

"Not if I ain't got to."

Andy didn't like the sound of that, so he chose to dodge the subject entirely. "Well . . . soon enough you'll be getting away from him."

Lasko shook his head slowly.

"What do you mean?"

"The Rexall Train ain't coming."

At first Andy couldn't take this in. He had already pictured the train so vividly in his mind's eye, right down to the cosmetics car and the maraschino cherry exhibit, that it seemed almost impossible that he might not see it for real.

"Why not?" he asked.

"*I don't know why not.*" Lasko's anger had flared out of nowhere. "It just ain't. Mr. Yee got a telegram two days ago. It's goin' to every goddamn state in the union 'cept Nevada. They're circlin' right around us . . . Utah, Idaho, Oregon. I guess we ain't worth it. I don't blame 'em. I wouldn't come here neither."

Andy made a murmur of sympathy. Or tried his best to.

So *that* was it. This explained why Lasko had been hiding out. It explained why Hegazti had been trying to soothe him with pastries. His dream of escape, preposterous as it might have been, had died overnight, so he was mourning it with wine and bile. It had nothing to do with the valise. Nothing to do with Andy either.

Andy slapped his hands on his thighs and rose. "I gotta go, Lasko."

"Why?"

"I just have to. It's late. I gotta get the truck back to Mama. I'm really sorry about the train."

Slack-mouthed, Lasko looked up at him. "You're leavin' cuz there ain't gonna be no train?"

"Don't be a nincompoop. I was never even *going* on the train."

"Why not?"

"You didn't *ask* me, Lasko. You just say things and strut around like a rooster. You act like I'm not even here. You don't even call me by my name."

Lasko stood up. "I did ask you—"

"No, you didn't. Never. I would've remembered."

Their faces were even now, inches apart. Andy was awash in the smell of wine and sweat and hair oil. The almost tactile smell of transgression.

"I meant to ask you," said Lasko.

"That's it? That's what you have to say?"

Lasko's eyelashes dipped like a raven's wing over a dark lake. " 'I meant to ask you, Andy'?"

Andy couldn't help but smile. "Too late for that now."

"You woulda gone with me, you mean?"

"I mighta."

"I thought you didn't like me."

"Why would I have agreed to anything if I didn't like you? You don't say 'Abyssinia' to someone you don't like."

Lasko stumbled forward like a bear hit with buckshot, wrapping his arms around Andy's shoulders. It seemed no more than a drunken display of affection, so Andy received him awkwardly. The truth was, he would have liked a kiss at the moment, a tender, uncomplicated one, the kiss of a prince in a movie musical. But there was no denying how good the hug felt. He wanted it to last longer than it did.

When Lasko pulled away, he looked Andy square in the eyes. "Wanna stay?" he asked huskily. "Wanna mess around?" One of his hands had already moved from Andy's back to the front of Andy's trousers, where, in the most perfunctory way, he began to rub Andy's pecker through the rumpled linen, as if it were a magic lamp from which a genie could be summoned on command.

"Stop," said Andy. "Don't."

"Boys can do this, you know." Lasko was still rubbing away. "We help each other out. It's what we do."

"Lasko, no."

"I'll suck you first, if you want. I don't mind."

"I'm going now. Let go of me."

"C'mon. We won't kiss or nothin'. I promise. We're buddies, right? We'll do it like men."

Andy swerved away from him to make good on his word, but Lasko seized his arm and yanked him back. "You think you're better'n me?"

Andy winced, shaking his head. "No," he said softly. "Just different."

"You ain't no different," Lasko snarled. "You're a godforsaken nance. Everybody knows about you."

"Nobody knows about me," said Andy.

He opened the door and went out. He knew Lasko wouldn't follow him, because their raised voices had already attracted attention from the house. Lasko's mother, the one who cooked the "World-Famous

Lamb" at the Martin, was standing by her back door, watching him in leery silence. Andy passed within yards of her, projecting innocence with calm, letting his dignity ascend from his wisteria toes.

"Good night, Mrs. Madrigal," he said quietly, heading into the night.

17

The Sudden Residence

Brian had Yelped a place for breakfast in Winnemucca, a diner on the main drag with an old-timey sign that looked promising. They could have eaten back at the Winnie, but they were chasing down their little mystery today, so bacon and eggs seemed about right by way of fortification. Plus he wanted to get Anna out of the barge, help her reconnect spiritually with her long-lost hometown—a fucking *challenge* on this strip crammed with mini-marts and 1960s motels. At least the diner hinted at a serious lineage, with its shiny pine walls and leatherette booths.

"You know," he said. "This coulda been here when you were here."

" 'Fraid not," said Wren as she held up the menu for Anna to peruse. "Nineteen forty-eight. Says so here on the back."

"Well, that's pretty old," he offered, somewhat deflated.

"I was in Minneapolis by then," Anna told him sweetly. "With a wife and a four-year-old daughter."

"Ah . . . right."

Anna gave him one of her private nice-try benedictions and turned back to Wren. "Dare we consider the raspberry crepes?"

"So how did that even happen?" asked Wren.

"What? Crepes in Winnemucca?"

Wren chuckled. "The wife and the daughter."

"Oh . . . at an army dance."

"No shit?"

"Fort Ord. Do you know where that is?"

"Monterey Bay," Brian replied, though he himself had not been asked.

"They used to train troops there," Anna continued. "I typed munitions reports for an alcoholic officer. I had a lot of drunks to deal with back then."

"So you met your wife at this dance." Wren was coaxing her back to the love story. Women, Brian had noticed, always want to know where people met. Even tough customers like Wren want to know. "What was it about her that made—"

"—a man like me want to get married?"

"Yeah."

"She was pretty," said Anna. "I was lonely. I was looking for normal, and she had more than her share of it."

"Did you have a sex life?"

"When I put my mind to it."

Brian made a secret screwy face at his wife. She made one back and handed him the menu with a flourish, as if to say "Leave us to our girl talk." They were in love with each other, these two. He had known it since Tahoe. It's exactly what he had hoped for, of course—Wren's full grasp of the primal force that was Anna—but he was already feeling a little selfish about having laid such a terrible trap.

Don't get too attached, he wanted to say. *I don't want you to hurt like I will.*

The waitress who took their orders was a willowy blonde with loopy earrings who asked cheerfully if they were "just passing through." The town did seem geared to people on their way to somewhere else, but Brian found himself touched by her low expectations, so he volunteered that Anna had grown up there.

"Really?" said the waitress, turning to Anna. "Whereabouts?"

"Out on Jungo Road," Anna replied discreetly.

"Gah. My husband works out there in the gold mines. We moved here from North Dakota last year. He's an engineer."

"There are gold mines on Jungo Road?" Anna's interest was clearly piqued.

"It's not what you think. Not like big chunks or anything—I wish. They leach little tiny bits out of the ground. With cyanide. In these big pits. Pays pretty good."

"I would imagine," Brian deadpanned, glancing at Wren.

The waitress, no dummy, seemed to catch his drift. "It's not harmful to the environment or anything. They've proven it. They've done tests."

Yep, he thought. The best money can buy.

She took their orders and left. When she was out of earshot, Wren leaned across the table on her elbows and let her pewter ponytail flick once for emphasis.

"Do not give her a hard time."

"Why not?"

"Because she's nice. And her husband works in a pit full of cyanide."

He couldn't help but grin. "You know it's evil, right? There's not more gold left to take, so they're poisoning it out of the earth. And when that shit spills, which it does on a fairly regular basis—"

"On the other hand," said Anna, "the crepes look a bit iffy."

Brian recognized this tactic, the sly way Anna had of deflecting his zealotry. He looked at her directly. "But this is out where you grew up, right? The very ground."

"Well . . . the very ground is now the Blue Moon Family Fun Center and Casino." She smiled coyly, widening her eyes. "No relation."

Wren chuckled. "What a hoot. We have to go out there."

"No, dear, we don't."

"Are you being a snob, Anna Madrigal?"

"No . . . it just seems to me that a place that calls itself a Family Fun Center and Casino couldn't possibly succeed at being either. Anyway, I've already seen it. Jake showed it to me on his magic slate. A virtual tour. Absolutely blood-curdling."

Brian smiled at her.

"I wouldn't fret over the cyanide," Anna added. "I'm sure they keep it away from the Family Fun."

Wren took a sip of her water. "Did they have gold when you were here?"

"Yes, but . . . mostly just rumors of it. It was all so . . . negligible." She seemed to meditate on that for a moment. "Pity Mama didn't know about cyanide. She would've jumped on that like a duck on a june bug."

Brian had rented a charcoal Jeep Cherokee for their tour of Winnemucca, so Wren insisted that Anna sit up front, the better to see the sights on her check list: the Catholic church, a local park, a Basque restaurant down by the Amtrak station. The first item, though—more crucial than the others, apparently—was the residence of Oliver Sudden at 2261 Sandstone Drive, so Brian had plugged the address into the GPS. On the way, however, he remembered something.

"You know they still have brothels in Winnemucca."

"You don't say," his wife said drily from the back seat.

"Aren't you a little curious?"

"I dunno," said Wren. "What about you, Anna?"

"We're on an adventure," Anna said, without really answering the question.

"It's on the way," Brian told them. "Down by the freeway. They call it the Line."

It was five minutes away, and easy enough to find once they arrived in the neighborhood. There were two homemade signs nailed at wacky angles to a dusty cottonwood. One had an arrow pointing to PARKING, the other to BROTHELS.

"Don't park," said Wren. "Just do a drive-by."

The Line was basically a mini-mall built of warping red plywood, its facade aping the storefronts of an old western town. Brian had seen this cheesy trick dozens of times in his travels. Sometimes the front disguised a gigantic box store full of Indian souvenirs; others were interstate rest stops designed to lure weary travelers with kids. He wondered if the Line was several broth-els or just one big warehouse full of flat-broke girls, patiently waiting to do anal for truckers.

There was a stretch limo parked out front, but no sign of life whatsoever.

"Do you think that's a customer?" asked Wren.

"I doubt it. Where would a limo come from?"

"Good point."

"It's probably theirs, is my guess. They use it to drive the girls around town. You know . . . to the casinos or something."

"Let's go," said Wren. "I'm getting the creeps."

Brian felt the same way. Was there anything more depressing than a sex joint at 10:00 a.m.—without lights or music or lust itself to transform reality?

"Our place was a lot homier," said Anna as they pulled away.

"I'll bet," said Wren.

Brian regretted having made the suggestion, so he forced some cheer into his voice. "Okay, campers, here we go! Let's go find Mr. Sudden!"

The GPS led them to what might have been a suburban neighborhood if the houses had not been so random. It was certainly someone's effort at suburbia: vinyl-sided shoe boxes attempting grandeur with a single tall window in the middle. Their lawns, defiantly green, stopped abruptly at the edge of the tufted desert.

"That's it," said Wren, spotting the number on a mailbox.

Brian parked on the road and turned off the engine. "I'll be right back. You should probably lock the doors. Just for the hell of it."

Wren gave him a quizzical look.

"You never know," he said. "It could be a meth lab or something."

Wren rolled her eyes at him. "In that case, shouldn't I keep the doors unlocked and the engine running?" She leaned forward to speak quietly into Anna's ear, sister-to-sister. "You haven't been Googling meth labs, have you?"

"Not that I know of," came the demure reply.

"I didn't mean you," he said, irked by their teasing.

"No more *Breaking Bad* for you," said Wren.

He climbed out of the Jeep and headed toward the front door, the sun falling hot on his neck. A fat-wheeled plastic tricycle in the driveway made him wonder for the third or fourth time if this place could possibly yield anything from Anna's past.

He rang a melodious doorbell.

A small dog began to bark inside. He could see it hurling itself into the air behind the lace on the glass panel in the door. Then there were footsteps, and someone appeared to scoop up the dog with one hand and open the door with the other. She was thirtyish and short, unusually short, with a heart-shaped face that tilted up at him like a shield against an alien invader. "Can I help you, sir?"

Sir. Nowadays that meant old man.

"I'm sorry to bother you," he said. "Is this the Sudden residence?"

She looked mildly annoyed. "Not really, no. That's my uncle's name. He lives with us. What's this about?"

If only I knew, he thought. "I have a lady here with me who thinks she may have a connection with him. She lived here a long time ago." He gestured toward the Jeep as if the mere sight of it would confirm his claim. Armed with so little information, he sounded like an itinerant scam artist. A dangerous one, to boot.

"He's not here," said the woman. "He's working today."

"Oliver Sudden, right?"

"Yes, Ollie. Oliver. Whatever."

"Is it possible for us to visit him?"

"If you're willing to drive. He's a greeter at the Blue Moon."

Brian was struck dumb for a moment.

"Do you know where that is?" asked the woman.

"The Family Fun Center?"

"That's the one."

He thanked her and almost sprinted back to the Jeep.

"Guess where we're going," he said to Anna.

18
No Two Ways

The octopus stole the show that first morning in Black Rock City. Michael had already seen it online, spewing fire at night, tentacles flailing ominously. It had been an awesome sight in the old-fashioned sense of the word, but somehow it had not prepared him for the high comedy of the great beast in daylight, this eye-rolling assemblage of garbage cans nodding to its fans like a showgirl in a supermarket.

"El Pulpo Mecanico," said Ben, as the octopus sashayed past their enclosure in its own churning eco-system of dust.

"Marcus Bachmann," Michael suggested.

Ben chuckled and returned to the task of assembling their camp stove. He was wearing the "cruelty-free" loincloth he had made at home. It was basically a string with a faux buckskin flap that managed to cover the crown of his dick while successfully containing nothing whatsoever. Michael was wearing his purple Etsy nightshirt. It had been custom-made for him by a seamstress in Turkey named Yosma, whose husband, a short, burly daddy with a mustache, had modeled this style next to a concrete Venus in their backyard. In their Etsy "convo" Michael had been tempted to tell Yosma (in the name of global goodwill) that his husband found her husband kind of hot, but Ben had nixed the idea as soon as Michael playfully proposed it. Words embarrassed Ben more than nudity ever could.

"Omigod, guys, you have to try Mystopia!" This was Shawna, with a childlike Christmas-morning madness in her dark brown eyes. Michael could see her mother there, the endearingly daffy Connie Bradshaw, who died a day after giving birth to Shawna. He would always regard Brian as Shawna's only functioning parent, but Connie lived on in Shawna's animated features and breathless delivery.

"What's Mystopia?"

"It's one of the camps—this lounge where they spray you with mist. Fucking heaven!"

"I dunno," said Michael, searching for the sunglass lenses to his goggles. "I'm not sure I wanna be washed by strangers."

"They don't *wash* you, they *mist* you. Like a big Evian spray bottle."

"He's thinking of the Human Carcass Wash," said Ben.

"Ah," said Michael. "So I am."

"You'd be able to tell the difference," said Shawna. "At the Carcass Wash you have to wash other people before they wash you."

"Isn't that always the way," said Michael.

He found the lenses in a plastic storage box and, after some effort, popped them into his goggles. Now all he needed was his nuclear-strength sunblock, his purple boots for the bicycle, the right silk scarf for the nightshirt, his CamelBak filled with water, his stovepipe hat, and . . . what else? He should have made a checklist for every step of this transformational journey to radical self-expression.

"You know what would be nice?" he said. "If you could just fly into here without the six-hour traffic jam. You could land right on the playa . . . have a fully stocked RV just waiting for you, with delicious meals and killer costumes and everything you need. Then you'd be free to wander and find your bliss."

Shawna gaped at him as if he'd just proposed genocide. "Ewww."

"They have that already," Ben told him. "It's called plug and play."

"And that's a bad thing because—"

"Because . . . you have to *earn* this experience," said Shawna. "Radical self-reliance is part of the deal. We're leaving the default world behind."

"Meaning everything that's not here?"

"Yes."

"And plug and play is just a bunch of CEOs and Republicans," Ben added.

"C'mon! Here?"

"Well, libertarians, at the very least. Rich people getting their freak on."

"A bunch of shirtcockers," said Shawna. "Gag me."

"Guess I'd better ask what that is."

"They run around in shirts with no pants."

Michael mugged at her. "As opposed to the half dozen *totally* naked people painted blue I saw on my way to the porta potties this morning?"

"It's complicated, Michael. It's a matter of intent. And commitment."

Michael picked up the manual with the schedule of events. "You're right. It's just hard to know where to start with my intent and commitment. Let's see now . . ." He flipped through the pages, reading entries at random. " 'Valerie Hummingbird Birthing Your Inner Voice' . . . 'Cirque du Cliché Morning Soiree' . . . 'Kunda Your Lini' . . . 'Fake Jamaican Accent Hour' . . . 'Dr. Scrote's Circumcision Wagon and Calamari Hut.' "

Ben laughed, still tinkering with the stove. "You made up that last one."

"I swear to God." Michael held out the manual as proof.

"That is fucking hilarious," said Shawna.

"Maybe to you," said Michael.

It *was* funny, of course, so he laughed along with them. "Forget about the stove," he told Ben. "Let's go find someone who'll gift us some breakfast."

She laughed, but gave him a faintly reproving look. "Now don't be a Sparkle Pony."

"I won't," said Michael, "and you can tell me what that is after breakfast."

"There's a camp on the next plaza that serves bacon and Bloody Marys."

"I'm there," said Michael. "Soon as I find the right scarf."

They took their inaugural bike ride after breakfast. Michael was buzzed from the Bloody Marys, which helped to loosen him up as he attempted a bicycle for the first time in years. Fortunately, there were not that many other bikes to dodge as they pedaled down one of the clock-numbered streets toward the playa. He had not made a point of noticing street signs. He'd resolved simply to follow Ben and Shawna until he got the hang of things. He was happy to be their duckling.

"Lookin' good, Sofa Daddy." Shawna was shouting encouragement over her shoulder. It was hard to imagine *her* not looking good in anything, which in this case included a pink halter top, a pink tutu, and clunky boots trimmed in pink faux fur. It made her easy to spot whenever she briefly wove out of sight. His other reference point, his husband, was a brown leather bowler above a sun-freckled back. He had swapped out the loincloth for a pair of shimmering (and sheer) green harem pants.

And so it went for the duckling—pink, green, pink, green—until they reached the broad crescent-shaped esplanade bordering the playa. There, without warning, he was swept into a perfect storm of vehicles: hundreds, maybe thousands, of bikes and art cars, some of them as enormous as tractor trailers and crammed with naked pagans, others small and troublesome, darting out of nowhere, tricked out like land sharks or Blinky from Pac-Man or chattering false teeth or cocks. This was not good. His time-honored ineptitude could do serious damage here—and not just to himself.

He flashed on the night he reunited with roller skates as an adult. He had zombie-walked his way into a rink in South City on a newly created "gay night," only to cruise another guy so intensely that he crashed into him and drew blood. It had been *his* blood, at least—the usual bloody nose—and they had gone home together afterward, he and this beautiful doctor, this gynecologist, for God's sake. They'd had six good years with each other, off and on—six glorious years—before Jon had been erased by a horror so new that it had only just been given a name.

So, how am I lookin', Dr. Fielding?

What do you make of this old man in his nightshirt and top hat?

Am I grateful enough to still be here?

This rumination was all it took for him to lose sight of Ben and Shawna. Panicked, he began to wobble wildly on the bike, clutching the handlebars just the way you're not supposed to, before braking and dismounting in the middle of the traffic in full expectation of calamity. To his amazement, the other bikers parted around him with nonchalant grace, like skiers avoiding a tree. No one even yelled. Maybe the silver mustache helped. Maybe he'd just been the lucky recipient of Radical Geezer Tolerance or some other immutable principle of Burning Man.

He pushed his bike to the other side of the esplanade. Pink and Green were waiting for him in the relative openness of the playa.

"Are you okay?" asked Ben.

"I'm fine. Just had to stop for a second."

"It gets easier up ahead," Ben told him.

It occurred to Michael that this was the great perk of being loved: someone to wait for you, someone to tell you that it will get easier up ahead.

Even when it might not be true.

This time, though, it was. The deep playa freed them from the crush of others, and soon the three of them—*just* the three of them—were racing across a hard platinum plain under the noonday sun, scarves streaming like banners, arms held aloft like Evita, or the queens in *Priscilla*. The arm thing, of course, was mostly Ben and Shawna's contribution, though Michael shared their exhilaration. He had never ridden a bike with such sustained abandon. He felt like one of those kids from *ET*, lifting off into the sky while the orchestra swelled accordingly.

At the moment they were heading toward three enormous letters—EGO—floating in the hazy beige of the horizon. This was their third art installation of the morning, after the Hand Holding the Fish and the Shipwreck, and all of them had appeared as mirages demanding investigation. The dust had a way of doing that, of teasing with its veils. So now they were off in

pursuit of the giant EGO—the superego, as it were—
and Ben was shouting something over his shoulder. It
sounded to Michael like "loose hand," which he found
disturbing, though not particularly informative.

The explanation came from the playa itself, when
his wheels hit a patch of alkali powder—"loose sand"—
that brought his bike to a dead halt,

Just. Like. That.

He hit the playa hard, but of course it was "loose"
in that spot, not the cracked, unyielding pavement that
made bike riding such a breeze. He had been spared by
the very thing that brought him down. Had he been
on some suitably friendly drug, he might have pondered that paradox for a while, lying there in the desert's silky embrace, but he felt filthy and achy and, yes,
embarrassed, even among family. He sat up to prove
that he wasn't dead. He was still sitting there, slurp-
ing from his CamelBak, when Ben and Shawna pushed
their bikes onto the scene.

"I give up," he said with a crooked smile.

"Now you're getting it," said Shawna.

He laughed. They all laughed. Surrender had been the
theme of her Burning Man orientation. He wondered,
though, if she was also referring to something else.

A blue moon was on the way, after all. There was
fertilizing to be done.

After the bike trip, Shawna went to visit her friends at Chakralicious, so Ben and Michael returned to their tent for a nap. Ben's youth—and, okay, sure, his natural athleticism—made him more active than Michael, but he insisted on an afternoon nap. Michael was grateful for that. Not to mention Ben's love of a quality air mattress. The entire floor of the tent was thick, cushioned relief from the playa.

It was too warm to cuddle, so they lay side by side with their feet touching, listening to the murmurs of siesta time. Michael was still fretting over Shawna's dreams of a playa pregnancy, so he approached the subject head-on.

"Did you get a chance to talk to her?"

Ben knew what he meant and, thankfully, did not pretend otherwise. "There haven't been that many chances, honey."

"I thought maybe when we were on the Shipwreck." Michael had waited in the captain's cabin, slightly nauseous from the heat and the crazily tilting decks, while Ben and Shawna went off to explore the rigging. They had been gone long enough for him to start feeling one with the tableau, as if he were the captain himself, every bit as dusty and abandoned as the old maps and sea chests surrounding him.

"That was hardly enough time," Ben told him. "How long does it take to say thanks but no thanks . . . and I'm sorry my tactless husband didn't handle this as well as he should have?"

Michael had hoped for a smile, but all he got was another question:

"And you're sure that's what I want to say?"

The uncharacteristic sarcasm in Ben's tone stung Michael. He kept his gaze on the dome of the tent for fear of what he might find in Ben's eyes.

"Tell me then," he said calmly. "Tell me what you feel."

"Now he asks," said Ben, as if he were talking to someone else.

There was a loud gas-jet roar somewhere outside the tent. Michael recognized it as the octopus, shooting flames for the sheer, frivolous hell of it.

"You don't *want* to have a baby with her, do you?"

Ben took a moment to answer. "Having a baby with her and giving her the chance to have one are two different things."

"No, sweetie. They aren't. She's not going anywhere. She'll still be a part of our lives. It will be your baby, no matter what kind of spin you put on it."

"She doesn't expect me to parent," said Ben "Or you or anyone else. She's been really clear about that."

"Do you really want a baby around? Do you want that sort of life?"

Ben sighed. "There's going to be a baby around no matter who fathers it. She wants to do this, and she's a part of our lives. You said so yourself."

"And you just said 'fathers.' "

"What?"

" 'No matter who *fathers* it' is what you just said. You would be that baby's father, Ben. There's no two ways about it."

A long, brooding silence before Ben finally said, "Haven't you ever thought about having a kid?"

He asked it so earnestly that Michael tried to answer accordingly.

"Not since I knew how it felt to be in love. That was all I wanted after that. That's all I want now."

Ben rolled on his side, his face golden in tent-filtered sun. "Seriously, you've never imagined it."

"Oh . . . well . . . imagined it, sure. In my early teens. But it was just to give them cool names. I had a Zachary and an Atticus, as I recall. I had a Tallulah decades before Bruce and Demi thought of it."

Ben gave him a drowsy smile. "Tallulah Tolliver? Really?"

Michael smiled back. "I know. If you say it fast enough, it becomes an al-Qaeda war cry."

They had moved off topic, but Ben seemed as glad about that as Michael was. And Michael knew that Ben would commit to nothing, spermwise, unless Michael had agreed upon it. Such was the nature of their marriage.

"Let's grab a snooze," Ben said, taking Michael's hand.

As he drifted into sleep, it occurred to Michael that Brian might be the only person who could talk some sense into Ben and Shawna. Her own father, after all, would understand how this arrangement would be a familial minefield. But Brian wasn't here. He was somewhere north of here, holed up with his new bride in an air-conditioned RV, taking Mrs. Madrigal on a cryptic Trip to Bountiful.

19
As Boys Do

It had been ten days since Andy last saw Lasko. School had let out for the summer, and Andy had stayed away from Eagle Drugs. He didn't hate Lasko for what had happened that night in the Madrigals' garage. He was just embarrassed for them both, and sad that his very first courtship (for that's what it had been) had ended in ugliness. Lasko had wanted Andy—no doubt about that—but Lasko had wanted a boy, and Andy had not been up to it. Had Andy mustered the nerve that night to show Lasko his Wondrous Wisteria toenails—just unlaced his shoes and flat-out showed him—Lasko might have saved face, knowing he was more of a man than Andy, and the tragedy might have been averted. But Andy had kept the truth to himself, as boys do, leaving Lasko the rejected pansy, humiliated and broken.

Andy would not figure this out until many years later, when he was no longer in Winnemucca, no longer Andy. That summer his focus was on his own heartache. He would not give a moment's thought to the fact that Lasko's mother had watched him leave the garage. Nor would he think about Lasko's volatile father or the reason for Lasko's banishment. If he dwelled on anything from that night, it was *Richard Halliburton's Book of Marvels*, which, in his haste to flee, he had left behind.

June was high season at the Blue Moon, so Margaret stayed busy in her cabinette. Andy missed her company. He went to several movies alone at the American—his favorite being *Love Before Breakfast*, with Irene Dunne—but they lacked the zest that came from hashing things over afterward with Margaret. At night he stayed in his room, curled up next to the Lux Radio Theater, sometimes in the dress, sometimes not. He had less reason to worry about Mama now that the house was busy and Gloria Watson was ensconced in some girl's camp in Utah.

He felt so old that summer, older than he would ever feel again. His youth had grown decrepit, and there was nothing in sight to replace it, neither college nor marriage nor foreign travel nor work beyond some flunky job in town where they would still be calling him Mona's boy. Missing college was the hardest part. They never talked about it, but Andy knew that Mama didn't have near enough money to pay for a proper education. And even if she did, it was stashed away somewhere, a puny grubstake for her dreams of gold. That's why Mama was all-fire set on Gloria or someone like her, someone who would take Andy off her hands for good.

Mama loved him—he knew that—but it wasn't a useful love.

You cannot be loved by someone who doesn't want to know you.

Delphine's mother had died of influenza in Louisiana, so she'd taken the train to the funeral with Mama's blessings—one of the reasons Margaret was working harder now. Delphine's absence gave Mama a chance to paint her cabinette (or rather, have Andy paint it), since Delphine had made a mess of it doing some phony voodoo routine for a customer that involved, among other things, the sacrifice of a chicken. She'd been quick about it, she claimed, and the chicken had already been "condemned to dinner," as Mama sometimes put it, but Mama had been infuriated, knowing that other customers might not take kindly to the bloodstains on the walls.

Andy had scrubbed those stains with a whole bottle of Lysol, only to be left with big brown continents on the cream-colored walls. So tonight, because it was hot and noisy in the house, he had gone to Delphine's cabinette with a brush and a bucket of paint he'd bought that morning at Melarkey Hardware. He had chosen the color himself, the same shade of wisteria that secretly inhabited his socks. It was a good color, exotic but not flashy, and it would complement Delphine's olive skin.

He painted by the light of Delphine's ballerina lamp while listening to her Victrola. Sometimes his brush-strokes kept time with the music (right now it was Billie Holiday's "Did I Remember?"), and he twirled to his heart's content, knowing Margaret wasn't there to warn him of the inherent dangers. It was delicious to be surrounded by this flagrant color, without apology or deceit. He sang along, when he knew the words, applying them to his own melancholy.

> *You were in my arms, and that was all I knew. We were alone, we two. What did I say to you? . . . Did I remember to tell you, I adore you . . .*

He couldn't remember the rest of that verse, but someone outside the cabinette finished it for him. Heroically basso. Just like in the movies.

> *. . . and I am livin' for you alone!*

The voice was unmistakable. It was as if he had somehow summoned it. He went to the door and peered through the little diamond-shaped window. Lasko was twenty feet away, a dark figure smoking a cigarette under the blue neon moon. Andy opened the door and stepped out. Lasko turned slowly to face him.

"What are you doing down here?"

"I live here, remember?"

"I mean, out here in the fuck shacks."

Andy hesitated. "I'm painting this one. Were you looking for me?"

"That's a laugh!"

Another pause. "I'm sorry I hurt your feelings, Lasko. I didn't mean to, because I like you . . . and I'm sorry if—"

"Well, I ain't sorry. I got me some poontang tonight."

Andy felt a terrible dread growing in his chest like a tumor, making his throat go dry. "You like Lady Day too, huh? You know the words."

Lasko ignored his effort at diversion. "Papi told me the old one was the best. More grateful for the ol' whanger, ya know." He seized himself between the legs the way he had once seized Andy. "Her pussy's loose, but she's got some nice gams."

"Shut your trap, Lasko."

"What? I ain't said nothin' bad. I didn't call her nympho or nothin' . . . like some people do."

Andy walked slowly toward him. He tried his best to sound calm. "You know who she is, don't you?" It wasn't so much a question as a revelation, spoken aloud, so he could actually believe it himself.

"Sure." Lasko flicked his still-lit cigarette to the ground. "She's got a reputation."

"That's not what I mean. She's the friend who gave me the valise. You knew that, didn't you, when you came? You remembered her name."

Lasko snorted. "Wish I had me a prosty for a friend."

Andy was so close now he could smell Lasko's breath. "You stole from her, Lasko. That's as low-down as it gets."

Lasko gave him a curdled smile. "It's not like she ain't gettin' her money back." He grabbed himself again. "One night at a time."

Andy's hands shot out and seized Lasko's shirtfront, curling it into his fists, yanking him closer.

"You stay away from her, you bastard!"

Lasko seemed too stunned to reply.

Andy shook him once, really hard, then shoved him away in disgust. Lasko stumbled backward, his knees finally buckling under him. His head hit the concrete base of the sign with a sound too soft not to be alarming.

Andy saw blood on the side of his face, slick as the cover of a dime novel under the blue glare of the neon.

He'd had the last word. He must have cracked Lasko's skull.

"Oh, God. . . . Lasko?"

Lasko didn't answer, didn't move. Andy could hear everything around him but Lasko: a car on the highway, a customer braying in the house, a dove cooing on top of Violet's cabinette. Then, after an eternity, Lasko propped himself on an elbow and pulled a handkerchief from his pocket to blot the side of his face. There was a long scrape there—a deep, ugly graze, but not as bad as Andy had feared.

"Let me help," he said.

"Get away."

"I just need to—"

"I'm warning you!"

Andy wondered if Lasko was about to lunge. All that pugilistic stuff, the fake fighting that he had found so endearing, could have held real fighting in its heart, a secret cruelty waiting to be unleashed. But Lasko just staggered to his feet, bloody handkerchief pressed to his head, and lurched toward the parking lot.

He was a fraud as a tough guy, a real impersonator. His cruelty was there all right, plain as day, but it was not contained in his fists.

Andy watched Lasko leave, watched until he climbed into a truck with MADRIGAL PLUMBING barely visible through the rust of the door. His father's truck. Andy heard an anguished squeal from a woman in the front seat.

Hegazti? Had his sister been waiting for him?

The truck pulled slowly out of the lot, passing Andy and the neon moon. Lasko leaned out of the window, still holding the handkerchief to his head.

"You better stay upstairs. Cuz I'm comin' back."

"No, you're not," Andy said quietly.

"Next week. She wants me to."

"No, she doesn't."

"Ask her. She can't get enough of me."

Andy was quiet for a moment. "Margaret," he said finally. "Her name is Margaret. You can't even say *her* name."

Lasko's lip curled. "Pussy don't need a name."

The truck pulled away. Lasko shouted his exit line out the window.

"Abyssinia!"

In those days, there was a law in Nevada decreeing that prostitutes could not work in counties where members of their family resided. It was a sensible law, Anna thought, one that had no doubt prevented a lot of accidental heartbreak, not to mention a few multiple murders. Andy had been exempt, however. Margaret might have been more mother to him than his own mother, but, having no legal offspring or relatives of her own in Humboldt County, this wheat-haired angel who had read him the Winnie-the-Pooh books was free to hurt anyone she pleased.

He stopped at the door of her cabinette. After a moment's hesitation, he entered without knocking. Margaret was standing there in her chenille bathrobe.

"Oh, lamb . . . you gave me a fright." She laughed at herself merrily. "You don't know what happened to my Lysol, do you?"

He didn't hear the question. He smelled Lasko's spunk, ripe in the air.

"That guy who was here—" he began.

"The Basque boy."

"Yes."

"He's the one who hocked the valise. I lent it to him, and he hocked it." His legs were trembling, so he clamped his hand on the doorjamb to make sure he could finish what he had to say. "He came here to get back at me . . . to hurt me."

Margaret sat down on the edge of the bed, her knees pressed together, her face contorted in disbelieving empathy. "Why would he do that?"

Andy spoke directly to her summering Swedish eyes. "Because I wouldn't be a boy with him."

She blinked at him, uncomprehending.

"Because I wouldn't do what boys do with each other in private."

Margaret absorbed that for a moment, nodding slowly. "Oh . . . well . . . I guess that makes sense."

"I liked him, but I couldn't. I mean, I never . . . and I couldn't. And now he thinks he has to prove he's a man. He has to go out and get some . . . some . . ."

"Snatch," said Margaret, nodding solemnly.

"Revenge."

"Well . . . that too. Same difference." She gave Andy a weary smile, then patted the bed, signaling him to sit down.

He remained standing. He could not let this be settled so easily. "Don't you get it? I told him you'd given me the valise. He knew your name, so he came here and fucked you. That's like fucking . . . I dunno . . . my mother or something."

Margaret's eyes went wide and watery. "Andy Ramsey, that's the sweetest thing anyone's ever said to me." She found a hankie in the pocket of her bathrobe and dabbed at her eyes for a while. "Just the sweetest. Don't go tellin' Mother Mucca, though. It would hurt her feelings."

"Who?"

Margaret nodded. "Ain't that rich? Violet started calling her that. I'm doin' it now myself. I ain't takin' her guff anymore." She tucked the hankie away. "Listen, lamb, that boy may have it in for you—I don't know—but his Papi placed the order with me personally. Said his son needed fixin'. Paid in advance, too. Plenty."

Andy nodded. "Seventy-five dollars?"

Margaret drew back. "Now how in the blazes—"

Andy just glowered at her.

"That's how much they got for the valise?"

"Bingo."

Margaret's shoulders were completely slumped, but she still managed to shrug them a little. "Oh well. What goes around comes around."

Andy's mind was elsewhere now. He was thinking about the plumbing truck in the parking lot, Hegazti waiting there, a reliable witness that Lasko had done the deed. The old man had been thorough. Fixing Lasko had been a family affair.

"You can't let him come back," he said.

"Oh, sweetheart. . . . We've already taken their money."

Their money.

"And he's not such a bad kid."

Andy couldn't believe his ears. "You should hear how he talks about you!"

Another what-the-hell shrug from Margaret. "You should hear how they *all* talk about me." She studied him and his pain. "If it makes you feel any better . . . he wasn't havin' a real swell time. He's just like you, lamb. I'm sure of it."

"He's *not* just like me! He's stupid and vindictive and childish."

"Well, not in that way maybe, but—"

"How can you stand it, Margaret?"

"What?"

"Men. Night after night. Putting up with their meanness."

She fiddled with the cord of her bathrobe. "I like 'em, I guess."

"Well, I don't. I want my friends to be women when I get outta here. Men don't even know who they are. They're such cowards."

"I reckon that's true," said Margaret with a sigh of resignation.

Andy finally sat down next to her. "Just don't see him again." He could feel tears scalding his cheeks. "Couldn't you do that?"

"Oh, lamb." She reached over and squeezed his hand. "You won't even know when it happens. And it won't mean nothin', you know that. This boy's a lost soul, and . . . I got so much mothering in me. Just like I got for you. You understand?"

He understood all too well. Sex had never been Margaret's only gift to the world. She had a vast, promiscuous kindness that had made him jealous, in small ways, even as a child. There had never been anything like this, though, nothing that had torn through his heart from the inside. She had let Lasko into the nest, and she wanted Andy to know it. He yanked his hand away from her, sprang to his feet.

"Andy, lamb, listen to me—"

But he was already out the door, heading for the house and ready for revenge.

In the parlor Mama was banging out a tune for the customers. It was easy enough to slip unnoticed into Mama's office, where he grabbed one of her envelopes and a sheet of her fancy stationery—the one with a howling pink tomcat in a top hat. He took them up to his room, latched the door, and began, furiously, to write.

Dear Mr. Madrigal,
I am sorry to have to write such a letter, but I feel
I must explain your son's injury. He came by my
establishment last night and made an indecent
advance toward my son. My son is all man, and
gave him what for. I will speak of this matter

publicly if your son ever returns to the Blue Moon.
He is not welcome here.

Sincerely,
MONA RAMSEY

P.S. I mean the sheriff!!

Letter in hand, Andy crept out of the house and into the truck. It took him twenty minutes to reach the Madrigals' house. He knew there was a strong chance that Lasko had taken Hegazti directly home, so he waited in the shadows beneath the big lighted LOTHING sign and watched Lasko's garage room for signs of activity. It was completely dark, so he crossed the backyard and went to the porch, where a mailbox and a door buzzer were all he needed to carry out his plan.

Only one had been strictly necessary, of course. Delivery would have been enough. They would have found the letter in the morning, and the message would have been conveyed. But Andy, in his pain and jealousy, wanted the satisfaction of being a *witness.* He wanted proof that he had stood his ground and fought back like a man, that this story had not ended with Lasko's heartless "Abyssinia."

He opened the mailbox, slipped in the letter, rang the buzzer, and ran like crazy.

Breathless, he took refuge in the truck, which was hidden behind a stand of cottonwoods. It wouldn't matter anyway, if someone saw the truck, since it belonged to Mama, and that would only confirm the authenticity of the letter. Andy was banking on his belief that no one would contact Mama. There would be too much shame and dishonor involved. This would be a family matter conducted in private.

Someone opened the door and stepped onto the porch. Even from this distance Andy could hear the momentous squeak of the mailbox.

The first voice he heard was Hegazti's. "Papi," she was calling, "Papi!"

The porch creaked under the heavy tread of the man of the house. Hegazti was speaking to him in Spanish, presumably translating the letter.

It serves you right, thought Andy. You had your way with my family. I'll have my way with yours.

Mr. Madrigal's growl grew into a bellow. "BELASKO! BELASKO!"

Lasko answered feebly from somewhere inside the house.

That'll keep you away, thought Andy. That'll keep you away for good.

How right he had been.

20

The Temple of Juno

A blue moon—the second full moon of the month— was rising over Black Rock City when Shawna set off on her own to look for Otto. She knew already he was part of the temple crew, so she made that her first destination, so she could praise him on his communal effort when she came to look for him at Seltzerville, the camp he shared with a dozen other street clowns. There was no way to do this but to do it. No phones, no tweets, nothing. Just this roulette of random souls, cycling through the watercolor twilight on their way from somewhere to somewhere else.

Once in a blue moon. As in rarely, but sometimes.

It was what she adored about Burning Man: the way one thing could lead you to another like an undertow. You threw yourself into it, and it took you from there, swirling you into moments so rich and rare that you could almost forget you had ever written LOL or OMG on someone's Twitter feed. Burning Man wasn't a link to life; it was life itself, immediate and astonishing. All those weeks of planning and ticket scrounging had led to this sweet release into the wild and woolly Now.

That's why it made sense to stop at the Hug Deli on her way to the Temple of Juno. Because it was *there*, this hand-painted sidewalk stand in the middle of nowhere, fake as can be yet completely archetypal, like something Wile E. Coyote would erect as a ruse for the Roadrunner. The menu at the Hug Deli included, among other items, the Warm and Fuzzy Hug, the Beverly Hills Air Kiss Hug, and the Gangsta Hug, with side orders of Pinch, Tickle, and Back Scratch. She ordered the Long Uncomfortable Hug, because she thought that was funny, thereby prompting a nut-brown Venice Beach–looking dude to hold on to her, earnestly pokerfaced, for a seeming eternity.

"Are you uncomfortable yet?"

"Fairly, yes."

"Excellent. My work here is done."

She laughed and mounted her bike, pedaling away from the zany mirage as her gratuitous hugger shouted "Namaste" in her direction.

Insemination should be so easy, she thought.

The spire of the Temple of Juno appeared in the dust as fragments of filigree, looming so high in the sky it could have been someone's last hallucination. It felt Asian, but not entirely, with a courtyard that made it sprawl like a kingdom. It took ten minutes to reach, pedaling hard, so she needed a long swig on her canteen once she had chained her bike out front. There were dozens of others joining her, freed from their wheels and continuing their pilgrim's progress toward the structure.

It was plywood, this temple, blond and raw up close but intricate as lace, a computer-hewn patchwork assembled by Otto and a multitude of others, people who had built something magnificent to be burned in a week on the premise that simple creation was its own joy, and everything, *everything*, must be released.

The more she thought about Otto, the more he seemed like the perfect guy to ask for sperm. He was strong and sober and kind. He'd been nice to her the night they ran into each other at Martuni's. He had even joked about the two exes who had come later. She had let him down gently, after all, when he started getting serious, and that had been four whole years ago. He seemed to have let her go as thoroughly as he had let go of Sammy, his monkey puppet—minus the ritual cremation.

But the real bonus was the fact that he was moving to Ottawa in a month. (He liked the sound of Otto from Ottawa, he said, and it was easy to find eco work in Canada.) The sheer geographical distance would lessen the chance of him forming an emotional attachment to the child. And maybe he'd be totally cool with the idea, expecting nothing in return for his contribution. Seltzerville was an easy bike ride to Dusty Dames, where the insemination would be staged. Or held. Or whatever.

She hated all the language of this, the mechanics. She wanted to focus on the end result, so that one day she would be able to tell the apple of her eye that she had loved her/him long before he/she had even been a seed. That she had dreamed of him/her in a place so profoundly infertile that life itself was imported for one magic week, and that love and art were the only intentions. Once pregnant, she would not (she swore) be one of those women who natter away about the future to their growing bellies, but she wouldn't mind having a word with the kid right now. She would tell her/him that the coast was clear, that it was beautiful here.

She flowed with the others into the temple, where beams of light slashed through the lacy walls like swords through a magician's cabinet. A great wooden pendulum—an inverted pyramid—swung almost imperceptibly above a mandala of humans arrayed beneath its point. Dust was the constant here, making everything velvety and sumptuous. The walls were covered with felt-tip scribbling that would have seemed defamatory without the knowledge that this was the soul of the space: poignant and pithy (or not so pithy) farewells to dead friends and old lovers, lost pets and bad vibes, anything that needed remembering and releasing through fire.

The people beneath the pendulum were in their own orbits of bliss or grief, which Shawna did not want to invade. Instead she made her way upstairs, reading the inscriptions that caught her eye, moved by the sheer accumulation of loss.

Grief-fiti. That's what it was.

She stopped on the landing and found a clear space on the wall, claiming it benignly with her presence, as she would a good spot on a beach. She was digging in her knapsack for a felt-tip marker when someone approached her with his own, presenting it to her with a courtly flourish. He was her age or thereabouts, and so coated in dust that the fabric-store fur of his Pan legs was indistinguishable from his own smooth flesh. His horns, in much the same way, merged with his head.

"Thanks," she said, "but I may be here for a while."

"Please," he said. "Keep it."

And with that he was gone—somewhat theatrically, but thrillingly just the same. She wondered if he had blessed her on the spur of the moment or if felt-tip markers were part of his official gifting. But even if he had a whole sack of those suckers stashed somewhere, it was a cool thing to do. It was good to give people things they needed. To be there for them in the moment. It showed you noticed.

She went to the wall and began to write in bright green ink:

Dear Connie Bradshaw,
We've met only once. You held me in your arms
and looked into my eyes. I wish I could remember
that. My friend Michael says you were kind and sort
of daffy and liked guys a lot. I do, too. And gals, by
the way. ☺ Something tells me we would get on
great. I've heard what you went through to give me
life, and I REALLY FUCKING APPRECIATE
IT, CONNIE. I'm living for us both now.

Your daughter,
SHAWNA HAWKINS

P.S. Would you like to be a grandmother? Wouldn't
that be fantabulous?

When she was finished, she left the temple and strolled around the courtyard. Night was falling swiftly. The lights in the temple made it glow like candlelight through old scrimshaw. She sat on one of the courtyard benches and wondered, idly, which parts of this other-worldly palace Otto had helped to build.

Juno, goddess of fertility and overseer of childbirth, protector of women and preserver of marriage.

Could there be a better place for her tonight?

She had been there for ten minutes before she noticed the writing on the wall behind her. It was rendered in the same green ink she had used for her own.

WANT TO BE A MOTHER? NEED SEED FROM A NICE GUY? THAT'S WHAT I'M GIFTING THIS YEAR. NO STRINGS ATTACHED. SEE NEXT BENCH.

It wasn't like her to blush, but the message felt so intuitive of her situation. She was like one of those starving wretches on *Survivor* getting a tree-mail message promising doughnuts and milk. She looked around the courtyard furtively—*guiltily*—to see if she was being watched. There were several dozen people there in the indigo gloaming, but none of them seemed especially interested in her.

The nearest bench was unoccupied, so she walked there and checked it out, using her pocket flashlight to examine the graffiti. Much of it was written in green ink, so the color was obviously not exclusive to the faun in the temple. The marker might have been provided by the temple crew itself. The anonymous benefactor could be anyone at all. Anyone.

His handwriting, however, was instantly recognizable from the other bench: loopy letters with open *O*'s. This time he had written:

HEALTHY EX-MORMON RESPECTS ALL WOMEN. NO
CONTACT DESIRED. TOP TIER OF TEMPLE, PLAYA
SIDE. INFO UNDER RAIL. LOOK 4 HEART. PROMISE
NEVER TO SEE YOU AGAIN.

Three minutes later, as she headed back to the temple, she thought, It's a good thing I'm not fucked up. It's a good thing this is my first e-less unmollyfied Burn in . . . well . . . ever. Otherwise, I might invest this moment with something falsely mystical, something beyond the lark of a treasure hunt in the desert. I might see it as a viable option, too, a natural progression of the Hug Deli, a great big why-the-hell-not.

She knew better than that. Especially sober. Otto would almost certainly end up being her go-to guy, because sperm was not a fast food proposition.

Except of course, that it *was*. What else was it if not that? It was always a thing of the moment, best served warm. And anonymity had certain advantages in this situation. Someday soon she would have a spouse, someone under the same roof who would love the Kid as deeply as she did. Why burden that person with a third person—some long-gone retired street clown boyfriend in Canada, for instance? It muddled things unnecessarily. Ben would never have been a problem in that regard, since he was already part of the package, already inextricable from her life.

What the hell was she talking about? *Yes, a very good thing you aren't fucked up tonight, missy.*

Reaching the mezzanine of the temple, she followed the railing until—yes!—she found a plain green heart without an inscription. It was almost too easy, this game. She sank to her butt on the spot and used her flashlight to inspect the underside. She found a smattering of words there. Green capital letters. *Eureka.*

IMMACULATE CONCEPTION

CAMP COINKYDINK

5:30 AND JASMINE

ASK FOR DUSTPUPPY

Here was the thing:

She didn't have to see Otto right away. She didn't have to see him at all, in fact, since he didn't even know she was coming. You couldn't break a date that had never been made, could you? She could tell him tomorrow how much she admired and respected his work on the temple. Tonight there was curiosity to be satisfied. Maybe—just maybe—there was a fourth option, beyond Ben and Caleb and Otto.

Camp Coinkydink was out toward the scattered edge of things. As Shawna pedaled across the gleaming playa under a silver-dollar moon, she remembered something Mrs. Madrigal used to say:

"Your regrets, my dear, are all about the things you *didn't* do."

21
Hazard of The Profession

Anna waited on a circular settee in the lobby of the Blue Moon Family Fun Center and Casino. An enormous arrangement of roses (artificial but convincing until she touched them) erupted volcanically from the center of the settee. She smiled at this effort—the wrongheadedness of it—since cut flowers had not been allowed in the original Blue Moon. Mama had very few superstitions (not even the acceptable Catholic ones), but she had clung to the orthodoxy of her profession. Cut flowers were seen as omens of death in a brothel, emblematic of beauty cut down in its prime. You did not bring roses to the girls without catching hell from Mama.

Brian and Wren were talking to a young woman at the counter. Behind them, in a room with a glass wall, children were frolicking in a pit of brightly colored balls. Their muffled squeals merged with the bells and whistles of the one-armed bandits in another room. Innocence and adult pleasures were efficiently segregated here.

Not like the old days at all.

She remembered the afternoon when she finally felt remorse for having written the letter to Lasko's father.

Andy had driven over to Eagle Drugs with an apology already forming in his head, somehow believing— a full week after the fact—that he could fix things with a kind word to Lasko or a confession to his father.

I should have brought pastries, he had thought. Or a pack of Camels.

He hated to think how Lasko might have suffered because of his offhanded wickedness. Lasko's banishment to the garage could have already assumed a dreadful new coloration—beatings, humiliation, who-knows-what. A man who had ordered his son to be "fixed" by a prostitute was capable of much more than that.

Andy had known there was little chance of finding Lasko at the drugstore—his father had no doubt removed him from public scrutiny—but he had gone to the Rexall in the hope that a conversation with Lasko would prove more benign in the presence of his boss, the even-tempered and professional Mr. Yee.

Mr. Yee, however, had been in a state when Andy arrived, muttering to himself as he swept shards of glass from the checkered linoleum floor.

The pharmacy had been robbed that morning, the old man said with a scowl. Some hooligan had broken the window and stolen pills from the cabinet.

"What sort of pills?" Andy had asked, suddenly sick with panic.

"Barbiturates!"

"What's that?"

"Sleeping pills . . . Sorry sonofabitch!" Mr. Yee, still sweeping furiously, saw Andy's stricken expression and collected himself long enough to offer reassurance. "Not your fault, son. If you see your buddy Lasko, tell him I need help pronto."

But it *is* my fault, thought Andy as he raced through back streets and alleys toward the hideous truth that he already knew.

It's nobody's fault but my own.

He was thinking that as he reached Lasko's garage.

As he entered that dim, dirt-floored room and smelled the rancid vomit and saw the body slumped like a sack of potatoes.

As he looked at that face, already gray and waxen with death.

As he choked down his sobs to keep from being heard in the house.

As he spotted the *Book of Marvels* and snatched the incriminating evidence from the shelf above the bed.

As he sped across the bridge toward the Blue Moon Lodge and the soft consolation of Margaret's arms.

There had never been a moment when he wasn't thinking it.

It's nobody's fault but my own.

Brian and Wren were striding toward Anna, both of them smiling, apparently successful in their search for Mr. Sudden. An ember of shame lodged in Anna's chest was searing its way to the light of day—or the light, at any rate, of a ridiculous theme park where whorehouses were fun for the whole family. It had not been fun, God knows, but it had not been like this place. There had been life at the Blue Moon, however lurid or dull, and there had been radio romance and a long-lashed boy who danced in pirate pants and probably loved her for a while. It might have been fine with no more than that had she not been so vindictive, so childishly selfish.

She had to ask herself if she was still being selfish. This last-minute quest for peace of mind could easily wreak havoc on an innocent, someone nearly as old as she who might not welcome—not to mention deserve—this antediluvian drama. It was far too late for confession, really; the confessors had all left the building.

"He's in the back," said Brian, "on his coffee break."

Wren extended her arm. "C'mon. He's expecting us."

Anna found herself frozen to the spot.

"Oh," said Brian. "Maybe you'd rather do this alone?"

"Forget that shit," said Wren. "She needs us."

"Do you?"

"I do, yes. I don't want to explain this a second time." She took Wren's arm. "I'm sorry I've been so vague, dear. It's all a bit of a rat-fuck, I'm afraid."

They made their way to an undecorated room where Mr. Oliver Sudden was seated at a folding table with his red plastic cup of coffee. He was a wiry fellow with a handlebar mustache—apparently real, if overly waxed—and the obligatory striped shirt and sassy arm garters of the casino's male employees. Seventy-five, she guessed. An extrovert built for greeting the public, aware of his roguishness.

He rose the moment he saw her inadequate locomotion.

"Here, sweetheart, let me help."

"Keep your seat," she said. "These two have it covered."

He scrambled toward a cluster of upholstered furniture at the other end of the room. "Bring her over here then. It's more comfortable."

Brian and Wren lowered her into an armchair, but not before her capricious old body had chirped out the tiniest fart.

"Oh, dear," she said. "Can't take her anywhere."

"Didn't hear a thing," he said. "Sit down, folks, please." He motioned Wren and Brian toward a plaid sofa, then turned back to Anna. "Did that just yesterday, by the way. In front of a lady from Texas."

"Oh well," Anna said with a dismissive wave. "Texas."

He chuckled and sat down on the arm of the chair next to her. "I hear you got some questions for me."

"I may be barking up the wrong tree."

"Bark away. That's what I do all day. Answer questions. 'Course mostly it's about where the bathrooms are."

She smiled. She liked this man.

"I'm wondering," she said, "if you used to work at the old Blue Moon. The one that was a brothel."

His mouth fell open in wonderment, exposing shiny white dentures. He grabbed the curl of his mustache as if it were the only way to close his mouth.

"Now how the hell did you know that?"

"My daughter met you. Back in the seventies. She remembered the name. Said you did chores around the place. Handyman work. We talked about you before she died."

Mr. Sudden's brow furrowed. "I'm truly sorry to hear that. Your children aren't supposed to go before you do."

She gave him a forgiving smile. "They say that, don't they? But it's not true. Children do it all the time."

Anna could see that afternoon so clearly. Nineteen ninety-nine. The crumbling folly on the mound above the manor house. The aching green of the Cotswold hills. The ragged chaise where Mona had held court above her kingdom, pale as a powdered queen.

There was tactful hesitation from Mr. Sudden. "I don't understand. Was your daughter . . . one of the ladies at the Blue Moon?"

"No . . . but she worked there for several weeks. Answering phones. I don't think she even used her real name."

He nodded sympathetically but without recognition.

"Red hair? Very frizzy. Like they wore it back then."

He shook his head. "Sorry."

"I wouldn't expect you to remember."

"I'm surprised she remembered me."

"I think it was the name, to be honest. It doesn't let you forget it."

A blinding flash of Clark Gable teeth. "I was a late baby. My mother wasn't expecting me. Her last name was Sudden, so . . . how could she resist?"

She studied him for a moment, assessing the kind placement of his features and something deeper and darker in those wide-spaced eyes.

"Margaret," she said softly, as if it were a prayer.

He was understandably flummoxed. "What?"

"Your mother's name was Margaret Sudden."

His hand went to his mustache and held on for dear life. "You knew her?"

"I did, yes." A slight nod was all it took to jar the tears from her eyes.

Which made her cross with herself. This was supposed to be *his* moment, not hers.

"I grew up at the Blue Moon Lodge," she added. She found a tissue in her sleeve and dabbed at her eyes. "Your mother read me the Winnie-the-Pooh books. She made me a dress for my sixteenth birthday. I loved her a great deal. More than I loved my mother, in fact."

His head tilted as he squinted at her. "Should I be remembering you?"

"No, no." She tucked away the tissue. "It was before your time. If you don't mind my asking, what year were you born?"

"Nineteen thirty-seven."

"Yes . . . before . . . just barely."

"So . . . you grew up there? How do you do that?"

"Happily, for the most part."

He smiled. "I meant—"

"My mother ran the joint. Mona Ramsey?"

He gaped at her. "Holy shit! *Mother Mucca?*" His eyes dropped in penitence. "Sorry. Meant no disrespect."

"None taken, dear. I know they called her that after I left. She was a tough old coot, wasn't she?"

"She was just a businesswoman," he said.

Anna smiled at him. "I suspect you and I scrubbed some of the same toilets."

He seemed to muse on that for a moment. She could practically hear the wheels turning in his head before he finally spoke:

"You're the daughter who ran away! Ma told me about you!"

"Did she?" Anna could easily have corrected him, but she didn't think it generous under the circumstances. There was too much left to share with this indulgent stranger. Besides, she was touched by Margaret's early alteration of Andy's gender. Margaret had known Anna well before Anna had become Anna, and apparently she had honored that reality after Andy fled town.

"Did she tell you what happened?"

A quick shake of his head. "Just that . . . you ran away. And nobody knew where you went. She was pretty broke up about it."

Damn you, tears. Stay away.

She glanced over at Brian and Wren, who were watching this interrogation with increasing fascination. She gave them a faint conspiratorial smile before addressing Mr. Sudden again. "Did you grow up at the Blue Moon yourself?"

"Oh, no. Ma left as soon as she got pregnant. I grew up in Portland. Had a wife and kid, but . . . they left after a while. A little problem with speed." He tapped those brazen white dentures. "I moved back here after Ma died in the seventies."

"And why—if you don't mind—did you do that?"

He shrugged. "Guess I wanted to see where we came from."

"And my mother gave you a job."

He nodded. "Part-time, but . . . she was a good egg. I was a train wreck back then. Musta been when your daughter met me."

"Most certainly," said Anna.

There was a tidy silence as she tried to compose the next question. She had already seen what she needed in the molten eddies of his eyes, an ancestral *something* that summoned her former life like no landmark could ever have done.

"Did your mother . . . did she ever talk to you about your father?"

He shook his head with a melancholy little smile, as if the answer were obvious. "I don't think she ever knew. Hazard of the profession."

"Mmm . . . but she was very careful most of the time."

"You knew her that well, eh?"

This was no time to bring up Lysol, but that's what Anna had on her mind. The foolproof yellow potion that kept babies at bay. The stuff Andy had used to clean chicken guts off the wall of Delphine's cabinette the night that Margaret was bedding Lasko for the sake of his manhood. It didn't have to have happened that night, but it could have, since Andy had taken the Lysol from Margaret's cabinette.

"I think I knew your father," she told Oliver Sudden. He just widened his eyes dubiously, so she continued.

"He was just a teenager, and he took his own life. I have plenty of reason to feel guilty about that, and I would very much like to apologize to someone before I die. I'm afraid you're the most logical candidate, because . . . well . . . you're alive. That's just the way it is, I'm terribly sorry. May we take you to dinner, Mr. Sudden?"

He blinked at her, then turned to Brian. "Is she always like this?"

"You have no idea," said Brian.

22
Candystriper

The Monarch was being a pain in the ass. It had worked perfectly before they dismantled it in Oakland, so the fuck-up had obviously happened on Jake's watch, during the reassembly in Black Rock City, something to do with the exposed gears and the dust. The beeotch had been wobbling all over the proving ground at Trans Bay, shaming the fuck out of him. He was glad that he was so high up (in the Pod Formerly Known as Anna's) that no one, not even Amos, could see him blushing.

"It's veering to the right now," he hollered.

"I know," said Amos with a note of strained patience in his voice. He was manning the left pod, one of three connected to the wheels. He was also in charge of the wings, which had just proven unflappable in the worst sense of the word.

"We can't take this out on the playa," Jake groaned. "We look like a wounded duck limping into the reeds."

Amos knew better than to agree with him. "It must be fixable. Let's have Incandescence take a look." Incandescence was the Burn name of Lisa Gelb, the asshat in the right pod. Nobody liked using that stupid name, since it made you slow down for it, just the way she did. She had been a sergeant in the army before her transition, and she wanted your attention all the time.

In-can-des-cence. Hup-two-three-four.

Amos was obviously enjoying himself, using Lisa to goad Jake out of his funk. Jake didn't feel like being goaded out of anything right now. This overgrown tricycle had lost its reason to live even before it got here. He had not made it to hold a poster of Anna. He had made it to hold Anna. He had made it to give her wings.

Now the Monarch itself seemed to sense that the game was over.

Lisa was looking up at him expectantly. "Lemme at it, dude," she said. "I think I know how to fix it."

Of course you do. And if you don't, you'll make some shit up.

Jake hopped out of his pod and monkeyed down to the ground. "Have at it, Incandescence. She's all yours. I'm through with this shit."

"You leave it to me, little feller."

This was provocation, pure and simple, but before Jake had a chance to respond, Amos had taken Jake by the arm and led him away from the scene.

"Why are you being such a dick?"

"*Me?* Did you hear what she called me?"

"She's pissed. You haven't let her anywhere near the Monarch since we got here. What harm can it do to let her have a shot at it?"

"You watch. She'll take total credit for it for the rest of the week. She'll act like she saved the day."

"There are worse things that could happen." Amos raised his brows knowingly, irritatingly.

"Like what?" asked Jake. "Being spared a lot of blank stares on the playa?"

"C'mon. Who cares?"

"It won't work without Anna here."

Amos shot him a WTF look.

"Not the machinery—the whole concept. That poster makes it look like a friggin' memorial or something. Like a Chinese funeral procession."

Amos chortled. "It would be working fine if it were Chinese."

"You blame me, don't you?"

"No. I don't give a shit, personally."

"You're judging me about something."

"Well, I think you're kinda being a man about machinery."

"Is that right?"

"Yep. Can't relate, sorry. It's like a bad NASCAR movie. If you want that kind of butch, you'll have to find another cis queer."

He felt the beginnings of a smile, so he crimped it into a smirk.

"Let's go to Center Camp," said Amos. "I'll buy you a drink."

Burning Man's commitment to gifting and radical self-reliance dictated that only two items were available for purchase in Black Rock City: ice and coffee. Jake enjoyed both nods to corrosive capitalism in the form of a large iced soy latte in the big tent at Center Camp. Then he and Amos cuddled up on a lumpy beanbag angled toward one of the performance spaces. The beanbag was what had attracted them, not the zoned-out guy on stage reading from a stack of papers. If not for his ponytail and Utilikilt, he might have been Christopher Lloyd in *Back to the Future*. His audience was skimpy and scattered, but they gave him their attention, hooting and clapping whenever he stopped long enough to signal that a response would be appropriate.

Amos frowned. "Do you think that whole thing's a poem?"

"Sounds like it. About GMOs."

"Oh, you mean like—"

"Yeah, genetically modified . . . whatever."

"Organisms."

"Right."

They were silent while the guy on stage droned on. *I spit on your alien corn. I curse your zombie wheat, your amber waves of evil . . .*

Finally Jake said, "It was smart of them to put the poetry next to the caffeine."

Amos chuckled and pulled Jake closer. "Feeling better?"

Jake conceded that he might be, that coffee worked miracles.

"You know," said Amos, "if Anna were here—"

"—it would be totally fucked. I know."

"Well—not that bad, but . . . she'd be feeling bad for you . . . and you would be feeling guilty. For no good reason. So—you've been spared all that."

"The sucky part," said Jake, "is that Marguerite and Selina get to be right."

Amos hesitated. "They don't have to know that."

"No?"

"Fuck no."

The guy on stage had become louder and more sing-songy. He had begun to chant, in fact.

Canto, Monsanto, canto, Monsanto.

"What does canto mean?" Jake asked.

"It's a verse in an epic poem."

"A long one, in other words."

"Look at that stack of paper, Jakey."

"Let's just wander away casually the next time they clap. We don't want to insult him. He's only got eight people listening."

"You think he's noticed?" Amos stood up, dusting off his butt. "C'mon. I've got some Mormon underwear you gotta take a look at."

That did not happen right away. They had errands to run before dark, and the last thing Jake wanted was to come back early and find Lisa—*fuck Incandescence*—still grunting away over the Monarch, telling anyone who'd listen how fucked up the reassembly had been. So they headed off to Arctica, one of the two camps where ice was sold, to buy cubes for their evening cocktails. A lean silver-haired woman of sixty or so was whaling away with an ice pick, her back turned to them. Jake should have recognized her—he *would* have, anywhere back in the city—but here she was completely out of context. The pigtails threw him too. And the pink-and-white-striped dress. The whole getup, really.

"Jake! It's Mary Ann!"

"Oh, hi." He laughed and hugged her awkwardly across the counter. "You look so much like . . . Dorothy, right? I didn't even—"

"I'm a candystriper, actually." She swept her fingers along the edge of her dress as if that would explain everything.

Jake shrugged. "Sorry. You know I suck at the femme stuff." He was rocking from foot to foot, nervously aware that it was his turn to introduce Amos. What would he call him with someone new? Was it too early for boyfriend?

"This is Amos Karpel." He made a feeble hand-wobbling gesture between them. "Mary Ann Singleton."

Amos gave her a sleepy smile. "I'm trying to make the connection between the uniform and the ice."

"Oh . . . well . . . there is none. I just work Arctica for the hoot of it. People are always so glad to see you. Mostly though I work the night shift at the medical tent." She arched a well-penciled eyebrow. "Totally untrained. Hence Candystriper." She wiggled a silver pigtail at him. "My playa name. World's oldest teen volunteer."

Amos smiled. "So what do you do?"

She shrugged. "Clean 'em up. Talk 'em down. Whatever the doctors want. There's a lot of dehydration and puncture wounds. You'd be surprised how many people step on rebar. I'm always saying 'gross,' which doesn't help a whole lot. I have to pretend that Candystriper said it in character, not me." She tilted her head in acknowledgment of her silliness. "Don't worry. Jake will explain me later. It's lovely to meet you, Amos. You're very cute. How many bags, gentlemen?"

They ordered four bags, all they could fit in their bike trailer. "We can give one to Lisa," said Amos, "if things work out with . . . the Monarch."

Jake gave him a withering look.

Mary Ann glanced between the two of them. "Is there royalty here or something?" She leaned closer and lowered her voice. "I'm very discreet. That's the way it's done. Anne Hathaway was here last year, and she just—walked amongst us."

"The Monarch is an art car," Amos explained. "A Monarch butterfly."

"Oh . . . of course . . . wow . . . like down in Pacific Grove. That's sounds amazing."

"We made it for Anna." It tumbled out of him just like that. He wanted Mary Ann to know. She went way back with Anna, and she would get it.

"*Is she here?*" She sounded more aghast than excited.

"No, it's just . . . a tribute."

"Oh—well . . . that's good. This would be a little rough on her."

"That's what everybody keeps saying."

Mary Ann loaded two bags of ice onto the counter. While Amos was transferring them to the trailer, she made a hasty hand signal to Jake that asked, *Are you two an item?* Jake reddened on the spot, and the exchange was not lost on Amos.

"We'd better be," he told her, grinning.

"Well, let me tell you something." Mary Ann put her hand on Jake's shoulder. It was chilly from the ice and felt good. "This is one of the finest men I've ever met."

"Mary Aaann," said Jake, sounding, even to his own ears, like a kid saying "Mooom."

"Shut up, Jake. I'm saying this." Her hand remained on his shoulder. "This man literally saved my life."

"I did not literally save your life."

"Okay then—my sanity. It was the worst moment of my life, and Jake was there—*so* there—being kind and strong and comforting."

"Makes sense to me," said Amos.

There was no way to change the subject but do it himself. "So what are you doing here? I mean, it doesn't seem like your sort of—"

Mary Ann drew back in mock indignation. "What? I don't look like Burning Man material?"

"Well, I wouldn't have—"

She laughed, cutting him off. "DeDe and D'or and I are doing a plug and play, so just shoot me now. We're the Ladies of Woodside. That's what the Candystriper thing is all about. I'm doing penance for my luxury. And I should be, believe me."

"Nice RV?"

"Huge. Oh my God."

"How huge?"

"Reba McIntyre huge. You guys should come over. Hang out. Take a shower." She gave him a wicked look. "I won't tell. Your radical self-reliance is safe with me." She leaned into him, as if she were about to offer him drugs. "A sit-down barbecue with cornbread and cole-slaw and chocolate cake. And showers."

Amos's face was hard for Jake to read. Was he charmed by her energy or slightly repelled by it? "Get thee behind me," he said, smiling.

She threw another bag on the counter. "I wasn't going for Satan."

He laughed. "Nowhere close."

"There's no virtue in missing out," she said.

A long, confusing silence hung in the air.

Jake jumped into the breach. "Anna's been loving the Volcano."

"Oh . . . good. It's not too much for her to manage?"

"Well . . . I do that for her."

"Of course. That's so sweet."

"Not that often, but . . . sometimes before bed."

Mary Ann smiled at him wistfully, sharing Mrs. Madrigal for a moment, then shooed them both away "Go! Make delicious cocktails! There's a line here!"

As Jake and Amos left with their wagons, Mary Ann hollered a final imperative. "And marry him, Amos . . . if you get half the chance."

"Do you hate her?" Jake asked as they unloaded the ice back at Trans Bay.

Amos thought for a moment. "I sort of *don't*."

"Yeah—me too."

"How did you save her life . . . or whatever?"

"Do you remember that shed I showed you at Michael's house?"

"Where the old guy killed himself?"

"Yep. . . . She was with him."

"What?"

"He shot himself in front of her. I showed up a few minutes later. All I did was call the police and let her cry on me. I guess it was kind of a bonding moment."

"I would say . . . yeah."

"That and our hysterectomies."

Amos remained unruffled. "She had one too? Not for the same reason, I take it."

"Hers was for cancer. Just a few months before mine. She spent some time with me in the hospital. I've never forgotten it."

"Then *I* won't," said Amos, giving him a tender look.

The Mormon underwear made its debut as soon as night fell. Amos came slouching through the tent flap, his chest hair spilling from the scooped neckline, his circumcised cock straining parabolically against the thin polyester blend of the fly.

"Excuse me, sir. May I speak with the lady of the house?"

Jake told him he must have the wrong house.

"Okay, then, what am I supposed to say?"

"In the first place, they're not in their underwear when they come to the door. Or *just* their underwear, anyway."

"So what did this guy say? The one who used to sit on your lap in his underwear?"

"I don't remember. Just be yourself, Amos."

Regrouping, Amos shook out his arms like a runner before a marathon. Then he grabbed his cock and snarled out his words backwoods style.

"I spit on your alien corn," he said. "I curse your zombie alfalfa, your amber waves of . . . whatever."

Jake laughed and threw a sneaker at him.

23
Life After Me

Michael and Ben had done molly twice in the course of their eight years together. One time during a hike in Pinyon City, the other during a Norah Jones concert in Golden Gate Park. It was a snuggly drug, like the old ecstasy, which had once carried a warning label about impromptu elopement while under the influence. The new ecstasy, on the other hand, was laced with speed—or so they had heard—so it was vital to obtain pure MDMA if you had any interest whatsoever in avoiding tooth loss and eventual madness. Ben knew a guy who knew a guy, so they ended up with several doses of molly for the trip to Black Rock City. One of them they would take on the night of the temple burn (a more spiritual experience, Ben said, than the actual burning of the Man); the other they were taking tonight at Comfort and Joy.

You could spot this camp from almost any place in the "gayborhood." Silky pink and orange banners— the colors of a desert sunset—streamed from poles around the perimeter of the village. It felt medieval, but not the granite-dark, ominous medieval of *Game of Thrones*—more like the Necco-colored fairy scenes in *True Blood.* This *was* a fairy scene, come to think of it— or rather a faerie scene—so it seemed to Michael as welcoming a place as any to wait for the molly to come on. He was not quite a faerie—just as he was not quite a bear and, in his distant, slim-hipped 501 youth, not quite a clone— but he liked the gentle energy of faeries. They had lots of sofas, too, here at Comfort and Joy. That was a big plus.

"Is that the orgy tent?"

Ben shrugged. "That's not quite the word for it. It's really laid-back and mellow. A lot of cuddling. Like the club in *Shortbus.*"

"As I recall, the people in that were fucking their brains out."

Ben rolled his head over and smiled at him. "You don't have to go in. *We* don't have to. We can stay right here on the sofa."

"For a while, at least, okay?"

"Of course."

Silly old coot! Michael had been in hundreds of sex spaces over the course of his adult life. Thousands, maybe, if he counted glory holes and Lands End and back rooms and the woods along Wohler Creek and Dick Dock in P-town and the Warm Sands resorts of Palm Springs and, okay fine, the men's room at Penn Station one sultry midnight in the late 1970s. It had been as easy as falling off a log. Or falling onto one, as the case may be. So what was so different now?

You are old, Mr. Mouse. Nobody wants to see you doing it. And if they do see you, you'll be met with rolling eyes and wrinkled noses.

If he were to express this to Ben, he would receive a reprimand, since Ben still found some fun in this body and wanted no part of Michael's sporadic self-loathing. But this tent, for some reason, filled him with irrational fear. It felt like the end of something, the whimper instead of the bang. It was as daunting as his very first gay outing when he climbed the stairs to the Rendezvous on Sutter Street to confront the unimaginable sight of male couples slow-dancing to Streisand.

How many more shots did he have at this? With Ben even? With anybody?

"Look!" cried Ben. "Let's try that!"

It was an open-air walkway hung with silvery Mylar streamers. A simple concept, but one that enchanted as soon as you were in the midst of it.

That was still the trick, wasn't it? *Just jump into it, babycakes.*

"Woohoo," said Michael, turning around for the return flight through the streamers.

Ben laughed. "Did I hear a woohoo?"

"Must've been somebody else," said Michael.

Back on the sofa now. An indigo dusk. A breeze tickling the pastel banners. Ben slumped against him, still shirtless and warm. A palpable unwinding.

"You feeling it?"

"Oh, yeah," said Michael.

"Nice, huh?"

"Mmm." He kissed the side of Ben's head. "Let's just live here."

"We couldn't have Roman here."

"Oh, fuck, you're right."

"What good is a city without dogs? It's doomed to be temporary."

"So right."

"He would love it though. All these funky crotches to sniff."

"I hope the Dood is happy with the new dogsitter," said Ben.

They let time pass between them like a breeze.

"I've been so selfish," Michael said after a while.

"About what?"

"The whole baby thing. I wasn't being honest with you. I wasn't grossed out by the idea of you helping Shawna out. I was just scared."

"Of what?"

"Oh . . . people making plans for a future I won't be part of . . . the whole idea of Life After Me."

"There is no life after you," said Ben.

"Well, that's what I think, but the universe may have different ideas."

Ben chuckled.

"It took so long to find you, Ben, and now I don't want it to change. I want it all set in amber. I want us and nobody else in the most selfish way you can possibly imagine. I can't help it—I'm old-fashioned. I believe marriage is between a man and a man. And if there's a baby to be taken care of—frankly—I want it to be me."

Ben said nothing.

"You see?" said Michael. "Selfish. Even a little creepy."

Ben pulled him closer. "I understand, though. I might be the same way."

"If you were old?"

"Yes."

Michael tweaked Ben's nipple. "I'm not *that* old."

"But, sure . . . I think of life after you . . . I do."

"Of course you do. You'd have to. Who wouldn't?" He paused. "What do you think of exactly?"

"Oh . . . living in Europe maybe."

Michael saw it: Ben selling his armoires in some trendy Roman neighborhood. Trastevere, say, or near the Piazza Navona. Ben's sandy hair flecked with a gray that matched his eyes. Ben going home on a Vespa to a roof terrace and a man.

"What would he be like?"

"Who knows? Somebody younger, maybe."

"Younger than me?"

Ben chortled. "Younger than me, doofus."

"Why would you do that?"

"I dunno. Because I haven't before? Because you've shown me it's possible?"

"Well . . . thank you . . . but that wasn't my intention."

Ben gave Michael's leg a shake.

"The young can be difficult," Michael added.

"So I've heard."

"And Rome is expensive."

"Who said anything about Rome?"

"Holy shit, those flags are beautiful," said Michael. "Just rippling across the sky like—what?—sorbet and cream?"

"I'll be there, Michael."

"What?"

"I will be with you. I'm here with you now, and I will be with you then."

Michael hesitated. "That's not what I meant."

"Yes, it is. How many times do I have to marry you before you get it?"

He leaned and kissed Michael.

"Is this the drugs talking?" asked Michael.

"No. But the drugs are asking the questions."

Michael chuckled. "We could do it in Ohio now."

"What?"

"Get married."

"Do you really want to get married in Ohio?"

"Not especially, no. I just want to Be. Here. Now."

Ben laughed. "Good. Call Shawna. She'll be so happy."

"We can't call her. We can't call anyone."

"That's right."

"I *am* here now."

"You are. And so is he."

Ben was pointing toward a buff and nearly naked youth prancing past their semicircle of sofas. " 'Evening of the Faun,' " said Ben.

The guy had goat horns sprouting from a mop of blond hair. His legs were trousered with some sort of faux fur through which an actual penis was spiking heroically. It wasn't huge, but it was finely formed and completely stole the show.

The guy pranced closer and stopped.

"Greetings," he said.

"Greetings," they replied, almost in unison.

"Do you mind?" He was asking to sit down.

"No . . . sure . . . of course." They shimmied apart to let him sink onto the sofa between them.

The faun pulled a goatskin wine bag from around his neck and guzzled from it before offering it first to Michael, then to Ben.

Seeing their hesitation, he said, "It's water."

They both accepted swigs and returned the bag.

"You can hold it if you want."

He meant his cock. Michael glanced at Ben and grinned.

Shrugging, Ben seized the guy's cock at the balls and squeezed it.

"Nice," he said.

"Thanks." The faun turned to Michael. "Your turn, Daddy."

Michael obliged him—because . . . why the hell not? The shaft was warm and roped with veins, a fistful of life.

Another endorsement seemed redundant, so Michael said, "I used to have a pair of those."

The faun gave him a clumsy, boyish leer. "Bet you still do."

"No." Michael laughed. "The pants, I mean. I had a whole Pan outfit. Long time ago."

"No shit?"

"Home Yardage. Mock chinchilla." He was still holding the guy's cock, having just noted that it was markedly thicker at the base. "I never thought of this, though. The open-air thing. I guess because I had to ride a cable car to the party."

The faun giggled, but that's the way it had happened. Mary Ann had sent him on his way that night. Squeaky clean out of Cleveland, she had already begun to accept his brand-new randiness as if it were her own. "Go find a nice billy goat," she had told him with a playful shove, and in some ways that was the version of her he still maintained, the smart girl creeping up on adventure with one eye covered, not the liberal rich lady from Woodside taking Zumba lessons at the Zen Center. He had come to like the latter-day Mary Ann, but never with the intimacy of old. She probably felt the same about him—that stodgy old queen fussing in his garden, holed up with his younger husband in the Castro.

"Those are nice, too," said Michael, letting go of the cock to touch the guy's horns. "Did you make those as well?"

"No," said the faun with a grin. "Those are real."

24

Immaculate Conception

On her way to Coinkydink, Shawna stopped at an installation that had caught her eye from a distance. It reminded her of one of those carnival Tilt-a-Whirls, a slanted spinning disk that held its contents by centrifugal force. In this case, though, the contents were not people but little bonfires that scattered sparks as they orbited through the night sky. It was a simple concept—all iron and fire—and its operation was even simpler: two people on the ground alternately throwing muscle into a giant crank. Two people, it suggested, could do wondrous things working together.

Was she totally out of her mind, chasing down a stranger who had lured her with graffiti and promised to disappear? Had this offer of no-strings-attached sperm so caught her fertile imagination that it had destroyed her ability to reason?

She stood for a while and watched the whirling embers, partially to absorb their magic, partially seeking postponement of potential folly.

That was when Otto appeared.

"Well, hello, ladylove."

He had called her that back in the day. Ladylove. It had bothered her with its faintly sexist overtones and corny echoes of his stint at the Renaissance Pleasure Faire. Tonight, however, she found it curiously reassuring. Go figure.

"Oh, hi," she said. "I was just heading to Seltzerville."

"To see *me*?"

"No. Ronald McDonald." It was a nervous response, but it came off a little snide, so she added: "I wanted to tell you how amazing the temple is, Otto. Really. Just stunning. You guys did an amazing job. Seriously. It's the best one ever."

He pressed his hands together and touched his fingertips to his red rubber clown nose. She thought for a moment that he was going to say "Namaste," and was hugely relieved when he didn't. She could not have suppressed the laugh.

He turned and looked at the flaming Tilt-a-Whirl. "This is unbelievable, right?"

"Truly," she said. "So primal and . . . elemental."
She scrounged for something else to say. "So how's
Ottawa coming along?"

He shrugged. "I'm still going."

"Well, that's good. I mean . . . I know how much
you want to."

He nodded. A long silence followed.

"Do you think we could talk for a bit?" she said
finally.

"Sure. What about?"

"Just . . . things. I'd like to get your take on
something."

"You wanna go to Seltzerville? It's not far."

"Perfect."

Otto looked genuinely pleased. "We can kick back.
Drink some tea. Ada makes a smokin' herbal tea. Calls
it Moose Juice."

Shawna blinked at him.

"It's kind of an Ottawa joke."

She nodded, taking it in. "Ada is from Ottawa?"

"Oh, sorry . . . thought I mentioned that at
Martuni's."

"Nope. Nothin' about anybody being from Ottawa.
Nothin' about *her*, actually. You mentioned two other
exes since me."

He smiled sheepishly. "Takes a while to get it right."

"Yep. Sure does. I'm glad, though. That's cool, Otto."

"Yeah." He nodded with a look of surprising tenderness. "It is."

She had to go to Seltzerville; there was no way around it. And there was no way she could ask Otto for sperm with an adoring Canadian clown-lass hanging on his every word—not to mention his leg. So they sipped that nasty tea and spoke with concern about a sixteen-year-old girl who had reportedly gone missing from her parents' camp, prompting the rangers to seal off the exits to prevent any attempt at abduction. Shawna wondered out loud who would bring their teenage daughter to BRC in the first place, only to realize how priggish and judgmental she sounded. She hated pretty much everything about herself at that moment.

When she had finished her tea, she bade them farewell and headed off in the direction of Coinkydink. Otto's new ladylove had been a sign, she decided, the final indicator that anonymity was the only way to go—at least, a form of modified anonymity in which she could actually lay eyes on the sperm donor and get a sense of what sort of person he might be. It wasn't so much a question of his physicality (though a degree of attractiveness would be nice) as the need to assess his spirit.

Coinkydink took a while to locate. There was no signage at all, just a ragtag circle of tents that she found troubling. She had not expected (nor had she desired) some grandiose Temple of Immaculate Conception, but this place was laidback to the point of disinterest. She had to ask around before she could even identify it.

"You've found us," said a petite brunette with a gleam in her eye.

"Oh, thank God."

" 'There's no such thing as Coinkydink.' "

"What?"

"That's our camp slogan."

"Well—I was beginning to think it might be true. I'm looking for someone named Dustpuppy."

The woman frowned. "Sorry, I don't think . . . oh, wait . . . that might be Jonah."

"Might be?"

"I just got here. I don't know everybody's playa name yet."

"Ah."

"Do you know what he looks like?"

"Sorry, I don't." Shawna considered explaining the reason for her visit, then decided against it for fear of compromising the contract. Dustpuppy might not be out to his campmates about the nature of his gifting. After all, it would not be an anonymous act if other people knew about it. Not to mention the fact that the whole damn thing could be a hoax, a wild-goose chase perpetrated by a prankster.

"I'm afraid everyone's gone right now," said the woman. "They took off in our art car."

"And you're here all by your lonesome?" Shawna had just noticed the perky coral nipples punctuating the woman's loose fishnet top.

"I don't mind," said the woman. "I'm glad for a little peace and quiet."

"I know what you mean."

"You're welcome to wait here for Jonah."

"Uh . . . well, thanks. I'm not even sure that Jonah is the one I'm looking for. Could you tell me what he looks like?"

The woman shrugged. "Youngish. Blond. Kinda cute." A kittenish smile flickered across her face before she added: "For a guy."

Shawna smiled back, letting her know she got the message.

"I know you," said the woman.

"Oh yeah?"

"Shawna Hanson, right?"

"Hawkins, actually."

"Right. I saw you on *The View*."

"Oh . . . yeah. That was fun. Whoopi was fun, anyway."

The woman stood there for a moment, bouncing on her heels, hands thrust in the pockets of her loose linen trousers.

"So," she said at last. "I haven't read your book."

"I won't hold that against you," said Shawna.

They did it in Juliette's tent—that was her name, Juliette. Their lovemaking was all meandering mouths and fingers, with no purpose at all beyond pleasure. No bicycle couriers were involved, no artisanal twat cozies. It was way uncomplicated and hot. And there was something about Juliette that smelled alluringly of home.

They lay there together, sticky and dusted as fresh pastries.

"Holy shit," said Juliette.

"I know," said Shawna.

"Where do you live?"

"I'm staying in the gayborhood."

"Not Beaverton?"

"No—just with some guys. I mean—gay guys. What's wrong with Beaverton?"

"Well—those gals are kinda tough."

"Nothing wrong with tough sometimes."

"No—I guess not. Anyway, I meant . . . where do you live in the default world?"

"Oh. San Francisco. Valencia Street."

"Me too. Well . . . Sixteenth, just off Valencia."

"Uh-oh."

"Why uh-oh?"

"Well . . . you're just around the corner. I might come a-callin'."

"That would be nice," said Juliette.

"You're single, then?"

"Yep . . . in the way *you* mean, at least."

"I don't get it."

Juliette reached down and touched her faintly rounded belly. "Next year there will be two of us."

Shawna was struck dumb for a moment.

"If that's too much for you," said Juliette. "Just say so now. I promise I won't be offended."

"No," said Shawna. "It's not too much for me at all."

She moved her hand to Juliette's belly and let it rest there as she gazed through a patch of tent mesh at the bursting blue moon she'd been promised.

Immaculate conception.

Maybe there was more than one way to do it.

25
A History of Boys

They were seated at the common table at the Martin Hotel when Brian realized that Anna was weeping. Wren had noticed it too and caught Brian's eye with a look of pained concern. Mr. Sudden, however, was completely oblivious as he swabbed up the remains of his lamb gravy with a bread roll. Wren grabbed a paper napkin out of a plastic holder and handed it to Anna without comment.

"I'm so sorry," said Anna, dabbing at her eyes. "This is tiresome of me."

"Don't be silly," said Wren.

"One should not cry over a piece of tin."

Brian looked at the wall behind her. It was an archaeological hodgepodge of knotty pine, gloppy paint, and battered pressed tin from an earlier era. "Does that bring back memories or something?"

"Just all my baby fears and dreams. Do you see it?"

Brian moved to her side of the table and studied the tin, finding nothing of particular interest.

"Look at the pattern," said Anna.

"Okay . . . flowers."

"No. Look again."

Brian finally saw it—or *them*, rather. "Jesus Christ."

Mr. Sudden glanced up from his plate, suddenly taking an interest. "Our Lord is in the tin?"

"No," said Brian. "These days he only shows up at Chick-fil-A."

Wren gave him her don't-provoke-people look.

"It's more like—private parts," he added.

"Pussies and peckers," said Anna, turning to Mr. Sudden with a nostalgic smile. "That's what your father called them. He's the one who showed this to me."

Now Mr. Sudden was out of his seat, checking out the pattern in the tin. Wren joined him immediately, peering over his shoulder.

"Well, damn if it isn't," said Mr. Sudden, widening his eyes at Wren.

They had aroused the curiosity of other customers, who were straining their necks for a closer look. Anna urged her family to take their seats again. "I'm sorry," she said. "I was being sentimental. I didn't mean to cause a fuss."

"Why did he show you this?" asked Mr. Sudden.

"Oh—just something boys do. He used to work in the kitchen here. It was his naughty little secret. We were both sixteen." She sighed. "So young."

"And he killed himself."

"Yes. That summer."

"And . . . why do you think you had something to do with that?"

"I know I did. I told Lasko's father he was gay. It must have been the final straw. His father was a terrible, angry man, and . . . the shame was too great, I suppose. He took an overdose of sleeping pills."

Mr. Sudden hesitated. "So . . . *was* he gay?"

Anna nodded. "I think so, yes."

"But he was sleeping with my mother."

"She was trying to turn him straight. His father had actually paid her to do that. People thought that would work. Back in the days of yore."

"So his family already . . . suspected he was gay?"

"Yes . . . I think he had a history of boys. But I was the one who confirmed it."

"And why would you do that?"

"I was jealous. Jealous of them both. So I wrote a letter, pretending it was from my mother, and told his father that Lasko had made a pass at me."

"I'm sorry, sweetheart. You're losing me again. How would that make him gay?"

"Because . . . I was a boy back then."

Mr. Sudden blinked at Anna for a moment, then turned to Brian.

"She was," said Brian.

He wasn't sure if Mr. Sudden believed a word of this, but it didn't matter. What mattered was that Anna had finally unburdened herself.

After dinner, while Wren drove Mr. Sudden home to Sandstone Drive, Brian and Anna waited in rocking chairs on the porch of the restaurant.

"So," he said, as an Amtrak train thundered past them, "it wasn't an anagram at all. You named yourself after Lasko Madrigal."

"Yes."

"He didn't treat you very well."

"No, he didn't, but . . . I saw his goodness for a while, and taking his name was a way of bringing him back to life. I always thought the name was lovely. It has its own music, doesn't it? Especially in Spanish."

"MA—DRI—GAL," intoned Brian by way of demonstration, drawing out the a's with basso seductiveness.

She winked at him to prolong the silliness but said nothing further. The two of them sat there in silence, meditating on the red and green lights along the tracks.

"How long did you stay here?" he asked.

"After he killed himself?"

"Yeah."

"Not long. A few weeks. Long enough for the fuss to die down. His family wanted everything hushed up, and . . . I was a big part of the Everything. There would have been trouble if I had stayed."

"Even though nothing happened between you and him?"

She nodded wistfully. "Even though."

"But you were ready to leave, right?"

"Oh yes." She gave him a crooked smile. "I just needed a little boot in the ass."

He chuckled. "So your mother never knew where you went until Mona brought her back to Barbary Lane."

Anna nodded. "I know it sounds cruel, but she would have tried to drag me back, and she would have expected some answers. I couldn't explain myself to someone who didn't know me. I couldn't explain myself to me back then."

"I'm glad you ran away," said Brian. "We wouldn't have had you otherwise. *I* wouldn't have had you. I would have totally . . . missed out on you."

Anna gave him a tender smile. "You are the dearest man, Brian Hawkins."

Embarrassed, he made light of the moment. "Oh, pshaw!"

"*Pshaw?*"

"Isn't that what you used to say?"

"Maybe *you* did. I'm much too young for *pshaw.*" She reached across the gap between the rockers and took his hand. Her long, slim fingers were cool and silky. "Do you know what I wish, Brian?"

"What?"

"I wish we were all back at Barbary Lane. Just for an hour or two. The whole family. Sitting in the garden and telling our stories."

Brian chuckled. "That might be a little disconcerting to the stockbrokers who live there now."

Anna smiled, still holding his hand. "We would invite them down for a toke." She looked distracted for a moment. "Oh—I've been meaning to ask you." She pulled an envelope from her blue velvet drawstring bag and handed it to him.

"What is it?" he asked.

"Just a note from Amos. And three tickets to something."

"Who's Amos?"

"Jake's new beau. The one who gave us our bon voyage."

Brian examined the contents of the envelope. The note read:

Anna,
We would love to have you with us, if you're
feeling up to it. There's room for an RV in our
camp. Brian will be able to explain.
    Amos

The tickets were to Burning Man.

Anna's eyes were on him now. "So explain," she said.

"It defies description," he told her.

Nevertheless, he tried.

Back at the RV, he and Wren tucked Anna into bed. "I suppose," she said, gazing up at them, "it's not a very practical idea. Going to this Burning thing."

"Not really," he said. "We'd have to go hundreds of miles south and then head north again. We're in the same state, but that's about it."

"Ah—I see. Oh well."

"I'm sure you'll get a full report from Jake—and Shawna for that matter."

"She's going, too?"

"Yep," said Wren. "With Michael and Ben."

"Goodness. Everyone."

Brian was starting to feel like a shit, but someone had to be the grown-up here. "They'll be back in a week," he told her. "We'll have a dinner somewhere and get a full recap."

"A week might be too long," Anna replied vaguely.

He was about to tell her that a week would fly by in no time when Wren rose abruptly and left the room. Great, he thought. My wife is pissed at me now.

He turned back to Anna. "It's just that it's a harsh environment. We don't have enough food or water or anything. It takes serious preparation."

"I understand, dear. I've just had this feeling, that's all."

"What sort of feeling?"

"You know . . . spooky old me."

He brushed a wayward strand of hair from her forehead. "Listen, lady. No premonitions until we get you home."

"But they're not about me," she said.

"What do you mean?"

"Pumpkin—" Wren was calling from the front of the RV. "May I have a word with you, please?"

"Go," said Anna, releasing him from further discussion.

Wren was at the dining table, hunched over her laptop. "Take a look at this," she said. It was a MapQuest map of the region with a road already highlighted. "We don't have to head that far south. There's a direct route between here and Burning Man. You just head out past the Blue Moon and keep driving. It's a straight shot."

Brian studied the map for a moment.

"See?" said Wren triumphantly. "Looks like it's only a hundred miles or so."

"Yeah, a hundred miles of totally bad-ass road. It's all dirt, baby. Probably rutted too. That's Jungo Road. Where those evil gold mines are."

"So? What's a few cyanide pits between us and them?"

He shrugged. "Okay—fine. Just make sure our cell phones are charged."

She turned and gaped at him. "Wow, that was easy."

"I can't fight the two of you," he said.

"She's up for it, then?"

"She's having one of her feelings again."

"Feelings?"

"An intuition, apparently."

"About what?"

"I'm afraid to ask."

In the morning they didn't head directly to Jungo Road. At Anna's request they went to the twin-towered Catholic church in the heart of town. Anna had been christened at St. Paul's, she explained, wearing a long white gown that Margaret had made for the occasion. She remembered the church and wanted to see it again.

The building, however, was locked.

Anna's face briefly registered disappointment. Then, spotting an iron gate by the side of the church, she wobbled past a shabby grotto into a cemetery full of plastic flowers and tombstones old and new. It wasn't a dauntingly large space, but the sun was brutal, so Brian became concerned when Anna kept moving.

"You wait here in the shade," he told her. "What are we looking for?"

"Madrigals," she said.

Wren jumped at the challenge, scouring the inscriptions on the stones with such enthusiasm that she hit pay dirt in less than three minutes. "Here's someone named Hegazti Madrigal," she hollered to Anna. "He died in nineteen ninety-three."

"She," said Anna.

"What?"

"Hegazti was a she."

"Oh, sorry."

"Are there any others nearby?"

"Doesn't look like it."

"Wait." Brian had spotted a stone that was flush with the ground. It was no bigger than a shoe box and weatherworn, but its inscription was easily readable.

BELASKO MADRIGAL
1920–1936

Wren gasped at the discovery. Brian wasn't sure whether his tone should be celebratory or funereal, so he returned to the shade, where Anna was waiting, and escorted her back to the grave marker. She stood there for about a minute, smiling tenderly at the granite reality, before murmuring a word that made no sense to him.

"Abyssinia," she said.

26
Worlds Beyond

B en and Michael were swapping sleepy grins, since the kid in the Pan outfit had conked out on Michael's chest in the big tent at Comfort and Joy. There was no way to move without waking him, so Michael was accommodating his weight to the point of numbness. "He's so peaceful," he murmured. "I hate to disturb him."

"There's no rush," said Ben, realizing how blissful that simple fact made him. He could spend an eternity here in this cushioned puppy pile of lantern-lit men, watching his husband holding this goat-legged kid. The kid's hand was resting on Michael's Buddha belly, receiving its benediction even in sleep. The oceanic sounds of sex still ebbed and flowed in various corners of the tent, but the three of them were contentedly beached, for the moment at least, on a warm and golden shore.

The kid stirred and rubbed his eye with his fist.

"Hey," he said, as if he had just discovered them.

"Hey," said Michael, kissing his forehead beneath the horns.

The kid rolled over languidly and nestled between the two of them. His once-prancing penis was now a silky pink mouse napping in his faux fur loins. He seemed to be startled, briefly, by the jungle growl of an orgasm in a far corner of the tent, but his lips soon plumped into a smile of understanding.

"I have a feeling," he said, "I'm not in Snowflake anymore."

Michael chuckled. "I have a feeling you've said that before."

"Maybe."

"I used to say it about Orlando."

"Where's Snowflake?" asked Ben.

"It rings a bell," said Michael, "for some reason."

"Arizona," said the kid.

"Right."

"How does that ring a bell?" asked Ben.

"Probably our alien abductions," said the kid.

"I don't think that's it," said Michael.

Ben laughed.

"They were for real," said the kid. "They made a movie out of it."

They were quiet for a while. The kid was holding Ben's cock—not in a particularly insistent way but idly, halfheartedly, as if it were a toy he might get around to playing with again. Michael noticed this and smiled benignly at Ben.

"Are you guys a couple?" asked the kid.

"You bet," said Michael. "Husbands."

Ben looked over at the man he'd been with for eight years, the man he'd married twice just to make it stick. Michael's generation—its history of fighting disease and bigotry—sometimes made him grumpier than Ben would like him to be, but he knew what he'd found in Michael: a gift for intimacy like none Ben had ever known. Michael, for all his messiness, knew how to connect with him completely.

"Don't you ever get jealous?" asked the kid.

"Oh, yeah," said Michael. "Truly, madly, deeply jealous."

"So?"

"So it's not as big an emotion as the one that holds us together."

The kid rolled his head toward Ben. "Do *you* get jealous?"

Ben hesitated just long enough for Michael to laugh. "Hell, no," said Michael. "He knows he's got me for life. I *try* to make him jealous, but I have no luck at all."

The kid grabbed Michael's cock with his other hand. "Bet I could do it."

Ben laughed. "How can I be jealous of someone who doesn't have a name?"

"Dustpuppy," said the kid.

"Cute," said Michael. "Kinda perfect, in fact."

Ben agreed that it was. Everything about this man was suited to their molly moment. He seemed closer to a spirit than a human being, the uncomplicated embodiment of youthful lust and sweetness. Ben remembered the kid's reference to alien abductions in Arizona and amused himself with the thought that Dustpuppy had been sent to them on assignment from another planet, an escort for worlds beyond.

"I have to sit up," said Michael. "You guys stay put."

"What's the matter?" asked Dustpuppy.

"Your foot?" asked Ben. He was well acquainted with this scenario. Michael's lingering gout had a way of making his limbs go numb. "Here," he said, grabbing a nearby bolster and propping it against a tent pole. Michael settled against it and issued a groan of relief as he extended his foot and shook it like a dust mop.

"Better," said Michael. "Thanks, sweetheart."

Dustpuppy looked distressed, so Ben tried to put him at ease. "It's his circulation," he said, gathering pillows in his arms. "Here . . . we can all sit up." He made a big pile against which the three of them reclined like drowsy pashas.

Ben found himself slipping in and out of sleep. The last time he awoke, Dustpuppy had gone (headed off, no doubt, for a mission on another planet), so Ben snuggled closer to Michael, who murmured his contentment unintelligibly.

Someone across the tent was playing a small stringed instrument. It had a medieval Anglo-Saxon sound.

"The music of our people," Ben said with a smile.

Another murmur from Michael.

"What is that?" asked Ben. "A lyre or a lute. I've never known the difference."

"What difference?"

"You know—between a lyre and a lute."

There was no response from Michael, so Ben looked directly into his eyes. They were open but unblinking. "Are you okay, honey?"

"I'm fine."

"No, you're not. Look at me, Michael . . . Michael?"

"I'm fine." Michael's eyes rolled back, exposing the whites.

"Sweetheart . . . damn it!"

Michael's whole body was shaking now, a series of small convulsions that made him lurch forward off the pile of pillows.

Ben looked up and yelled to no one in particular, "Help us, please! Is there a doctor here? Somebody, please help us!"

The music ended abruptly. Several people sprang to their feet and rushed to offer aid, standing in a circle around them. Some of them were naked and still had semi-erections—a detail that Ben would remember and recount for years to come.

Michael was blue and unmoving. His breathing had stopped completely. His legs were wet with urine.

Ben held him in his arms and began to cry out of sheer helplessness.

He could not leave this man, so he could not run for help.

"Stretch out!" said someone behind him. "Get him flat!"

So Ben complied, lowering Michael to the dusty carpet, arranging his limbs with such care that he might have been preparing him for ritual anointment.

Do it right, he told himself. Assume he's alive.

"I'm here, babe," he said. "Don't worry. We're taking this ride together."

No response. Michael's hand was cold and stiff as Ben held it in a frantic pantomime of ordinary life.

"Get Hawkeye!" someone shouted.

"I'm on it!" said another. "Where is he?"

"Next door at Celestial Bodies. He's a ranger. He's got a walkie-talkie!"

Ben just kept talking quietly to his husband's inert face. "They're getting Hawkeye, sweetheart. He's a ranger."

Nothing.

"He's got a walkie-talkie."

Nothing.

"I love you, Michael. Do you hear me? I'm here, and I'm not going anywhere. I promised you that, didn't I? I'm here, baby, right here, so listen to me, okay?"

But Michael was beyond listening.

27
In Her Mind's Eye

The road was so rutted that Anna was jostled awake several times in the course of the hundred-mile drive. There was very little to be seen outside the window beyond the powdery emptiness in the headlights of Brian's motor home. She had asked to be wakened when they passed through Jungo, but that moment never came, since Brian said there had been no evidence of the town's existence. Not a train track, nor a station, nor a skeleton of planks that might have passed for Mrs. Austin's general store. *Time* magazine (and the gold lust of President Hoover) had made Jungo a new El Dorado, but the town had long since vanished, its bones picked clean by the other time, the lowercased time, whose truth was more reliable in the end.

Wren was sitting on the floor the last time Anna awoke.

"Yes, dear?"

"Are you okay? It's awfully bumpy."

She agreed that the road was a bit of a washboard. "The bed is comfy, though. It almost absorbs the shock."

"Frankly," said Wren, "I'm a little nauseous. Just hoping you aren't."

Anna explained that her stomach was ironclad and always had been.

"Lucky you," said Wren.

"I hope I'm not being a nuisance."

"No—no . . . I'm curious about Burning Man myself. And Brian promises a nice flat road on the way back."

It would serve no purpose, Anna realized, to explain her real motivation for requesting this side trip. Her gift for premonition—whether morbid or pleasant—had often fallen short of the mark, so she knew it was best to keep her mouth shut. Even if—heaven forbid—there proved to be a reason for her growing dread, there was nothing they could do about it now. She would only cause them early anguish.

Still, it was hard to forget the times she'd been right.

Lasko, for instance, had been leaving the world just when she had decided to ask for his forgiveness. And forty years later, on a Christmas Eve at Barbary Lane, she would know the very moment that life left Edgar

Halcyon, her one great love. She would not be with him at the time, but she would feel it—a warm breeze of bay rum and Harris tweed that swept through every pore of her body.

This time, though, she was seeing a tent. A big tent scattered with bright pillows, like something out of the Arabian Nights. And people she didn't recognize were scrambling around frantically and shouting the word *doctor.*

"Where are you right now?" asked Wren.

"Nowhere I should be, apparently."

"I hear you. The mind wanders when you're on the moon. This has to be the most desolate place I've ever seen. There hasn't been another vehicle since we left Winnemucca. I just tried calling a friend and—nada. We're fine, though. We have more than enough Kombucha to survive the trip."

Anna smiled at her. This woman was such a generous, uncomplicated spirit. How perfectly suited she was for leading Brian out of his vagrant gloom.

"Anyway," Wren added, "Brian says we'll be in Gerlach in a half an hour. That's the town at the entrance."

This moment of consolation was punctuated by another walloping bounce from the motor home—and the sound of Brian hollering "Whoa, Nellie!"

Wren rolled her eyes. "I have no idea where that came from."

"I think," said Anna, "from Michael."

"Really?"

"An old cowboy show on television. Someone said it to a Jeep."

Wren grinned. "I'm sure the Nellie part was what amused Michael."

There had been plenty of talk about butch and nellie in those days. Anna in fact had worried that Michael would embrace one or the other to such a degree that the natural blend could not occur. She need not have fretted. In no time at all an entire orchestra of gender traits were at Michael's command, and he took joy in the mix. He had once been fond of referring to himself as the Butchinelli Brothers.

Anna managed a smile. "He brought you into the family, really."

Wren shrugged. "Does meeting me in a bar count?"

"It better . . . or nothing will."

Wren laughed. "You're right, though. I would never have met Brian without Michael. He was one of those people you take to instantly. So full of life and mischief you could just eat him with a spoon."

Anna looked away, afraid that her face would betray her feelings.

"I hope we can find him," said Wren, "in the midst of that madhouse."

"Do we know it's going to be a madhouse?" asked Anna.

"Well—Brian says it's going to be festive and very busy. But Michael's staying with Shawna, and we know where *she's* staying. Once we park with Jake and Amos, we can put out the word. Word has a way of spreading there, apparently."

I can feel it, thought Anna. I can feel the word spreading out from that tent like bright red syrup in a cone of shaved ice.

How awful it was to eavesdrop without being there, without being able to act. She asked Wren to help her sit up in the bed.

"We can move you to a chair if you like."

"No, this is fine. I just need to look out at something."

Wren plumped a pillow behind her and gazed out at the gray blur beyond the window. "Even if it's nothing, huh?"

Anna nodded. *Even if it's nothing.*

Wren, sensing something wrong, stayed with Anna for a period of silence, broken only by another "Whoa, Nellie!" from Brian as the vehicle hit another rut.

"For God's sake," Wren hollered, "don't break an axle."

"I'm workin' on it," her husband hollered back.

The tent seemed more subdued now. Fewer players in the scene. The cause for the commotion had apparently been removed.

This might have been calming to Anna, but somehow it wasn't.

28
Something Else Afoot

Mary Ann's shift at Arctica had left her bone-tired and aching. Who knew ice could be so fricking heavy? She had tried to push through to the end, but one of her coworkers had noticed her exhaustion and insisted that she go home and rest. If he had known that "home" was this air-conditioned Hollywood-style trailer with a comfy king bed and a wafer-thin television, he might not have been so sympathetic, but she accepted his compassion without protest. There was no way she could face the medical tent tonight without a little down time. And possibly a filet mignon.

It was good to be tired this way. She remembered the old tired, the tired that had dogged her before her cancer was diagnosed, and the tired that had drained her after her surgery. But she had been cancer-free for four years now, so she had reason to savor her ordinary old-person weariness. There were worse things in life than the usual aches, and she had known them, thank you very much.

She stretched out on the bed with her flute of prosecco and congratulated herself on having accepted DeDe Halcyon-Wilson's invitation to occupy this pleasure craft. DeDe's and D'or's RV was next door, so there was plenty of opportunity for fellowship whenever she wanted it. She just didn't want it right now. She wanted to sip her prosecco, and meditate for a while, and maybe have a modest shower and a nap. As she lay sorting out the order in which these events would occur, she noticed the ever-deepening drifts of playa dust on the floor. You could not get away from the stuff, however elegant your quarters. It walked right in the door and sat down.

She knew how plenty of Burners felt about plug and play. She had seen the barely concealed contempt on the face of Jake's new boyfriend, Amos. To this young hipster, she was just one of those decadent trustafarians who let other people shop for their costumes, or *make* them even, who let other people cook for them and build their art cars. All of which might be true to an extent, but it was still hurtful. In the end, everybody faced the whiteouts. It was a very democratizing thing, the dust.

Besides, it was not like they were sponsored by Halliburton or something. This camp had been organized by dinky little *Western Gentry* magazine, or more accurately, westerngentrymag.com, the online presence of the society publication. It was hardly the evil empire. The magazine had not been especially intrusive either, beyond photographing the inaugural organic barbecue, when Mary Ann's Steampunk Duchess costume had been looking (if she did say so herself) pretty darn rad.

No, she had not made it herself. So the fuck what.

The next time she spoke to Amos, she would try to give him a better idea of who she really was. She wanted him to know that. She wanted him to like her.

She had a feeling he'd be around for a while.

She was in the midst of meditation when someone rapped energetically on the side of the RV. She considered ignoring it, then finally rose and opened the door.

It was Shawna with another young woman.

"Hola, Mary Ann."

"Omigod. What are you doing here?"

Shawna rolled her eyes just the way she had when she was six—toward someone else. "She's been saying that to me my whole life."

Mary Ann smiled and extended her soiled candy-striped arms. "You know what I mean. Come in. Give me a fucking hug."

They embraced with an audible double sigh, much to Mary Ann's relief.

"Mary Ann—Juliette. Juliette—Mary Ann."

"I'm the friend formerly known as mother," said Mary Ann, shaking Juliette's hand. "I adopted her at birth, but I left her with her dad when she was little."

"Wait till she gets through the door, Mary Ann."

"Oh—sorry."

"She overshares," Shawna told Juliette.

"Like you don't," said Mary Ann, grinning. "Seriously—how did you know I was here?"

"Jake and Amos."

"Of course. I gave them ice at Arctica." She closed the door and led them into the lounge, which, with its rounded corners and buried purple lights, reminded her vaguely of Virgin First Class. "Okay, no cracks about bourgeois decadence."

"Not a peep out of me," said Shawna.

"By the way," said Mary Ann, gesturing for them to sit down. "I don't think Amos likes me very much."

Shawna shrugged. "Nobody does at first."

Juliette gaped at Shawna. "Dude."

"It's all right," said Mary Ann. "We understand each other."

"I like you already," said Juliette.

Shawna, Mary Ann noted, seemed unduly pleased to hear that.

They gabbed and laughed and drank prosecco, and Mary Ann broke out the prosciutto-wrapped melon the nice *Western Gentry* staff member had left in her fridge that morning. Shawna's pretty friend seemed to be a fairly recent one, maybe even a hookup, but Juliette was bright as a button and obviously smitten with Shawna. Who could blame her? Shawna had always been a charmer, and now, of course, she was sort of a celebrity. Certainly much more of a celebrity than Mary Ann had ever been during her run on *Mary Ann in the Morning*. Shawna had already been on *Letterman* several times; Mary Ann's fame had never crossed the Central Valley.

Mary Ann knew she had no right to be proud of Shawna, but she was. She was proud of the spunky seven-year-old she could still see in this woman. She was proud of the woman who had survived abandonment so many years ago. Better yet, she *liked* this woman who had faced her trials and written about them so bravely, who picked her lovers as adventurously as she picked her clothes.

She knew that Shawna liked her as well. That had happened precisely because they had both scrapped any effort at reconciliation. There had been nothing to reconcile after all these years, only a new foundation to be built. It helped that they loved people in common: Michael, Ben, Jake, Brian (yes, Brian), and, of course, Anna.

Still, she was puzzled as to why Shawna had pulled this surprise visit today, especially in the company of someone Mary Ann had never met. It could have been merely a matter of air-conditioning and comfortable seating—Mary Ann would not have blamed her for that—but there was something else afoot that eluded her.

Shawna and Juliette left after a two-hour visit. Shawna lagged behind for a few extra words.

"Thanks for this."

"Hey," said Mary Ann. "It was fun. She's a nice girl."

"It may not be anything," said Shawna. "But I wanted you to meet them."

"Them?"

Shawna blushed—a rare occurrence. "Her, I mean, of course." She looked away, flustered. "Come join us down at Dusty Dames tonight, if you feel like it."

This was Mary Ann's first invitation to the funkier world beyond *Western Gentry*. She was profoundly touched that it had come from Shawna.

"Oh, thanks," she said. "That would be wonderful, but I've got night duty over at the medical tent."

29

The Marvelous Present

For Brian, Black Rock City was the same, only different. The same bursts of color and whimsy, but noticeably bigger and slicker, like the leap between the old Vegas and the new Vegas. Wren and Anna, on the other hand, found everything fresh and captivating. They kept their faces pressed to the windows like toddlers at a Macy's Christmas display. Brian was relieved to see Anna looking more cheerful; something had been clouding her spirit on the hard road from Winnemucca.

He might have been more cheerful himself if he hadn't been absorbed by his search for Trans Bay, the camp where Jake and Amos were staying, where there was supposedly a parking spot waiting for them. If he could find the fucking camp. As usual, the signs were hard to read out here, and some of the camps blurred into each other like stalls at a crowded flea market. You would think, he told himself, that a camp run by transgender activists from San Francisco would announce itself with a little more aplomb, but maybe he was just stereotyping under duress.

"I'm sorry," he told the ladies in back. "It's around here somewhere. I know you're ready for a decent night's sleep."

"We're fine," said Wren. "This is just mind-boggling."

"Oh my goodness, look at that!" Anna was pointing to an art car crossing an intersection ahead of them. It was an enormous pedal-driven tricycle, a butterfly with orange-and-black wings that flapped as it moved. The wings were lighted in such a way that they glowed like amber glass. Brian laughed with joy.

"It's a monarch," said Anna. "Do you know about monarchs?"

"Just what they look like," said Brian.

"I'm clueless," said Wren.

"They migrate like birds," Anna explained. "They're the only butterflies that do. But the distance of their migration is so enormous—thousands of miles—that they can't make the journey on their own. They only live for two months."

"So—how do they do it?"

"They don't. Their children do it. Their grandchil-
dren. Somehow they know exactly where to go and
specifically where to land. Somehow—it's in them.
The new generation winters in the same tree every year
without ever having seen the tree." Anna paused as the
butterfly tricycle rounded the corner and disappeared
into the swirl of traffic. "They don't need their elders
at all. It's a miraculous thing."

Brian knew she was talking to him, but he didn't say
a word. He didn't trust his voice not to crack.

"They're poisonous," Anna added, "so they're tough
little bastards. Nobody would dare eat them. They're
flying caution signs—look at them, orange and black,
pure Halloween. But they survive, and their pattern is
so familiar it's imprinted on our brains like something
generic—like plaid. Am I making any sense?"

Wren murmured her understanding.

"They have two months," said Anna. "That's it. But
some part of them must know that they're part of this
endless continuum, this . . . community after death.
And even if they *don't* know, *we* know, and that itself
takes your breath away."

"It does," said Wren, a little too fervently. "I believe
in that."

"It's not a metaphor for heaven," said Anna.

"Well, why not?"

"Because I'm too old for that shit."

"Oh, now—"

"Tell her, Brian."

"She's too old for that shit."

Wren laughed. "You two!"

"I'm not too old for *this*." Anna gestured to the carnival sparkling outside the window. "Thank you, Brian, for the marvelous present."

He wasn't sure if she meant present as in gift—this side trip into Black Rock City—or present as in now, this moment, the marvelous present.

Either way, he was glad to be thanked.

He found Trans Bay a few minutes later. Someone named Lisa directed him curtly to a space at the back of the camp, where she barked orders as he angled the Winnie into its assigned spot. She was friendlier, though, when he was finally in place. She clamped her hands on the door and congratulated him on his expertise.

"I've been moving this barge around for a while," he told her.

"Amos said you might be coming," said Lisa. "We were beginning to think he was bullshitting us."

Brian smiled at her. "We had a few other errands to run."

Lisa seemed to hesitate. "Look—do you mind if I ask—" She cut herself off.

"Go ahead," he said. "You're entitled, whatever it is. We're grateful for the hospitality."

Lisa placed her wide, sturdy hand on her heart, as if to keep it from escaping, then lowered her voice. "Is Anna Madrigal in there?"

Brian smiled at her. "The one and only."

"Oh my Jesus fucking God." The words were uttered reverently, like a prayer of adoration. "She saved my life in Eye Rack."

Brian's first thought was about Lisa's grotesque pronunciation, one of his major irritants these days. *We invade a country, bomb the shit out of it, kill hundreds of thousands of people, and we still don't have the decency to say its name right.*

"You must be thinking of someone else," he said. "Anna's never been to—"

"No, man, she was right there on my iPad in Eye Rack."

My iPad in Eye Rack.

"There was an article about her on this transgender blog, and—she made me see how I could be old and happy. She made me want to live and come home to Sunnyvale and . . . be myself. Oh shit!"

The "Oh shit!" had come in response to the tears plopping down Lisa's coarse, pockmarked cheeks. Brian yanked a couple of Kleenexes from the box Wren had installed on the dashboard and handed them to Lisa. "Here ya go, soldier."

"Sergeant," said Lisa, mopping up before blowing her nose noisily. "Don't let her see me like this. I need to pretty up first."

"Roger Wilco," said Brian. (He wasn't sure if that was the proper army lingo, but Lisa didn't correct him.) "In the meantime, can you help us find Jake and Amos?"

"Oh, sure. They're right over—oh shit, they left on the art car."

"Do you know when they'll be back?"

"Well . . . you know how *that* is. Or do you?"

"Yep. I do. I'm an old Burner."

Lisa left, and Brian joined the ladies in back. It felt good to kick back, to enjoy the sensation of having landed somewhere after sixty miles of rutted moonscape. The terrain here was virtually the same as Jungo Road, but there was life at least, and its throbbing expectant rhythms could be heard just outside. He sank into the armchair and pried the cap off an Anchor Steam. "Jake is away for a while," he said.

"Ah," said Anna, looking disappointed.

Wren tried to be helpful. "Does he have his cell on him?"

"Nobody has a cell," Brian told her. "There's very little reception, and the dust would destroy them."

Wren smirked as she gazed out the window at a knot of revelers heading into the night. "And even if you had one, there'd be damn few places to stick it."

Brian smiled at her, feeling an enormous surge of love. Home, for better or worse, would always be next to this woman. "Want a beer, honey?"

Wren puckered her lips at him—her technique for silently conveying love. "I'm fine, pumpkin." She glanced over at Anna with tender, nanny-eyed sympathy. "This one, though, could probably use a good night's sleep."

Anna shook her head decisively. "No . . . not yet."

"Don't make me get bossy," said Brian. "Jake and Amos will get back eventually, but there's nothing we can do until then but get lost out there." He had already tried, and failed, to remember the name of Shawna's camp, if he had ever known it in the first place. It was just common sense to stay put. If your car broke down in Death Valley, you stayed with the car and waited for someone to find you. Without exception. Especially if your car had a frail old lady inside.

"You don't understand," said Anna. "He's alone."

"Who?" asked Brian.

"Michael."

"*Our* Michael?"

"Yes." There was both urgency and impatience in her tone, as if Brian were deliberately misunderstanding her.

"Are you being spooky?" he asked.

"Yes, that's exactly what I'm doing. Listen to me, dear. He's leaving, and he needs someone with him."

30
Those Four Minutes

This particular someone had pigtails of plaited silver that evoked both Rebecca of Sunnybrook Farm and Baby Jane Hudson. They erupted from the side of her head with childlike gaiety, though her face was etched with her years when she smiled down at him. The smile placed her. It moved him past the nonsensical name tag and the pink-and-white-striped uniform into the realm of someone he loved.

"Mary Ann?"

"Call me Candystriper," she said.

"Where's Ben?"

"With the doctor. He's here. Don't worry."

"What are you doing here?"

"I work here."

"Am I dead?"

"Oh, gee, thanks."

"I just mean . . . this is surreal. You aren't medically trained."

"Go ahead. Rub it in." She paused. "All I have to do is draw a little blood."

"No fucking way."

She smiled. "I'm just here to cheer you up." Her cool, elegant hand swept across his forehead. "How am I doing, babycakes?"

"Not bad, so far."

"You scared the shit out of Ben, you know. You were out for four minutes. White as a sheet and limp. He thought you were dead."

This still made no sense to him. He remembered talking to Ben about lyres and lutes, he remembered Ben asking if something was the matter, he remembered Ben telling him the paramedics were on the way, he remembered telling Ben that it was an overreaction, that he had merely passed out pleasantly for a moment or two. He had not been there at all for the peeing and shaking and the going limp. He had not even believed it until one of the paramedics asked him to stand up and he felt the soggy cotton sticking to his leg. Then he had grown sheepish in the presence of these proficient strangers. "Your point is well taken," he had told them with a smile.

He remembered, too, the flickering film of his trip to the medical tent: the bouncy humiliation of the stretcher ride, the way the lights of the ambulance stole the thunder of the EL-wired bicycles that parted to let them pass. He remembered how the paramedic in the ambulance had slapped his wrists and complained jovially about his absence of veins, finally settling on a fierce jab to the back of his hand. He remembered watching the IV bag as the fluid—whatever it was—dripped into him. He remembered thinking: This could be serious. This could take me out right now.

"What do they think it was?" he asked Mary Ann.

"Apparently you had a little seizure."

"Brought on by what?"

"It happens sometimes when people pass out sitting up. Your organs get all squished up or something, so the body shuts down."

"You're shitting me."

Sofa Daddy had been the perfect playa name for him.

"I'm not supposed to talk about these things," Mary Ann whispered, "so act surprised when they tell you."

He rolled his eyes at her. "I'll do my best."

That was so like her, he realized. It stirred pleasant echoes of the old days at 28 Barbary Lane. *Mrs. Madrigal is throwing a party for your birthday, so don't go out cruising tonight, and be sure to act surprised when it happens.*

She had to be the first to tell you. It was her favorite form of intimacy.

When Ben returned, Mary Ann was gone. Ben kissed him on the cheek, then pulled a chair next to the bed.

"Did that freak you out?" he asked. "Seeing Mary Ann?"

"It did feel mildly hallucinatory. All of this does."

Ben nodded. "Do you wanna leave?"

"I might . . ." He didn't want to disappoint Ben, but he was craving clean sheets and hot showers. "Did the doctor say I should leave?"

"No. She just said to take it easy. No more drugs for a while, and keep hydrating. She suggested an MRI when we get home."

"For what?"

"Just to make sure it was nothing . . . out of the ordinary."

Michael felt drained and disoriented. At the moment, it was not hard to believe that something might be out of the ordinary. "I'm a little scared, sweetheart."

Ben smiled. "*You* are?"

"I'm so sorry."

"For what?"

"I dunno. For scaring you. For thinking you overreacted."

"Well . . . *that* you can be sorry for."

"It must have been awful, those four minutes."

Ben hesitated. "I said good-bye to you. I told you I loved you, and I said good-bye. Just in case you could hear me."

Awful, indeed, but immeasurably beautiful to the living Michael.

"Take me home," he said.

31
No Tidying Up

Word of Anna's arrival in Black Rock City had spread as if by smoke signals even before Jake and Amos returned to Trans Bay. As near as Brian could figure, Sergeant Lisa had a lot to do with it, since perfect strangers had been inscribing love letters to their icon in the thick dust of the Winnebago. Jake himself was misty-eyed at the sight of his roommate. "Shit," he said. "I'd totally given up hope."

"Oh, you must never do that," she said.

"How did you even find us?"

"Your friend," said Anna, casting her eyes toward Amos.

"Tickets and everything," said Wren.

Jake gaped at Amos. "You are so bad. And so rich, apparently."

Everyone but Amos laughed awkwardly, since no one seemed to know the full truth of this. Amos just ducked his head with a modest smile.

"Wait'll you see what we made for you," said Jake.

Anna widened her eyes. "For me?"

"I think," said Brian, jumping in, "it's time we let our ladyship go to bed. Everything will be a helluva lot more fun in the morning."

Anna ignored him. "You don't know where we can find Michael, do you?"

"Sure," said Jake. "They're over on Edelweiss. Want me to bike over there and tell him you're here?"

"Would you, dear?"

"Should I tell him to join us in the morning? We do a bitchin' breakfast here."

"A bitchin' breakfast sounds heavenly."

And with that Jake and Amos left, and Wren and Brian began helping Anna prepare for bed. She looked profoundly weary to Brian, but he also detected a certain restlessness as he pulled off her slippers and adjusted her sheets. The chill of a desert night had crept into the Winnie, so he pulled a blanket from the overhead compartment and placed it at the foot of the bed. "Just in case," he told Anna.

"You'll wake me, won't you, dear, when Jake gets back?"

"Of course," he said.

But fifteen minutes later, when Jake got back, the news was hardly worthy of a wake-up.

"I couldn't find them," he said at the door. "Nobody's seen them for a while."

Brian stepped out of the Winnie and shut the door. "They're gone?"

"It's possible, I guess. The car isn't there."

"Shit." Brian thought for a moment. "What about Shawna? She's supposed to be staying at their camp."

"I checked. She's off with some chick named Juliette."

"Of course she is."

He knew he sounded like a cranky old dad, but he couldn't help it. Anna wanted the family together, and he would do his damnedest to make it happen.

His damnedest was not enough. The next morning at Trans Bay's traditional flapjack breakfast—a long trestle table under a lavender awning—he broke the news as gently as possible. "It's looking like they may have left," he told her. "But we could still run into them. Same goes for Shawna. This place is like that."

"I understand," she said, a strangely placid light in her eyes.

"And we can stay here as long as we like."

"That's very nice of them."

"It takes a while sometimes for people to come together here, but that's the beauty of—"

"Brian, dear—you mustn't try to tidy things up. You'll just exhaust yourself."

"What?"

"There's no tidying up to be done . . . with the possible exception of this hat." She fiddled with the loose ends of the turban that Sergeant Lisa had presented to her as soon as they had left the Winnie that morning. "What I mean to say is . . . I've said all I need to say to each and every one of you. Michael included. It's in you now for good." She reached over and took his hand. "Do you understand me, dear?"

"I think so, yeah."

"There's nothing you have to say, nothing you have to do . . . and nowhere I have to be. It's all free time from here on out. For both of us."

Wren, sitting across the table, noticed this exchange and smiled at him. Then her beautiful lips went oval in amazement. "You are shitting me," she said.

He turned to see what she meant.

It was that monarch butterfly, looming above them like the inevitable.

32
The Ride

S he was amazed at the practiced grace with which
they placed her in the highest seat. Jake and
Amos led her up the ramp, holding her arms, while
Sergeant Lisa, quite literally, brought up the rear.
She landed in the pod (as Jake called it) much the way
she landed in her favorite chair at home. They gave
her a thermos of cold water and a pretty Edwardian
parasol and a silver bell to ring whenever she wanted
their attention. The ride would last fifteen minutes,
they told her, unless she wanted it to end earlier. The
three pods beneath her held Jake, Amos, and Sergeant
Lisa.

Then the machine began to move, and she heard a
squeal of delight from Wren and a manly hoot from
Brian and waves of applause—applause!—from the

people assembled along the road. She assumed they were clapping for this wondrous human-propelled creation with its flapping jack-o'-lantern wings until she heard the chants as she moved toward the blazing white ocean of the open desert.

Anna Madrigal, Anna Madrigal, Anna Madrigal ...

How on earth did they know?

She looked down and saw Jake beaming up at her, pointing to a sign on the front of the butterfly. She could not read it from this height and angle, but she assumed it bore her name. A name she had chosen herself, by way of reparation, all those years ago.

The glorious machine picked up speed. The wheels were singing to her now, the warm wind caressing her face like the softest yellow chiffon. She could feel the freedom in her hair as she raised her arms, ever so briefly, to the welcoming sky. The cheers grew dimmer, fading away at the moment of release. A single voice remained, redolent of love.

"Be good, lamb! Live long and be good!"

Margaret was running after her down the train tracks, blowing kisses and weeping copiously. She could barely manage it in those heels, but she was trying.

"Remember to call my aunt on the Embarcadero!"

"I will."

"And use the money for something nice!"

"I will."

"And don't forget to—"

Anna couldn't hear the rest, but she knew she would have to learn her own lessons now.

There was a city waiting for her.

About the Author

Armistead Maupin is the author of the nine-volume Tales of the City series, the first three books of which were made into a television miniseries starring Olympia Dukakis and Laura Linney. Maupin's other books include *Maybe the Moon and The Night Listener*. A stage musical version of *Tales of the City* premiered at San Francisco's American Conservatory Theater in May 2011. He lives in Santa Fe with his husband, the photographer Christopher Turner.

HARPER LUXE

THE NEW LUXURY IN READING

We hope you enjoyed reading
our new, comfortable print size and found it
an experience you would like to repeat.

Well – you're in luck!

HarperLuxe offers the finest in fiction and
nonfiction books in this same larger print size and
paperback format. Light and easy to read, HarperLuxe
paperbacks are for book lovers who want to see
what they are reading without the strain.

For a full listing of titles and
new releases to come, please visit our website:

www.HarperLuxe.com

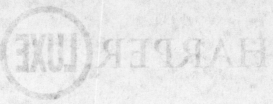